A new thriller from a master of psychological suspense!

"This I gotta see." With a cynical smirk, Dees reached across the table for the napkin, unfolded it and read the message scrawled on it. His smirk evaporated instantly. At first, Dees thought he'd made a mistake and he read it again, his lips silently forming each word. His skin suddenly paled, felt clammy. He read the message a third time, this time aloud, looking across at Rawlings just to make sure. His voice came out pinched and frightened: *"The masked dog is loose."*

Rawlings looked back at Dees, who kept clutching the greasy napkin, staring dumbly at the words that had devastated him so completely, filling his heart with horror.

Rawlings sighed. "Mondays are a bitch, aren't they, Dees?"

RAYMOND OBSTFELD

MASKED DOG

A GOLD EAGLE BOOK FROM

W⊕RLDWIDE

TORONTO · NEW YORK · LONDON · PARIS
AMSTERDAM · STOCKHOLM · HAMBURG
ATHENS · MILAN · TOKYO · SYDNEY

To Patty, a Queen of Hearts in a world of knaves.
You put the bop in bop-she-bop-she-bop.

First edition August 1986

ISBN 0-373-62101-9

Printed in Canada

Troubles...

The urgent top secret message came into Washington, D.C., at 11:34 A.M. Fat Boy, the Agency's mammoth new communications computer, decoded it by 11:37 A.M. Immediately a hard copy was rushed across the hall by Rosenbloom, who hadn't read the contents, but knew from the frightened expressions on the faces of those who had that his vacation plans for Yosemite, starting tomorrow, were *pffft*, down the toilet.

Rosenbloom caught up with Deputy Section Chief Godfrey on his way to the men's room and handed him the sealed envelope. Godfrey nodded curtly, spun around, then almost jogged back to his office, nervously balancing the envelope across both palms as if it were a ticking bomb. He laid it on his immaculate desk, polished daily to such a gloss that the envelope was reflected in the dark wood, and stared at it for a long and panicky moment.

Godfrey didn't want to take responsibility by opening it while Section Chief Rawlings was at lunch, but neither did he want to sit on it and get blamed later if something went wrong. So he buzzed Dees. Technically Dees had a lower rank, but the little bastard was annoyingly clever, thrived on responsibility and was hungry for Rawlings's job. When Dees and the envelope left his office, Godfrey sneaked out to lunch.

Dees followed procedure. He phoned the restaurant where Rawlings was eating, a greasy hamburger joint on Seventeenth Street—which meant the office would smell like raw onions and kosher pickles for the rest of the day. As he hung up the phone, Dees laid a roll of spearmint breath mints on Rawlings's desk and hoped his boss would get the hint.

Within ten minutes, Rawlings was marching through the busy office, his thick-knuckled hand strangling a greasy white bag containing the rest of his teriyaki burger and fries. He tossed the bag on his desk, knocking the breath mints onto the floor. Dees picked them up and placed them next to the bag, making sure Rawlings saw him.

"You're a snotty prick, Dees," Rawlings said. He reached into his bag to munch on a couple of limp fries.

"Your praise humbles me," Dees said in the flat ironic tone he knew rankled Rawlings.

Rawlings frowned. "So where's the Candygram?"

Dees held up the sealed envelope. "Shouldn't you get your man Godfrey in here for this? He's the second ranking official in this section. That's procedure."

"Fuck Godfrey," Rawlings said. "If he didn't have the balls to call me himself, I don't want him in on this. Besides—" Rawlings winked at him "—this might give you a chance to maneuver closer to my job, eh, Dees?"

Dees handed Rawlings the message. It was in a thick maroon envelope, signifying Highest Priority: Immediate Action. Rawlings tore open the envelope with clumsy fingers, the grease on them staining the paper. He unfolded the green-and-white computer printout and read silently.

Dees studied his section chief's square face for some reaction. Hard to tell. With those loose jowls and oversized teeth, Rawlings looked like a junkyard dog bred for bad temper rather than looks or intelligence. Dees knew better. Rawlings liked to play the crude bumpkin, but there wasn't a sharper mind in Washington. Except, Dees admitted, his own.

"Hmmmm," Rawlings said, and read the message again, his dark eyes narrow with concentration.

Dees waited. No point in asking what the message said. Rawlings would tell him when he was ready. Not before.

Rawlings closed his eyes and massaged the lids, as if a sudden headache had struck him. After a thoughtful pause, he muttered, "Calender."

Dees snatched the daily calendar from the desk and set it in front of Rawlings.

Rawlings brushed it away, annoyed. "Not that calendar, moron. *Calender*. Price Calender."

Dees looked confused. "What about him?"

"Get him."

"He's inactive. You know that."

"So? Inactive's only a word, Dees, easily changed. Like employed."

Dees ignored the threat. "Christ, why Calender? Even when he was active he was nothing special."

"He had his uses."

"As a mule, transporting."

Rawlings was folding the urgent top secret message into a misshapen airplane, one that didn't have a chance of ever flying. "Except once."

"Yeah, okay, once. But that was an accident. A fluke."

"Tell him that when you see him. Just don't ask him about his wife, okay?"

Dees snorted. "You got a dozen actives you can assign. Guys younger and in shape and trained. They can't wait to get out in the field and use code words and tiny cameras and all that nifty stuff. Price Calender never liked any of it, never."

"We didn't give him much choice."

"That's another reason to keep him out. Jesus, you know what he's doing for a living now? It's pathetic."

"Maybe. But he's perfect for this. Just this one."

"Perfect, him? In what way?"

Rawlings frowned. "Read his file."

Dees let the statement hang there a moment, not saying anything. He could see the section chief was getting annoyed.

Rawlings folded a couple of cold fries into his mouth. He smiled, his oversized teeth mashing the fries while he spoke. "Hell, Dees, what's worst case, anyway?"

"Worst case?" Dees said. "Well, you blow this operation—whatever it is—by using Calender, and I have to share the blame. Looks bad on my record. Or through some miracle, you succeed and stay in this damn office, and I don't get your job and the fat salary increase that goes with it." He reached across the desk, peeled open the roll of breath mints and popped one in his mouth. "Which means I can't afford the ridiculous payments on that Porsche I've been having wet dreams about. That's worst case."

"Or I could succeed and get promoted and you'd still get my job. And your Porsche."

Dees considered that a moment, then shook his head. "Nope. You're too old and you've made too many enemies around here for a promotion. I'm better off waiting for you to screw up and then trying to stay clear when your body hits the ground."

"You're a calculating bastard, Dees," Rawlings said with a grin, "but you're probably right."

Neither spoke for a minute. Finally Dees said, "He won't come, you know. Calender."

"Oh, he'll come."

"How?"

"Simple. We'll ask him."

"Just like that, huh? Tell him one more for the Gipper?"

"No," Rawlings said, scribbling something on the crumpled napkin from his lunch bag, writing around a smear of catsup. "Hand him this."

"Oh, sure. Just hand him a couple of words scrawled on a greasy napkin and he'll wing out to D.C. for God and country and Rawlings."

"No. For something else." Rawlings's face hardened and his crooked teeth clenched at some memory. His voice went uncharacteristically quiet. "Just give it to him."

"Right. Only this I gotta see." With a cynical smirk, Dees unfolded the napkin and read the message. The smirk evaporated instantly. At first Dees thought he'd made a mistake, and read it again, his lips silently forming each word. His skin suddenly paled, felt clammy. He read the napkin a third time, this time aloud, looking at Rawlings just to make sure. His voice came out pinched and frightened. " 'The masked dog is loose.' "

Rawlings swiveled around on his creaky chair and fed the paper airplane into the shredder. The compact machine whirred to life for the few seconds it took to chomp the urgent top secret message into ribbons. He looked over at Dees, who was still clutching the greasy napkin, staring dumbly at the words that had devastated him so completely, filling his heart with horror. Rawlings sighed. "Mondays are a bitch, aren't they, Dees?"

1

Price Calender saw her as he entered the bar, and froze in midstride.

Pretty, he thought. Okay, more than pretty, but still a couple of notches from gorgeous. Sitting there not looking at anybody in particular, keeping her eyes slightly far away to discourage guys from hitting on her. He watched her through the dim lighting and the haze of cigarette smoke that made the circular bar she sat at look like Alcatraz Island on a foggy night. He took a step closer. About twenty-five, with a slight overbite. Smooth skin, except around her eyes, where there were creases deep as clenched talons. The makeup almost hid them, but not quite. Price stared and thought, uh-huh, someone used to getting her own way. But still pretty, the way cobra-skin cowboy boots are pretty. Nice to look at, hard to keep.

Price stood in the doorway, waiting until he was sure she was alone. He didn't want to be surprised by some no-neck bull returning from the bathroom and anxious to fight.

He'd been out all day in the hot dry Santa Ana winds, hunting for a suitable present for his daughter's tenth birthday. He hadn't seen her in almost two weeks, and he thought it kind of funny that he was so nervous about seeing her tomorrow. Nervous, yet excited. The last time they'd been together was the day before her trip to the hospital. They ate lunch at Hamburger Hamlet, and she kept ordering things—more water, crackers, zucchini—because the waiter had a glass eye and she couldn't get enough of seeing it. Afterward that was all she'd talked about in the car—how much fun it would be to have a glass eye you could pop out and scare somebody with. Price had conceded it might be neat, and pretended to pop his out and lose it on the car floor. She'd laughed for miles.

Earlier that evening he'd felt moody and had canceled another date with waitress-undiscovered actress Dominique Duvall, formerly Karen Schneider of Anaheim. Instead he'd stayed buried in his sofa, watching the Lakers blow a close one with the Seattle Supersonics. Then he'd drifted down to Westwood for a late movie he sat halfway through before realizing he'd seen it already on one of the dozen flights he'd made last week. Now he was in Billy's for a quick nightcap. He didn't need to look at his watch to know what time it was. He always knew. The curse of insomniacs.

It was nearing midnight, and the place was still pretty lively for a Monday. Bruce Springsteen's voice pulsed over the din and some of the customers were swaying, snapping fingers, drumming on the edges of their tables. Billy, the owner, kept one of Price's old records in the jukebox, but it was rare for anyone to actually spend a quarter to hear it.

"Hi," Price said to the pretty woman, swinging a leg over the bar stool next to her. Christ, he thought, I look like John Wayne mounting a damn horse. He pointed at her empty wineglass. "Drink?"

"Yes, it is," she said, not giving an inch.

He thought about dropping the whole thing right there. Who needed this crap? Hell, he wasn't desperate, just a little lonely thinking about another long night without sleep. Tired of watching old movies he'd never heard of, drifting off during one, waking in the middle of another. Barbara Stanwyck suddenly replaced by Gloria Grahame.

She was searching her black clutch purse for something to light her cigarette with. Camel, he noticed, unfiltered. Price pushed his cheap lighter across the bar. It slid through a couple of interlocking wet rings before clinking up against her glass. He didn't offer to light the cigarette. "I'm Price," he said. Friendly, but not pushing anything.

She picked up the lighter without looking at him, roasted the tip of her cigarette, tilted her head back and blew a thin stream of smoke toward the expensive brass ceiling fan Billy had put in to give the place more of a *Casablanca* atmosphere. The fan just gave everyone a chill on the back of the neck, but no one wanted to hurt Billy's feelings, least of all Price, who owed Billy fifty bucks for the birthday present he'd bought his daughter today.

Now that he was closer, Price could see that the woman was older than he'd thought, maybe twenty-nine, thirty. Only a few years younger than he was. But also much prettier than he'd first realized. Maybe even beautiful.

She turned toward him, his lighter still in her hand, and smiled a set of the whitest teeth he'd ever seen.

"Okay, sport, what'll it be?" she said, her words clipped and precise, as if hiding some regional accent she was ashamed of. Mississippi, Kansas, Boston—he couldn't tell. "Speak up, buster. You wanna fuck, suck, snort, shoot up, wig out, dress up, strip down? You wanna get on top, underneath, want me to bend over, get on all fours and bark like a dog, smell my panties, wear my bra? Well? What's it gonna be?''

Price stared at her a moment. "Tell me, Sister Theresa," he said, "do the other nuns worry when you go out on Saturday night?"

"Wise guy, huh?"

Price grinned. He hadn't been called that in years, not since high school, when every teacher used the expression to describe Price and his elder brother, Derek. *Wise guys, the both of 'em. Come to a bad end.* Well, they'd been right about Derek, at least. And Price? Depended on who you asked.

"I don't like being laughed at," she said. Her eyes were fierce even in the haze.

"I wasn't laughing at you. Honestly."

"Like hell," she said, then flicked Price's lighter, touching the hissing flame to the cuff of his new shirt, which stuck out of the sleeve of his sport jacket. It ignited immediately.

"Goddamn!" he hollered, jumping up and swatting furiously at his flaming cuff. "Are you nuts, lady?" He smelled a sour stench, and panicked when he realized it was his own skin and hair. He was only vaguely aware that she was walking toward the front door as he grabbed a glass of melting ice from the sleepy customer next to him and doused the flame. Tiny ice cubes clicked across the floor like dice.

"Wow, Price," said the guy whose drink he'd grabbed. "Quick thinking."

"On the tab, Billy," Price called over his shoulder to the man behind the bar.

Hefty Billy Steeple shook his shaggy buffalo head and reached for a pen. "Fuckin' tab."

14

But Price was already through the front door, brushing past a couple just entering. "Wait, goddamn it," he shouted at the woman's back as she zipped out into the clear Los Angeles night. She was wearing a charcoal lamb's wool skirt and matching double-breasted sweater. Her blouse was some shade of red or pink that had a name you didn't need your lips to pronounce.

She was half a block down Westwood Boulevard, standing in the harsh light of a parking lot, fumbling in her purse for her keys or parking stub, or maybe some mace, for all he knew. His feet scuffed along the pavement as he ran toward her, holding his singed cuff up. She stopped rummaging a moment, turned to see him coming, and smirked with such contempt that Price momentarily wanted to slap the smugness from her face.

But he knew he wouldn't hit her, hated himself for even thinking it. He had never hit a woman. Except Liza R. And her he'd nearly beaten to death before they'd stopped him—two guys in expensive dark suits dragging him off her because she hadn't yet given up the information they'd wanted. But he hadn't cared about the damn information. He'd cared about something else. Well, she was dead now. He clenched his left hand. The second knuckle, which he'd broken with the same punch that had fractured her jaw, still ached when it was humid. In some climates he could barely play the guitar and had to rely on his lead guitar player, Trinidad, to fill in the famous riffs for him. The audiences didn't seem to notice the difference.

"Come for a piece of revenge, sport?" she said, smiling. "Punch my teeth out? Tear my blouse? Go ahead. But if I can pick, I'd rather you punched my teeth out. I've got dental insurance. But the blouse is a

Liz Claiborne, and I had to type a hell of a lot of accident reports to get it.''

Price felt his anger seeping out. He tried to whip up his fury again, concentrated on the stinging in his wrist, the smoky tattered cuff sticking absurdly out of his charred sport jacket. No use. He simply snapped his fingers and held out his palm. "You forgot to return my lighter.''

And she laughed.

Not sarcastically. Not drunkenly. Just a good hearty laugh, with her head thrown back and her fillings showing. "You made me laugh," she said with a great deal of surprise in her voice.

He scowled, holding up his blackened cuff. "Then I guess $32.50 was a small price to pay.''

She laughed again. She was wearing pearls; he hadn't noticed that before. They looked real.

"That's twice you've made me laugh," she said. "That means you must be married, living with someone, or recently separated and looking for someone to show pictures of your kids to. Or gay. Which is it?''

"None of the above. Widower." Not really a lie, but not exactly the truth.

She looked him over, head to toe, and for a moment he was worried that she'd recognize him. But people hardly did anymore.

"I don't sew," she said, "so I can't fix your shirt and jacket. I don't cook, so I can't invite you to my place for a snack.''

"Where does that leave us?''

She shrugged. "I'm a pretty good lay.''

He stared into her eyes. Nothing special there. Just plain brown, like vinyl luggage. But wait a second, there was something there sparkling behind the steady gaze. Something.

She shook her head. "Look, I'm sorry. Sometimes I'm kind of crass. I don't mean anything. It's just that you meet a lot of creeps, so I go into my tough-broad act."

"What usually happens?"

"If they start slobbering, I tell them to follow my car to my apartment, then lose them in traffic on Wilshire Boulevard. You can believe me or not."

"I believe you," he said, but wasn't sure that he did. He wanted to though, so he didn't press it.

"C'mon," she said. "We'll go to my place and I'll make you some herbal tea or decaffeinated coffee or something healthy. We'll figure out the rest later."

"Want me to follow you in my car?"

She smiled. "I'll drive us. I can bring you back to your car later. Okay?"

He nodded and followed her through the parking lot. There were only three cars left. Hers was the yellow Ferrari with the roof off.

"The only thing I got from my divorce," she explained. "This car and a miscarriage."

Price climbed in, feet sliding into the tunnel under the dash. "Nice," he said, remembering the year he'd made enough money to buy a dozen of these babies in assorted colors. Now he was glad she wouldn't see his battered red VW Rabbit, parked in the alley behind Billy's.

"What was her name?" she asked.

"Pardon?"

"Your wife. What was her name?"

"Liza R."

"R? Was that her middle initial or something?"

"No. Part of her name. Liza R. Her parents were a little funky. Original bohemians. Black berets, obscure jazz, Ban the Bomb, the whole bit."

"Bohemians, huh? That near Spain?"

Price looked at her. "No, I mean—"

"I'm *joking*."

She smiled at him, and he wanted to kiss her right then, hold her tight, not say anything for maybe fifteen minutes. Just hug. Not spoil anything by rushing. The impulse was unusual for him, and it surprised him.

The motor growled to life, then purred gently.

She said, "How'd she die?"

Price was silent.

"If it's too personal," she said, "too painful . . ."

"An accident. A car accident." Another lie.

She didn't say anything. She shoved the gearshift into reverse and backed out of the stall, swinging around the lot and nosing onto deserted Westwood.

It occurred to Price that he didn't know her name. He debated asking her outright or just waiting for her to tell him, letting her play it her way. Finally he just said, "What's your name?"

"You don't know?" She sounded surprised. "I thought—"

Suddenly a squeal of tires sliced the lazy Westwood evening as a white car swerved out of a dark alley toward the Ferrari. She stomped on the brakes, causing the car to fishtail slightly.

"What the fuck are you guys doing?" she yelled as two men in business suits jumped out of the brand-new Mustang and ran toward them, pulling heavy black guns out from under their jackets.

Price didn't move. He recognized the style, if not the men, and realized for the first time that he'd been expecting them all along. He hadn't known when or where, but sooner or later he'd known they'd show. Nothing to do now but hope they were good shots.

He wasn't good at suffering.

2

The husky men on either side of the Ferrari gestured simultaneously with their guns.

"Hands on the dashboard, assholes," one of them said. "Move."

"Slow and easy," the other warned.

Price immediately slapped both his hands on top of the Ferrari's soft leather dashboard. He wasn't sure why they hadn't just shot him and left. He didn't ask.

"You too, lady," the one on Price's side growled. He held his .38 straight out with both hands, his face frozen in a no-nonsense scowl. His partner was more casual, leaning on the driver's door with one hand, resting the barrel of the gun on top of the windshield. Grinning a little. Showing off for the pretty woman.

"Just a goddamn minute," she said. "Who are you guys?"

"FBI, ma'am," the showoff on her side drawled as if he had to reach all the way back to Dixie for each word. "Now we'd 'preciate it if you'd both just do like we asked. Pronto."

"Let me see some ID first, buster."

The scowling guy on Price's side was about twenty-five, his sharp narrow face dominated by black horn-rimmed glasses with yellow-tinted lenses. Even through the yellow tinting Price could see he was getting angry. "Just get out of the car, both of you, and follow us. Now!"

She said, "We're not going anywhere till we see some ID, pal."

Price didn't want her to get in trouble on his account. He was the one they were after and he accepted what they had planned for him. Oddly, he wasn't even frightened. He turned to her and said calmly, "It's all right. Do as they say."

"Listen to him, lady."

"Like hell," she said.

"Hey, bitch—"

"Take it easy, Bill." The showy guy on her side grinned. "These folks got their rights." He dug an ID wallet out of his jacket, flipped it open to reveal a plastic card with some official lettering and a tiny photograph identifying FBI Agent Terrance Fine. "Satisfied?" he asked her.

"Yeah, well, I just wanted to make sure," she said, sounding a little contrite.

"Sure," Agent Fine sympathized. "Good-looking lady like you needs to be careful. Now, ma'am, if you'll just shut your ignition off and you and the gentleman get out and come with us, everything will be explained shortly." They both stepped back from the car to allow the doors to open.

"Right," she said, nodding.

Price didn't like it. Why involve her? It was him they wanted to tidy up some old business from seven years ago. He was angry that they were dragging her into it. Not that he was surprised. Their arrogance was without limit.

Without hesitating, Price yanked the door handle open. The scowling guy with the tinted glasses stepped back, lowering his gun slightly. But before Price could swivel his legs out, the car suddenly rocketed forward, tires screaming and smoking for half a block. Price was thrown backward into the car, his door flapping closed from the jolt. His head snapped back into the chest of the woman he'd met only a short while ago. She shoved him roughly off her, explaining, "Gotta shift."

Two shots boomed out from behind them before she'd swung the Ferrari around the corner onto another street. One of the bullets plowed a foot of yellow paint off Price's door. The second bullet whistled between them, continuing until it punched through the display window of a Tower Records store, setting off a clanging alarm.

Price glanced over his shoulder as they squealed around the corner, and glimpsed both men jumping into their white Mustang. "They're coming after us."

"I figured," she said, shifting into fourth and running a red light. The Ferrari roared straight down Westwood to Wilshire, then went into a sliding right turn that almost sent them into a slow-moving Datsun. The Datsun blared angrily, and Price could see the teenage driver mouthing obscenities as the Ferrari sped away.

"Doesn't this thing have any seat belts?" Price asked, groping around for a buckle.

"Just my side," she said. "Yours is broken."

"Great." He looked back over his shoulder, saw the white Mustang take a turn too sharply, bumping up over a curb, scraping the front bumper along the pavement in a shower of sparks. "They're still coming."

"Don't worry," she shouted over the rushing wind, "I've lost more eager men on this run than the FBI has fingerprints."

Price held on to the dashboard with both hands, studying her out of the corners of his eyes. Her brown eyes were fixed on the road, occasionally checking her rearview mirror, but there it was again, that steely glint within the dull brown, almost as if she were enjoying herself. But he couldn't figure why she'd risk her life to help him. It brought out his old suspicions.

Losing the Mustang proved to be as easy as she'd boasted. Flicking off the headlights, she turned down a few dark residential streets, dashed into a narrow alley and coasted down a delivery well of a Von's supermarket among mountains of empty produce boxes.

They sat silently, listening. The sweet cloying scent of overripe oranges mixed with the heavier smell of rotting bananas. When they were both certain the Mustang was lost amid the creeping night fog and sleepy side streets of Santa Monica, she started the engine.

"What's your name?" Price asked.

"Jo. Without an 'e.'"

"Well, Jo, thanks for getting me away from those guys. I really appreciate it."

She looked at him, surprised. "You? I thought they were after me."

3

Jo jiggled the key, jiggled the knob, then jiggled the whole door. "It's stuck again."

"Want me to try?"

"No, damn it. I've been opening it alone every other day for the past week. I can manage one more time." She lifted the knob, shouldered the door and twisted the key at the same time. It turned, the dead bolt retracting. She smiled. "See?"

"Sure your friend won't mind?" Price asked.

"What if she does? What choice do we have?"

Price nodded and entered the apartment. Jo's bluntness was getting a little depressing.

"Have a seat while I feed her fish." She gestured at the worn sofa while she marched straight for the twenty-gallon fish tank next to the TV. She opened a small can of fish food and sprinkled it on top of the water. Three fat fish darted up out of the seaweed.

"What kind are they?" Price asked. "The fish."

"I dunno. Pretty, though, huh?"

Price squinted at them. He'd known he needed glasses for almost a year now, but so far he'd avoided going to an optometrist to confirm his suspicion. Yet even without glasses, those three fish looked unnaturally ugly. "Yeah," he said, "pretty."

"Heather's up in Mammoth skiing this week. That is, if she has any time to ski while looking for a husband. If she can't find one for herself, she'll settle for anyone else's." She laughed, that same explosive laugh Price had delighted in earlier. "Good thing Heather's my best friend. Otherwise I could be *really* bitchy. It's hard, you know."

"What?"

"Having a best friend with a name like Heather. I mean, she looks like a Heather."

"What's a Heather look like?"

"Guess."

He shrugged. "I don't know. Kind of blond. Pert nose. A little ditsy. Looks good in a bikini."

"That's our Heather. Disgusting, huh?" She twisted the lid back on the fish-food can and flopped down onto the opposite end of the sofa, putting her feet up on the coffee table. "Well, at least we have a place to stay while we decide what to do next."

"Maybe we should start by figuring out which one of us they were after."

"Okay." She gave him a wicked smile, and suddenly she looked five years younger. "What'd you do?"

He studied her eyes, trying to see if she was kidding him, didn't really recognize him. But she gave away nothing in her expression. "You go first."

"Okay. Full name—Jo Dixon Montana. Occupation—insurance secretary. Age—none of your business. Let's just say that if I were a wine, I'd be valuable—if I were a cheese, you'd throw me out."

"Didn't you forget something?"

"What?"

"Why the FBI would be after you."

"Oh? I thought you could figure that out from my name. Jo *Montana*."

Price thought about it a moment. "God, yes. Jo and Steve Montana. You're the astronaut's wife."

She touched a finger to her nose. "Splashdown. Only make that *ex*-wife."

"Sure, I read about you once a few years ago. Your husband was up there in a space shuttle, *Enterprise*, I think—"

"*Columbia.*"

"Yeah, right. Anyway, he's up there for something like a month—"

"Twenty-four days."

"And when he finally gets home, you'd sold the house and furniture and moved from Houston to Los Angeles. Took him two days to find you."

"It was my house, my furniture. My daddy left them to me."

Price heard a twang in her speech. "Haven't completely lost that Texas accent, huh?"

"Just when I get emotional. I've almost got it licked. You can't live in California and sound like a shitkicker, or everybody thinks you're dumb."

Price doubted many would make that mistake about her. He shook his head and laughed.

"What's so funny?" She frowned.

"Relax, I'm not laughing at you. I swear on my one good cuff."

"Then what's so funny."

"It's just that the whole time you were worried that I might recognize you, I was afraid you'd recognize me."

She raised an eyebrow. "Why would I recognize you? You somebody?"

"Thanks a lot."

"You know what I mean."

"Yeah, I know. I'm Price Calender."

She pursed her lips, nibbled the lower one as if deep in thought. Finally she shook her head. "Sorry, doesn't ring a bell."

" 'Rock 'n' Roll Drive-In.' 'Don't Tell Maggie.' 'Palisades Drag.' "

"Oh, Gawwd!" she squealed, and covered her face. She peeked through her fingers and grinned. "We used to dance to you all the time. Jimmy Tubeck finally got his hand inside my bra in his daddy's Buick while you sang 'Tattooed Tina.' Gawd. Whatever happened to you?"

"Nothing. I kind of lost interest for a while. Then the record companies lost interest in me. The past few years I've been touring again with my own band. Opening act in Vegas for Gladys Knight and the Pips. Or playing the Iowa State Fair on an oldies-but-goodies lineup. Nothing splashy, but it pays the bills. Hell, all my hits came in a two-year period. I wasn't exactly established on the pop scene."

Jo pulled the hem of her skirt up past her knee and scratched her shapely thigh through the panty hose. Then she flicked the skirt down again. "Funny, huh? I mean, most people think it's great to be famous, even for the little bit they were. But you know something?" A slow grin spread across her face. "They're right! It *is* great!"

Price smiled.

"Oh, sure, there's some bad stuff. Like once you've been famous it's hard to be taken seriously as anything else. I'm always going to be the 'astronaut's wife.' "

"Yeah." Price nodded. "Or being washed up by the time you're thirty-four. Spending the rest of your life on the comeback trail."

"Wondering if people are interested in you, or just celebrity hunting. So they can tell their friends they fucked the 'astronaut's wife.'"

They fell silent a few minutes, each staring at the three ugly fish.

Jo looked over at Price. "But why would the FBI want a washed-up rock 'n' roll singer?"

"'Washed-up singer.' What are you, Jo, the Bruce Lee of tact? I had some dealings with the government while I was still on top and doing all that world traveling. *Before* I was washed up."

"All right, I'm sorry. Geez, touchy."

"Things didn't work out exactly as planned and I walked away. They told me I couldn't walk away. I guess they finally got around to making good on their threat."

"What were you, a spy or something?"

Price frowned. "Nothing so dramatic." She waited, but he didn't elaborate. "What about you? Being the ex-wife of an astronaut doesn't qualify as a federal offense, does it?"

"You don't know Steve Montana. He's got friends everywhere. He walks up to some guy he's never met, they talk for twenty minutes, and suddenly they're best buddies. The guy'll do anything for him. It's spooky. I guess he still can't figure how I could've left him. He still calls and writes and begs for us to get back again. I think he's planning to run for office and he doesn't want this failure on his record. He's very anal that way."

"That doesn't explain those guys shooting at us."

"No, it doesn't. I thought Steve might've sent them to bring me to him. When I pulled away I didn't really think they'd *shoot*." She looked at Price. "I guess that leaves you and your mysterious past as the target."

"I guess."

Jo stretched her arms above her head and yawned, her mouth gaping. She made no effort to cover it or the foghorn sound that accompanied the yawn. She glanced at her watch. "Guess we better get some sleep. We should be safe here for a few hours."

"Now that we know they're after me," Price said, "you can take off. I'll lock up when I leave in the morning."

"I wish. But you forget, it was *my* car we made our getaway in. I think it's safe to assume they got my license number and are waiting at my apartment for us."

"Right. I forgot."

"Some spy."

"I wasn't a spy."

"Whatever. I think we should both stay here until morning. Then you can split. That way, when I go home and they question me, I won't know where you've gone."

"Makes sense."

She stood up, kicked off her shoes, slipped out of her lamb's wool sweater and started toward the bedroom. "Well?"

"What?"

"You coming to bed? It's a queen size, plenty of room." She grinned. "You've got enough troubles. No need for you getting cramps from sleeping on the sofa, too."

For some reason Price felt nervous—not his usual attitude with women. Maybe it was her bluntness, the way she seemed to say whatever popped into her head. Maybe something else. Whatever the reason, it didn't keep him from following her into the bedroom.

"Just what you'd expect from a Heather, isn't it?" she asked, nodding at the bed as she unbuttoned her blouse—the bed was lined with a dozen stuffed animals. Beneath the blouse was a bra the color of cranberry, which cupped pale breasts. She removed the blouse and laid it carefully over the wooden rocker by the window. The window and the rocker were both crammed with stuffed animals. "Sick," she said, shaking her head at them as she unzipped her skirt.

Price unbuttoned his shirt while watching her undress.

"It's hard to believe this is the bedroom of a woman known to have slept with two men and another woman at the same time. Right here in this same bed." She stepped out of her skirt and slip. She wore no underpants beneath her panty hose. The thick pubic hairs were matted into a dark patch. She placed her hands on her hips. "I mean, I know she's my best friend and all, but doesn't that sound a little kinky to you?"

"Sounds crowded," Price said. He was busy fumbling open his belt. He wished she'd say "gawd" again. He loved it when she said that.

A loud noise from the living room echoed through the apartment. The sound of the front door swinging open and slamming into the wall. Heavy footsteps marching toward them.

Absurdly Price zipped his fly. Then he looked over at Jo, but she didn't move.

Three men hustled into the room, two of them waving guns. The third man glanced at Jo, then at Price, his face expressionless.

Jo, wearing only her bra, panty hose and pearls, walked up to the third man and shoved her wrist with her watch under his nose. "Gawd, Dees, you know how late you guys are?"

4

The man in the two-thousand-dollar suit walked across the Manhattan schoolyard, each step grinding bits of broken glass under his five-hundred-dollar shoes. There was no point trying to avoid the glass—it was everywhere. Little gem-sized chunks of brown and green and clear from smashed soda and beer bottles that students threw in at night as a sign of contempt. Years of such abuse had given the blacktop a sheen of powdered glass that made the playground glisten in the sun like a mountain lake. Yet, despite the crushed glass, the man made hardly a sound as he walked.

There—the one dribbling the basketball was who he'd come to see.

She was the only woman among the group of five young men. She was hunched over, dribbling the ball with great control, using her lithe body to protect the ball. The young black kid guarding her was about seventeen, fifteen years younger than she, and about a foot taller. He reached in to swat the ball away and she quickly rolled to the right, cutting straight for the basket. A lanky Irish kid left his man to block her path to the basket. She could have passed the ball off to her unguarded teammate then, but the man in the expensive suit knew she wouldn't. She leaped into the air, her tanned muscled legs bunched for power, and slammed her hip into the Irish kid's jaw with a *thwack*. The kid staggered back a few steps as the woman lofted the ball toward the basket. It banked off the backboard and dropped through the chain net without touching the rim.

The Irish kid was leaning against the pole, wiping the blood from his mouth. He tested a few teeth to see how loose they were. Everyone gathered around him.

"You okay?" she asked him, her face furrowed with concern.

"Sure," he said, nodding, but a mist of blood accompanied his words. He squared his shoulders, assured everyone he was fine. They patted his back and butt, clapped hands and returned to the court.

The man in the suit watched from a distance. He wouldn't call to her, not wanting everyone to hear his lingering Slavic accent. There was no need to go closer, anyway. Though she hadn't looked directly at him or acknowledged his presence in any way, he knew she'd seen him. She missed nothing.

He stuck his hands in his pants pockets and felt the keys to his Mercedes, his Central Park apartment, his secret storage room. His possessions. It made the waiting easier.

The tall black kid she was guarding had the ball now. He faked to the left, caught her off balance, then went right. But she recovered quickly and reached in as he dribbled by, and pushed the ball away from him in middribble. The black kid tried to grab it back, but one of her teammates wrestled it away from him and made an easy lay-up. The black kid stomped his foot and swore.

The man in the suit smirked. He allowed himself to admire her body awhile, the lean tight muscles that flowed like some powerful river under her smooth skin.

Looking at her face, you wouldn't say she was beautiful exactly. The eyes were too large, the nose a little crooked, the hair a little wild. But in a roomful of *Vogue* models, she would be the one face you'd stare at most, the person you'd contrive to meet. That was part of what made her so valuable. And, of course, her special skills.

The man in the expensive blue suit had made love to her once, two years ago, the last time they'd worked together. He'd had sex with many women in his life, from diplomats' wives to thousand-dollar-a-night whores, exotic women from all over the world. None had been as adventurous, as energetic as she was. Despite the carnal pleasure, he remembered it as almost a contest of wills, a martial-arts match of throws and takedowns. One that he lost. Yet he'd give anything to lose again.

They'd never made love again. It was as if she'd lost interest. The next night he knocked on her door expectantly. When she opened it, she was standing there with another woman, sipping red wine. Both were in robes, their skins shining with a sweat produced only one way.

The assignment had been successful. They'd both received bonuses. He had not seen her since, but he'd thought of her often. The stories he'd heard about her since then from others in the business were even stranger, more mysterious. No one was foolish enough to ask her questions about her past directly.

The basketball game was over. She wiped her face with the hem of her T-shirt, exposing part of her bra. Then she waved to the street kids as they walked away. She was coming toward him now, and he noticed the kids all turn and stare at her as she walked away. They

34

grinned and whispered to one another and licked their thirsty lips.

"Nice suit, Alexei," she said, pinching the lapel between sweaty fingers.

"Alex," he corrected her.

She laughed. "That accent is still as thick as potato soup. I thought you were taking speech lessons or something."

"For three years now."

"Fire him, man. You've been robbed."

They started walking across the playground toward Sullivan Street. Greenwich Village was pretty deserted even for an early Tuesday morning.

"We have an assignment," he said sternly, trying to maintain some authority.

"No kidding." She was sarcastic, as usual.

"We must leave within the hour."

"No problem."

A young couple in jogging shorts and shoes ran by. The man and the woman waited until the couple was half a block away before they resumed their conversation. "You want the details now?" he asked.

She shrugged.

"The masked dog is loose."

She hesitated for only a second, then continued walking. "That could be dangerous." No fear, just professional challenge.

"Indeed, dangerous."

"I thought he had been destroyed."

"So did we all. Apparently you Americans are not as stupid as you sometimes seem."

She ignored him. He wanted to shake her from her smug attitude. He decided to play his trump card. "There's a secondary target."

"Oh?" Nothing unusual.

"You know this one."

"That will make it easier."

"Yes," the man in the blue suit said with a grin. "His name is Price Calender."

She stopped dead and turned to face him. Her eyes seemed even bigger now, her mouth thin and dangerous. He had expected some reaction, but nothing quite so intense.

"You're sure?" she asked.

"Yes, Liza R. I'm sure."

Liza R nodded. "Good."

5

Price Calender sat alone in a tiny white room in a large white building in downtown Washington, D.C., nursing a Dr. Pepper from the machine down the hall. He didn't need the caffeine to stay awake—Rawlings's grubby note had already taken care of that. He'd barely been aware of the flight, the drive from Dulles airport, the elevator ride. He thought only of the message on the greasy napkin. *The masked dog is loose.*

He looked around the small room. It had been seven years since he'd been in this building, in this room. Seven years since he'd had anything to do with these people. The two leather chairs were new; so was the fancy chrome floor lamp. And the end table. That was all the furniture the room could comfortably hold. The bullet hole he'd made in the wall seven years ago had been mended.

Price picked at the charred threads of his shirt cuff. There had been no time to change or pack. They'd hustled him straight from that apartment to LAX in time for a half-empty TWA nonstop to Washington. Dees on one side of him, Jo Montana on the other. There was no movie. No one spoke. Dees slept fitfully, waking abruptly when they were over Kansas as if from a bad dream. The astronaut's ex-wife read *The Fountainhead* by Ayn Rand. Price noticed she skipped ahead to the end, read the last few pages, then went back to

37

her marker in the middle of the book. That annoyed him almost as much as her tricking him back in L.A., but he didn't say anything. What for?

The tiny white room reminded Price of that shabby recording studio in North Hollywood where he, Trinidad and Barney had cut their first single, "Chains of Lace." They'd personally handed a copy to every deejay in L.A., with a ten dollar bill tucked inside the record sleeve for a selected few. Small-time stuff, considering what a lot of the deejays were pulling down from the major record companies, but Price had sold his VW·bug and borrowed another five-hundred from his grandmother to pay for the recording session. They *had* to make it work.

That was 1971—a bad year for rock 'n' roll. Sax man King Curtis was stabbed to death in a fight in New York City on Friday the thirteenth. Duane Allman was killed in a motorcycle crash in Macon, Georgia. Jim Morrison died of a heart attack and was buried in the Poets' Corner of the Père Lachaise Cemetery in Paris. Junior Parker, Gene Vincent and Donald McPherson all died. So did "Chains of Lace."

The record got some air time, even sold a few hundred singles, but not enough to interest any R and D guys from RCA or Columbia to handle national distribution. Trinidad took a couple hundred of the unsold singles from Price's garage and used them for target practice with his 12-gauge shotgun, his kid brother throwing them in the air and Trinidad blowing them apart. Barney decided to quit rock 'n' roll and go back to premed at UCLA. When he told his parents, they gave him a new Fiat.

Two years later, a month after Jim Croce died in a plane crash, Price and Trinidad were back in that same

crummy North Hollywood studio with two new guys—
Zip Larson and Kenny Edmunds—recording "Off-
ramp Life." This time it was picked up by some new R
and D whiz kid from Elektra, whose younger sister had
played "Chains of Lace" for him a couple of years back.
Six months after Mama Cass choked to death, "Off-
ramp Life" cracked *Billboard*'s top ten.

Two more hits followed, and a successful U.S. tour.
They were making plans for a world tour to promote
their new album. It looked like nothing could stop
them.

And then, one night after a sold-out concert at the
Universal Amphitheater in Los Angeles, he met Liza
R.

"My God, Price," Rawlings said as he entered the
tiny white room. "What happened to your beard?"

Price tilted his Dr. Pepper can at the patch of scalp
showing at the back of Rawlings's head. "What happened to your hair?"

"Fell out." He ran his hand over the spot, examined
his fingers to see if they'd dislodged any more loose
hairs, then smiled. "It's like a variation of Pinocchio.
Every time I tell a lie, another one drops out. Guess I
should be glad to have any hair left then, huh?" He
closed the door behind him and set his coffee mug on
the table. He studied Price, shook his head. "Hard to
get used to you without that Robin Hood beard. Practically your trademark, wasn't it?"

Price leaned back into his chair. No point in rushing
Rawlings. He had his own way. "It turned gray."

"Just your beard?"

"Yeah. About five years ago I started getting some
gray splotches on either side of my jaw. Three years ago
they were solid white, like I'd been dribbling oatmeal

down my chin. My audiences are in their thirties, coming to remember their wild youth, not be reminded of their graying parents." He picked a burned thread loose from his cuff. "Didn't much feel like dyeing it, I guess."

Rawlings chuckled. "Remember Patterson? The gung-ho kid who chauffeured your limo when you played Berlin."

Price looked surprised. "He was one of yours?"

"Of course. Yeah, I know he looked about eighteen, but he was twenty-seven. Anyway, he grows this thick black beard as part of his cover down in Argentina. I mean, this kid's seen *Serpico* a hundred times, is really into this authentic disguise stuff. He's infiltrated a group of Latin terrorists and is sleeping in their hideout. Suddenly the whole place goes up in flames. They've been firebombed by a rival group. Patterson's fucking beard catches on fire. Half a dozen of the others are killed, but he comes through without a scratch, except for his beard burning off. We jet the kid back here pronto, but his skin's the texture of a raw cabbage. The doctors graft on skin from his butt to his chin. Operation is successful, hardly see any scars. Only thing is, he's got these wiry little hairs growing out of his chin that look kinda funny." Rawlings chuckled again.

Price sipped his Dr. Pepper. The carbonation sizzled in the silence like static.

Rawlings leaned his bulk back into the leather chair. His smile hardened, leaving only those small dark eyes staring. "So much for old times, eh, Price?"

Price pointed at the smooth white wall. "I see they fixed the hole."

"What hole?"

"The bullet hole. Last time we saw each other I tried to kill you."

"Oh, was that you?"

Price smiled. "You haven't changed, Rawlings. Still the biggest bullshit jockey around. Lucky for you I was always such a bad shot. Missed you completely."

Rawlings pushed up his left sleeve. The tail of a white worm-sized scar stuck out above his hairy wrist. "Not such a bad shot, Price."

Price was startled. It had been a wild shot, fired in anger, not really meant to hit anyone, just to release his thundering rage. He'd seen the bullet bore into that wall next to the door. It must have grazed Rawlings first, though at the time Rawlings hadn't even flinched. A couple of agents had jumped Price and roughly dragged him out of there. That was the last time he'd seen Rawlings. Still, it gave Price no satisfaction to know he'd actually hit Rawlings, even such a minor wound. Yes, he'd been part of it, but Price had already killed the one he'd wanted dead. The one who'd deserved it. Liza R.

"How's the comeback doing?" Rawlings asked. "Any record deals in the making?"

"Let's get to it, okay, Rawlings? I got your note. I'm here. You've got a lot of explaining to do."

Rawlings fished around in his rumpled jacket pocket a moment, brought out a crushed pack of Winstons. The cigarettes looked to Calender as if they'd been bought the same day as the jacket, back around 1973. He shook one loose and offered it to Price.

Price reached for it, stopped in midair and shook his head. "No, thanks."

"No? Christ, you used to put away three packs a day back when you were touring."

Price couldn't believe how civilized they were acting with all this chitchat about record deals and smoking. Like nothing had ever happened. Yet there was some relief in talking to the only person still alive who knew everything that had happened back then. He looked at Rawlings and said, "I'm trying to quit."

Rawlings shoved the wrinkled pack back into his wrinkled jacket. "Commendable, I suppose," he said, sounding doubtful. He gave Price a long, hard once-over. "What the hell happened to you, Price? Your eyes have circles so dark you look like a fucking coal miner."

"Insomnia."

"How long?"

Price gave him a cold look. "Guess."

"Yeah, right. Seven years."

"On and off. Comes and goes."

Rawlings sipped from his coffee, his eyes staring into Price's over the rim of the cup. He made a sour face and set the cup back down. "They can put a man on the moon, but they can't make a decaffeinated coffee I like." He laughed, the laugh quickly degenerating into a weary sigh. "I guess you want to hear about it."

"Yeah, I want to hear about it."

Rawlings hopped out of the chair with a deftness not expected of someone his size. "I've got a VCR out in the hall. Let me wheel it in here. The tapes will explain everything."

"Why don't we just go to the screening room upstairs? There's more room and all the equipment's already set up."

"Security."

Price grinned. "Meaning you don't want anybody to know you've brought me in on this. Rattling old bones and all."

"That's what I said. Security. My job security." He opened the door, wedged it with one foot and tried to drag in the cart with the TV monitor and VCR while still holding the door. He struggled, banging the cart into the doorjamb a few times. His foot slipped a bit and the door bumped his butt. He looked over his shoulder at Price.

Price did not offer to help.

6

"Kind of a smart-ass, isn't he?" Dees said, tapping Price's face on the monitor screen.

Jo didn't respond. She didn't like Dees, his smug slick manner. She didn't like sitting here in this dark room two floors above the room Rawlings and Calender were in, watching them on the hidden camera. She didn't like the way she smelled after being on a plane for six hours, in a car for one and in this building for two. She didn't like the way she'd hustled the same guy who'd written a couple of her favorite old songs. She hadn't been totally honest when she'd told Price about Jimmy Tubeck getting his hand under her bra during "Tattooed Tina." Horny little Jimmy had gotten much farther than that.

The TV screen glowed blue in the dark room. In the upper left hand corner of the screen, the date and the time were displayed. Dees adjusted a couple of knobs, which made no noticeable difference as far as Jo could see, but he seemed satisfied after a while and nodded. His tinkering reminded Jo of the way her ex-husband would fiddle with the stereo for fifteen minutes just so they could hear one song. Balance, bass, treble, Dolby, equalizer and a dozen other knobs to play with as if he were still in the shuttle. He approached sex the same way, as if he were bringing her in for a landing.

"C'mon, Rawlings," Dees muttered to himself, "how hard is it to plug that sucker in?"

On screen, Rawlings was maneuvering the cart with the VCR and TV against the wall. He leaned over and jiggled the plug into the socket. *"This equipment's practically shot to hell,"* he told Calender. *"Turns out some of the personnel have been using it to tape TV shows while they were on duty."*

He was pointing to a red sticker pasted on the front of the cart. Jo leaned forward, but couldn't make it out on the small screen.

"Official Use Only," Rawlings read to Calender. *"We had to buy a shitload of these things and paste 'em on every piece of equipment in the building. It's not like Langley here—security's a little looser. You know what these stickers run? Cost the taxpayers $1,258. We're talking in the middle of a budget crunch."*

"This is a small room, Rawlings," Price said. *"How much more bullshit do you think you can squeeze in here?"*

Dees cackled and looked at Jo. "You believe this guy?" He shook his head, answering his own question.

Jo stared at the screen. The white digital readout of the time was superimposed right over Calender's face, so she couldn't read his expression. But his voice, even through the distortion of the speaker, sounded a little—she was probably imagining this—hurt. She remembered the look in his eyes when that prick Dees and his henchmen had finally arrived at the apartment. The plan had called for her to get Price outside the bar, and they would pick him up. But those two phony FBI punks had interfered, and Dees had ended up chasing after them. She'd had no choice then but to play it by ear. She hadn't meant for it to go as far as it

had, his standing there half-undressed when Dees arrived, but it had all come about so naturally, the two of
them drifting toward bed. Maybe too naturally, she
wondered.

Still, that look in his eyes when Dees came into the
bedroom. Not angry or betrayed, really. That's what
she'd expected; that's what she'd steeled herself for.
Obscenities at least, maybe some spit in the face. But
his reaction was unexpected: silence and a sadness in
the eyes, like disappointment. She would have preferred spit.

Jo pulled out a Camel and stuck it between her lips.
She rummaged through her purse for matches, found
Calender's Bic lighter. She thumbed it into a flame.

"No smoking in here," Dees reminded her without
taking his eyes from the screen.

"Forgot," she said, dropping lighter and cigarette
into her purse.

*"These tapes show some of what's been going on with the
Masked Dog Project over the past seven years, since you
were last involved."* Rawlings pried open one of three
brown vinyl cases and removed the black plastic cas-
sette. He slipped it into the Panasonic VCR, grabbed
the remote control unit and settled back into his leather
chair.

"One question first," Price said. *"And you damn well
know what it is."*

Rawlings shook his head. *"What do you mean,
Price?"*

Dees snorted. "Attaboy, boss. Don't give an inch."

*"I mean that the Masked Dog Project was supposed to
have been abandoned seven years ago. Completely dis-
mantled. And the Masked Dog was supposed to be destroyed. We'd made a deal."*

"I tried, Price. I was overruled. No appeal."

Jo nudged Dees. "What are they talking about? What's the Masked Dog Project?"

"Ssshhh," Dees said. "It gets better. Rawlings is so sincere and folksy, like Captain Kangaroo. God, he's good."

"Okay now," Rawlings said. *"This is what's happened to the Masked Dog since you last saw him."*

Jo watched him flick the Play button on the remote unit. At the same time a second monitor in front of her and Dees showed a similar picture. She noticed Price Calender leaning forward, his face now clear of the digital readout. His expression was intense.

PRICE HUNCHED FORWARD, squinting a little with his bad eyes. He planted his elbows on his knees, steepling his fingers around his mouth and nose like an oxygen mask. Watching the familiar faces fill the screen was like gazing through a portal to his past. A past that he had not been able to escape during the last seven years, even in sleep.

"This part's mostly background stuff. You already know it." Rawlings pressed the Forward Search button on the remote unit. The tape flickered by at an accelerated rate.

"No," Price said. "Let's see it all. It's like my family album, right?"

Rawlings shrugged, pressed a button. The tape resumed at normal speed. Candid photographs of all the individuals involved were presented, followed by brief biographical data on each. Dr. Frank Elder. Price Calender. Liza R. And, of course, Gifford S. Devane . . . the Masked Dog.

The profiles were remarkably complete. Yet there was much omitted from each, in some cases on purpose. In some cases because only the two men sitting in this room knew the complete facts.

"So, Dr. Frank Elder is still running the project, huh?" Price said, watching the doctor's bio flash in front of him. The photographs revealed a tall, gaunt, unsmiling man who obviously took himself very seriously.

"I'll update you after the tapes," Rawlings said mysteriously.

Price's own bio was accurate. Born in Riverside, California, 1950. Father sold advertising time for local radio station. Mother taught art history at University of California at Riverside. Both living in Florida now. They even had Price's first prom photo. His maroon tuxedo a size too small and his date, Darlene Hill, a size too tall. He'd liked leggy athletic women even then. They had photos of Barney, Trinidad and Price practicing in Barney's parents' backyard, next to the pool they'd promised to clean afterward as payment. The three of them playing at a high-school dance. A few dark and dismal joints in Los Angeles. A peace rally near the VA Hospital. Photos of the new group on tour. Standing with the Beach Boys. Joni Mitchell. Neil Young. The Eagles. Holding their gold and platinum albums. And some more recent photos Price hadn't known were taken. Price walking toward his one-bedroom Westwood apartment. Coming out of Billy's. At the San Diego Zoo with his daughter, Rebecca.

"Kept up on me, didn't you?" he said, controlling his anger.

"Standard procedure, Price."

"Oh, then it's okay...."

Liza R's face bloomed upon the screen and Price stopped talking. She was, as always, smiling. There was no hint of what lay behind that friendly smile, what she was really capable of. Price studied the face as if it were a jigsaw puzzle he'd assembled incorrectly. Everything looked right, but somehow, somewhere, he must have forced a piece to fit, throwing the rest of the puzzle off.

There was no accompanying bio. Just a paragraph informing them that whatever background information they'd gathered from acquaintances had not checked out upon investigation. As far as they were concerned, they had no reliable information as to her origins or anything that she'd done before meeting Price Calender that June evening at the Universal Amphitheater.

There were more photographs. Of her alone. In cut-off jeans and T-shirt, holding one of Price's albums, pinching her nose with her thumb and finger and making a sour face. Of the two of them, her head nestled lovingly against his shoulder while he played the guitar—probably that song he'd written especially for her. Of the three of them, Price and Liza R each holding one of Rebecca's tiny hands as they swung her over a puddle. Of Liza R dead. Bruised and bleeding. The way Price had left her.

Price stood slowly, moving between the screen and Rawlings. He clamped his hand around Rawlings's wrist, the one holding the remote control unit. Price squeezed until Rawlings's fingers opened, dropping the unit onto his lap.

"You're much stronger than before." Rawlings's bland expression showed none of the stinging pain he felt in his wrist. "All that Nautilus stuff must have helped."

Price squeezed even harder. A bone in Rawlings's wrist shifted.

"That hurts," Rawlings said calmly.

"I know." Price stared at the section chief almost a full minute. His eyes were glacial. Finally he released Rawlings's wrist, turned and walked out the door.

Rawlings remained seated, rubbing the numbness from his wrist. This was not the same Price Calender of seven years ago. He was a harder man, colder. Good, he'd need that. Rawlings glanced up to the section of wall where he knew the camera was hidden. "Don't go after him, Dees. He'll be back." Then to himself, "He's got nowhere else to go."

"WHAT'D HE SAY?" Dees asked. "Right after, 'He'll be back.' He said something."

Jo shook her head. "I couldn't make it out."

"Wow. You see what he just did to Rawlings? That guy's more nuts than I thought."

"Dees." Rawlings was looking at the camera again. "I think he's had enough memories for now. We'll skip ahead to the current stuff. Fill Jo in on the rest."

"Tote that barge, lift that spy," Dees said.

"Where'd he go?" Jo asked. "Calender."

"Let's find out." Dees punched a few buttons on the console and the image of Rawlings, sitting in the leather chair, jiggling his foot impatiently, was replaced by an overhead view of the corridor outside that room. It was empty. "Come out, come out, wherever you are," Dees sang, fiddling with more controls. Another corridor appeared on the screen, also empty.

"Not many people here today," Jo said. "This a slow day for the Agency?"

Dees shrugged. "That floor is always pretty deserted. You have to have a special clearance to gain access. It's where we brief and debrief people we don't want everyone else to know about. Don't worry, Calender can't leave the floor." He punched another button and a small room with a wall of vending machines and a microwave oven appeared. "Bingo," Dees said.

Price Calender was standing at the soft-drink machine, stuffing a couple of quarters into the slot. He stabbed a button and a can of Pepsi plopped down the chute. He lifted the tab, took a sip, then pressed the cold can to his forehead.

Jo studied his face, could almost feel the torment wringing his features. Suddenly she felt dirty and disgusted with herself, like a Peeping Tom. "Change it."

"Huh?" Dees said.

"Change the channel, or whatever you do. Leave him alone."

"Ten bucks says we see a real tear."

Jo reached in front of Dees, jostling him with her elbow, and jabbed a couple buttons. Price vanished from the screen, and was replaced with an overhead shot of the men's room. A man was standing at the urinal, shaking the last drops from his penis.

Dees turned to her and smiled. "My, my. So this is what an astronaut's wife does for kicks."

"Ex-wife," she corrected. "Now fill me in."

Dees adjusted the console so the screen was back in the tiny room with Rawlings, then turned around to face her. He picked fussily at the lapel of his beige sport jacket until he'd flicked something so small, Jo couldn't even see it. "These rooms are filthy. Nobody ever dusts

51

in here. Not like Langley, boy." He leaned against the console and crossed his arms. "This whole Masked Dog Project is before my time. I was out in the field then. I'd heard some rumors, some really scary rumors, but nothing clear. It wasn't until yesterday I got to read the file. And let me tell you—" he frowned "—it's worse than the rumors."

"So Price Calender was an agent?"

"Him? No way. More like a dupe."

Jo shook her head. "I don't get it."

Dees turned around, punched some buttons. The images from the videotape on the second screen began to reverse at a high speed. He stopped the tape at a close-up of Liza R. "Ta-da. Mrs. Price Calender. Liza R."

Jo stared at the face with a little jealousy. It was the kind of face that belonged to the girl all the boys would gladly dump their cheerleader or yearbook-editor girlfriends for. It wasn't the beauty; she was only marginally pretty, with that crooked nose and wild hair. It was the taunting expression, the feeling you got looking into those sharp eyes that this woman knew what she wanted and how to get it. That she didn't give a shit about rules or taboos. She wanted what she wanted, and if you hung around her, some of that energy might spill onto you like magic fairy dust. The sensuality and raw sexiness in that face were undeniable. Men would claw over one another to get near her. And women would admire and fear her. Jo could certainly understand why Price Calender had married her.

Jo gazed into the too-wide eyes with fascination. Jo had always been popular. In high school she'd been prom queen, in college homecoming queen. Her parents had raised her to be the perfect Texas lady, bred for marriage like the horses they raised on their ranch. She'd had plenty of opportunity, men calling with expensive gifts all the time. Her parents kept the gifts displayed in the den as if they were some kind of trophies she'd won playing tennis or golf. She'd even slept with a few of the men, thinking to get serious about them, but she couldn't work up the enthusiasm. Finally she'd had her fill of rich dinners and country-club chatter. She knew she had to do something. But what? What was she qualified to do with her degree in Romance languages, all of which she spoke with a heavy Texas accent?

Her father unknowingly solved that problem. Being a strong Republican booster, he hosted a fund-raiser for a Republican presidential candidate making a swing through the state. Jo didn't agree with either her father's or the candidate's politics, but since her mother was ill, she agreed to act as hostess. Bored and just a little tipsy, she forced one young man to dance with her. He turned out to be a Secret Service guard for the candidate. At first she asked him about his job to be polite, but as he spoke, she became fascinated. "Any women in the Service?" she'd asked. "Some," he'd said, winking. "But we're always looking for a few good women." Within six months, Jo Dixon was training in Washington.

"Think you've memorized the face by now?" Dees prodded.

"Yes."

"Well, here's another shot you'll want to remember." He fast-forwarded the tape, and the hypnotic face was replaced by another photograph of her. Only in this one she was on a stretcher, her eyes closed, her face bruised and bleeding. Her skin was ashen. "Yeah, she's dead."

"What happened?" Jo asked.

"Calender killed her. Ran her down with a Jeep."

Jo looked at him. "He what?"

"Don't look so shocked. I'm no great fan of Price Calender's, but if anyone had it coming, it was this lady here." He leaned closer to the screen, staring at her photo. "Damn shame. A woman like that..." He sighed. "Anyway, it scans something like this. Price Calender is your usual rock 'n' roll star. A couple of hits, money, groupies. The American Wet Dream, am I right? Okay, maybe he's not exactly like the others. One thing, I admit, he really takes his music seriously. Another is that no drugs are allowed, not even some friendly pot. He lays down this rap about not wanting to do anything to jeopardize the group, but the guy is basically straight, nothing stronger than a cigarette, some beer."

"You sound as if you disapprove," Jo said.

"You been to many Washington parties?"

"Enough." Hardly a day went by when she was here that someone didn't invite her to "an important Washington function."

"Then you've seen your share of joints and coke at these parties."

Jo nodded. "Sometimes."

"You approve?"

She'd shared a few joints with a congressional aide or two. She'd stayed away from coke, fearing she might like it. "What's your point, Dees?"

"Calender's group was one of the hottest, bridging the hippie protesters and ROTC nerds. He had it all, man." Dees shrugged. "Hell, I guess I just don't like him."

For some reason she didn't understand, that angered Jo. "Let's get back to the briefing."

"Right. Anyway, even Mr. Clean wasn't above an occasional dalliance with a nubile young groupie, though he wasn't involved with anyone. Until Liza R."

"She have a last name?"

"None we know about. The one she gave our boy Price was Benson. It doesn't check out." He twisted around to check the screen. Rawlings was glancing at his watch. Dees faced Jo again. "So one night after a smash sellout concert at Universal Amphitheater, this mysterious woman appears, toting a three-year-old daughter. The woman is gorgeous, intelligent, witty, sexy. Every guy at the party is trying to hit on her, but she only has eyes for our hero. They fall in love, get married, promise to rock 'n' roll forever, and he adopts her daughter, Rebecca." Dees advances the tape to a still of Rebecca. She has her mother's spunky good looks, but also a warmth to the eyes that her mother lacks. "Cute kid, huh?"

"Yeah," Jo said evenly. Kids made her nervous. While married to Steve, that's all he'd wanted. She'd tried at first, but the effort had resulted in a miscarriage. Later she'd realized their marriage wasn't going to match the shelf life of yogurt. But lately she'd become more aware of her own biological clock, and some maternal urgings she'd never felt before. They confused and frightened her.

"Well, Liza R goes on tour with the group, all over Europe and Asia. They're selling more records in Japan than the U.S. Price takes to being a husband and daddy like a religious convert. The guy and his daughter are inseparable. Everything's *Rolling Stone* heaven. Then the bad news. They come back into the U.S. and Customs officers do a seams-of-your-underwear search. They come up with enough dope to turn on more people than Marilyn Chambers.''

"I thought he was against that stuff."

"Price didn't know anything about it."

Jo nodded. "Liza R?"

"Liza R. She'd been dealing in every damn country. Hid the stuff in her daughter's toys and clothing. How do you like that?"

"It stinks."

Dees laughed. "It gets better. Price gets offered a deal—while he's visiting all these exotic places, his government wants him to make a few secret pickups and deliveries. Otherwise Uncle Sammy is gonna stomp his grapes. They'll all go to jail. Well, Price doesn't have any choice. He protects his family and his group and agrees. Only Price and Liza R and the Agency, represented by our own Mr. Rawlings, know about the deal."

"So Price became a courier."

"A mule," Dees said unkindly. "But here's the cute part. Guess who tipped us off about the dope in the first place."

Jo's eyes widened. "No!"

"Yup. Little Liza R. We didn't track that info down until later, after she was already dead. She'd made a deal with Rawlings's superior, and he didn't tell anyone until she was dead."

"So she *wanted* to go to work for you guys."

"Damn right. The dope was a red herring. She was after the Masked Dog Project."

"What the hell *is* that?"

"Patience, lady. Don't they teach that over in Secret Service?" He advanced the tape. A long unsmiling face stared out. It had the look of a man who preferred squashing flies with his thumb rather than a swatter. "This is Dr. Frank Elder, director of the Masked Dog Project. Friendly puss, huh? Say, didn't you go to Texas A & M?"

"Yes," Jo said.

"Well, he taught there once. Before your time. Taught psychology at two or three schools before his real gift emerged. Grant writing. Son of a bitch wrote a hell of a grant proposal. Started getting government money, and ta-da, a star is born. His most controversial project was to take a newborn child and begin videotaping his life from the moment of birth. His own son. Every moment of the child's life, waking or sleeping, was recorded for the first five years of his life. And I'm talking every single *second* of his life. His friends had to come over to his house to play—he wasn't allowed to go to theirs."

"Gawd, poor kid."

"The cameras inside the house were hidden from view, and outside everyone thought the parents were just home-movie freaks. After the kid turned six, they had to send him to school, so the taping became less comprehensive."

"What was the point?" Jo asked angrily.

"Hey, don't bark at me. It wasn't my idea. Dr. Frank Elder had this theory that if you knew everything that happened to a person from the moment they were born, and fed it all into a computer, eventually you would be able to predict their behavior. No matter what choices the person has, you can predict what their decision will be. It worked, too, to a limited degree. He'd put half a dozen books in front of the boy and the computer could tell you which one he'd read. Put a bunch of different fruits in front of him and the computer could tell you whether he'd pick the apple or the orange or the peach. It wasn't completely accurate, but enough so that the ramifications were staggering. Imagine being able to predict what the bosses of the Soviet Union would do in a certain crisis. Or Castro. Hell, even our allies.''

"So that's what the Masked Dog Project is about? Predicting an individual's behavior?''

Dees took a deep breath. "Not exactly. Something a bit more, uh, unusual.''

"What about Dr. Elder's experiments?''

"Well, there was one thing about his son he wasn't able to predict.''

"What?''

"The kid put his dad's .22 to his temple and . . .'' Dees squeezed an imaginary trigger.

"Accident?''

"Suicide. No doubt. Dr. Elder diagnosed it himself.''

Jo felt queasy. "And this is the man you have running the Masked Dog Project.''

"Up until the Masked Dog escaped yesterday.'' Dees advanced the tape again. The face appearing this time was pasty, square-jawed, with unsettlingly shifty eyes and black curly hair thick as penthouse carpeting. Thin lips. "That's Gifford S. Devane. That's the Masked Dog.''

"What's he done?'' Jo asked.

"He was a doctor. Pediatrician. Had a nice little practice over on Long Island. *Star Wars* wallpaper, copies of *Highlights* and *Humpty-Dumpty* in the waiting room. A chummy rapport with kids. His wife was quiet, never went out much. Good reason why—he used to beat the shit out of her. Knocked her around the way most guys knock off a couple beers—for relaxation. Broke both her arms at different times, fingers, toes. Didn't like her nail polish once so he ripped the whole nails off two of her fingers."

"Christ." Jo swallowed a bitter taste.

"That's not the good stuff. Turns out he'd been molesting his patients for years. Little girls from three to twelve. Oral copulation, anal intercourse, everything you can think of. He'd threaten them with a hypodermic needle, warn them that if they told anyone their mommies would bring them back so he could give them a hundred shots all over. You know how kids love shots. Anyway, finally one kid tells and the cops do a little investigating. They go to Devane's office to arrest him, but the bastard escapes out the back. He's half nuts with anger now, thinking his wife finally turned him in for beating her. She's sitting home, watching *Days of Our Lives* or something, when he comes bursting through the door and starts slamming her around. By the time the cops get there he's jumping on her spine. He gets twenty-five years in jail. She gets life in a wheelchair."

Jo shook her head, confused. "What's a man like that have to do with a top secret government project?"

"They needed volunteers. Hard-core prisoners. Guys with nothing left to lose. Gifford S. Devane was one of them."

"Volunteers for what?"

"A drug. A drug that will change the way war is fought, the way countries negotiate, the way the world works."

"Somebody putting cocaine back in the Coca-Cola we export?" Jo said.

"Don't think *that* hasn't been discussed a few times. But, no, this isn't anything quite so sane as that." He rubbed something out of his eye, examined his finger, found nothing, brushed it against his jacket, anyway. "The name of the drug is so top secret they won't even tell us. Afraid someone might figure out how to make it from its name. But I can tell you some of its infamous history. Like most evil, it started innocently. Some researcher in Akron working on a drug to help tranquilize the more violent of the mentally handicapped, yet still allow them to learn. The results were remarkable. The patients remained calm, yet weren't drugged into a stupor. And their learning rate was amazing. Naturally the Pentagon found out."

"Someone had been applying for grants again?"

"Of course. You'd think these scientific geniuses would have learned there's no such thing as a free lunch, wouldn't you? Nope. They get their grant, but they also get a few extra government researchers. And soon the whole program is moved out to Washington. The Pentagon wants to know whether it's possible to develop a similar drug that will make soldiers unafraid, yet still able to function. They'd seen a lot of stoned-out troops in Vietnam charging gung-ho through the swamps. They want that same enthusiasm, but with normal reflexes. They bring in Dr. Frank Elder, now minus his son and newly divorced from his alcoholic wife, his predicting computer on the back burner. He pledges to refine a drug that will 'throw a hooded mask over the dogs of fear within each of us.' Hence the name, the Masked Dog Project.

"Under Dr. Frank Elder's supervision the project flourishes. A form of the sought-after drug is finished. It does indeed suppress any fear. Mice run straight into the jaws of waiting cats, to the thunderous applause of Pentagon staffers. And there is a nice side effect—it somehow stimulates the subject's memory. They can remember more than before. The Pentagon can't write checks fast enough. Only one problem, Dr. Elder tells them—the drug makes the subject unmanageable. Unwilling to follow orders, highly independent."

Jo frowned. "They must have loved that."

"They'd expected a few bugs, which Dr. Elder assured them would be ironed out much faster if he had human subjects to work on. There was some talk of using volunteer soldiers, but a cooler head reminded them of the many legal suits pending, due to similar experiments with soldiers involving everything from truth drugs to nuclear bombs. They decided on prisoners.

"Enter Dr. Gifford S. Devane. Not a chance in hell of parole for this guy. Even other prisoners don't like him, call him Short Eyes. And no little girls in jail. So he volunteers with the promise of a reduced sentence, maybe even knock ten years off. And Dr. Frank Elder likes the idea of having a physician as a subject, someone who can answer questions with more than, 'Duh, it feels funny, Doc.' They try stronger doses. A couple guys die in convulsions. They try different combinations. One guy tries to escape by punching his way through the cement walls. By the time they stop him, there's just enough left of his fists to amputate."

"And Gifford S. Devane?" Jo asked, fascinated despite her horror.

"Son of a bitch is doing fine. They discover a couple more side effects. The stuff makes you stronger. Yeah, it's got some form of steroids in it to balance some mineral deficiency. Combine that with the fact that the very chemical that suppresses fear somehow also suppresses feelings of pain, and you've got something of a superman."

"A monster, you mean."

"Price." Rawlings's voice boomed through the speaker.

Jo and Dees faced the monitor, saw Price Calender entering the room. His face was blank, expressionless. He took his seat and waited.

7

"We'll skip ahead, I think," Rawlings continued as Price silently took his seat. Rawlings exchanged cassettes in the VCR. He rolled back into his chair and thumbed the Play button on the remote unit. The screen lit up.

Price reached across and snatched the remote unit from Rawlings's thick hand. He jabbed the Stop button and the screen went blank. "I don't need visual aids, Rawlings. I was there, remember? Just tell me what happened."

Rawlings looked surprised, but nodded. "Okay, Price."

"Let's start with our deal. In exchange for the Masked Dog files that Liza R stole from you and I recovered, you promised to dismantle the project."

Rawlings shrugged. "I lied. Maybe I could have persuaded, even blackmailed somebody into canceling funding. But I didn't. I only had so many favors I could call in, and I used them up when you left."

"On what?" Price asked.

"On your life. Certainly you must have wondered why no one ever came around to make sure you didn't sell your story to *People* magazine?"

"Yeah. I wondered."

"Well, wonder no more."

Price thought about it a moment. You couldn't trust anything Rawlings said, no matter how plausible. Still, Price was alive. That was a fact. And there was no other explanation. But he'd be damned if he'd thank Rawlings for not having him killed. "What else you got?"

"You remember what Devane was like seven years ago?"

"You kidding? Strong as an ox, the memory of an elephant and completely fearless."

Rawlings nodded. "Yeah, well, he's gotten worse. Or better. Depends how you look at it. Seems that this drug Dr. Elder was still refining, right up until yesterday, had a cumulative effect. What wasn't burned by the body was stored in the fatty tissues, like LSD or PCP. That meant that even though they kept the doses relatively small, the effects were building up in Devane. You know that the son of a bitch now has total recall and a photographic memory?" Rawlings took the remote unit back from Price, started the tape. There was Gifford S. Devane, even in lab greens looking rugged and jaunty, like a playboy mountain climber. He was smiling as he recited from memory several pages of Tolstoy's *War and Peace*.

"Jesus," Price said.

"So *he* thinks." Rawlings advanced the tape. "Here he is working out." Devane was stripped to the waist, curling a barbell loaded with weights the size of tractor tires. His body was frightening. There weren't any of the useless bulging muscles that swelled the bodies of most weight lifters like the sails of old whaling ships. His muscles were all flat, like slabs of rock arranged in overlapping layers, the muscle fibers straining against the taut skin as if they'd been twined with steel cable. They looked terrifyingly efficient. His stomach was ribbed with blocks of muscles that looked so solid a jackhammer wouldn't disturb them. The arms lifted the weights with a relaxed smoothness. He was still smiling at the camera, his twinkling eyes saying, "No problem."

"That's about four hundred pounds he's curling there," Rawlings said. "He's barely working up a sweat."

"He seems happy enough."

"Why not? He used to be a clever, educated, ruthless bastard who molested children and crippled his wife. Now he's a clever, educated, ruthless bastard who also has total recall, a photographic memory, the strength of ten men and feels no fear. What's not to smile about?"

Price said, "And he's escaped."

"And he's escaped."

"How?"

"You know how long Devane's been in that program? Almost ten years. Two before your wife tried to spring him and seven since then. He was the last human subject left. And like I said, he's clever. He's even charming, if you can forget the stuff he's done."

"That's quite an 'if.'"

"Not for Dr. Frank Elder. He liked showing off for Devane. And Devane knew how to play it up. The two were almost buddies. Devane even helped in some of the lab research. Of course, Elder didn't tell us any of this. It's all come out since the escape. Anyway, Devane just waited, smiling his way into Elder's ego, until Elder was a little too relaxed about security one day. And that was it."

Price sighed. "And Elder?"

"Oh, Devane killed him. Practically twisted his goddamn head off. Like a screw-top."

"How many others?"

"Four others killed. It was a mess. And, no, we don't have any idea where he's gone. But with his brain and his new abilities, he's going to be difficult to find."

"You mean impossible."

Rawlings pointed the remote unit at Price. "That's why you're here. Devane is smart as they come, but the drug hasn't changed his basic personality. He's got the use of that computer memory, but he still carries a grudge. The same thing that sent him back to his wife when he thought she'd turned him in will bring him back to you. As far as he's concerned, you're responsible for his being in prison these past seven years. When you killed your wife while she was trying to bust him out, you did him wrong."

"That's not why I killed her."

"I know. He doesn't."

"Tell him."

Rawlings shook his head. "Even if he did know it wouldn't matter. He'd come after you, anyway. That's how he is. Obsessive. He was that way before the experimentation—he's even worse now. With a guy like him, all loose ends have to be tied up." Rawlings grinned. "And let's face it, Price, you're a loose end."

Price studied the screen, Devane's eyes.

"Thing we got to do, Price, we've got to show you to him and bring him out now."

"What's the rush?" Price said.

"Aside from the damage he's already done and is capable of doing, what kind of work do you think a man like that's going to go into to support himself?"

"Some kind of crime, I guess. Something that pays well."

"And what pays the best?"

Price thought about that. Robbing banks? Too risky. Most of those guys get caught. Computer crime takes too long to set up. No, someone with Devane's abilities could do a lot better for himself. "Assassination?"

"That's the way we figure it. The guy could work free-lance and make a fortune. But there's another problem."

"Yeah," Price said. "It shouldn't take word too long to reach Moscow. They'd give a pretty ruble to have him, if not working for them, then in their laboratory where they might work up the same drug."

"Word's already reached them."

"I see. Those FBI guys in the Mustang?"

"KGB."

"I didn't think the FBI could afford new Mustangs. One of them does a sweet Southern accent, though."

"Zinov. A bit of a showboat, if you ask me." Raw lings glanced at Price. "You gonna help?"

Price stared at the freeze-frame jiggling on the TV screen. Devane's smiling face and cruel eyes glared out while his arms bulged with four hundred pounds in midcurl.

Rawlings continued, "One other thing—not crucial for your purposes, but it might help you decide. The drug has one other small side effect. It heightens sexual drive. Elder said it has something to do with the DNA's compulsion for reproduction. In an ordinary human it would mean nothing more than going out with a lot of women. But with Devane's sexual history..." He shook his head, his lips stretched tight against his oversized teeth. "Now that he's out, he's liable to do anything."

"Don't lay that on me," Price said. "I don't owe you guys anything."

Rawlings didn't respond, but Price knew what hung in the air between them. Price could refuse, but they'd use him, anyway. Eventually Devane would come after him, and they'd be there, waiting. Only that way Price wouldn't be in on the plan and the chances of him, or someone around him, getting killed were greater. He really had no choice.

Price leaned toward Rawlings and began counting off on his fingers. "I want a life insurance policy of five hundred thousand dollars, with Rebecca as the beneficiary. Guaranteed, no riders, no bullshit. Effective yesterday."

"Okay."

"I want a gun powerful enough to stop that creature, and I want some target lessons, starting today."

"You got it. Hand-to-hand, too, if you want."

Price looked at the screen, at Devane's clifflike muscles, then gave Rawlings a look.

Rawlings nodded. "Yeah, right. Forget that."

"I want to be informed of what's going on at all times. Don't double-deal me, Rawlings. First sign you're setting me up and I rabbit down a hole so deep Devane will be speaking Russian by the time you find me."

"Don't worry. There's no reason to keep anything from you. We're in this together. We're assigning Jo Montana as your personal bodyguard. She'll fit in without attracting attention."

"Hardly. She's a goddamn astronaut's wife."

"Ex-wife," Rawlings corrected. "Besides, she was with the Secret Service before she was an astronaut's wife. That's how she met Steve Montana—guarding him during a speaking tour. Now that she's with our agency, she's even more effective. Everyone thinks she's just some astronaut's ex-wife."

"Maybe," Price said. "Only she's a little old for the rock scene. Most of the girls are a lot younger."

"Makeup."

"Makeup won't hide those lines." Price scratched his chin. "Maybe we can tell everybody she's a druggie. That'll explain her wrinkles."

"Whatever." Rawlings stood up. "Let me go and round up some of my staff, get the wheels in motion. Insurance policy and gun, right?"

"Yeah, and one other thing. I want to be back in L.A. by tomorrow morning. I've got an important meeting."

"Oh?" Rawlings grinned. "RCA? Columbia?"

"My daughter."

"I DON'T KNOW," Dees said. "I like your wrinkles."

"Shut up," Jo said. She watched the monitor; Price sat there humming "California Dreamin'," staring at Devane's smiling face frozen on the TV screen. Momentarily the horror of everything she'd learned in the past few minutes was drowned out by an overwhelming desire to torch Price Calender's other sleeve. She looked too old, huh? Too many wrinkles?

Rawlings bustled through the door without ceremony. "Okay, you heard what he wants. Get it."

"The insurance policy, too?"

"The whole five hundred thousand dollars."

"Yes, sir." Dees saluted.

"You understand your assignment, Jo?" Rawlings asked her.

"Well, uh, dress like some drugged groupie?"

"No, no."

"But I thought he said—"

"About looking old and the wrinkles? He did that for your benefit. He probably knows you're up here watching. He may be an amateur, but he's not dumb. He just wanted to get you back for what you did to him in L.A."

"Oh," Jo said, unconvinced.

"So what's your job?"

"Guard him. Protect him."

"No," Rawlings said. "It's to make sure he *feels* guarded and protected. Safe enough to expose himself so Devane will come after him. Devane's the one we're after."

"You don't want me to protect Calender?"

"Sure, if you can. But not at the risk of losing Devane. If it means getting Devane one inch closer in one of our guys' gunsights, then let him kill Calender." Rawlings looked at his watch. "Now get ready. You're heading back to L.A. today."

Jo was a little afraid of Rawlings, his bulldog face and absolute confidence. She spoke up, anyway. "I don't like it. He should be told."

"He's not a baby. He's had enough dealings with us to know where our loyalties lie."

"That's bullshit."

"That's business."

"I formally protest," she said, "for the record."

Rawlings grinned. "What record?"

8

Charlie Katz answered the knock at his kitchen door while popping open a can of Coors. His liberal sensibilities made him feel a little guilty about drinking a nonunion beer, but after one cool sip, he figured, screw it, I'm a dentist, not a union organizer.

When he opened the back door he almost choked. "My God, Giff," he gasped, beer misting from his lips. "What are you doing here?"

"Long time no see, Charlie."

"Geez, yeah. Long time. Christ." Charlie was vaguely aware he was sputtering.

Gifford S. Devane just smiled, his big teeth bright in the morning sun. "Aren't you going to invite your old neighbor in?"

"Huh? In? Sure, Giff. Hell, yes. Come on in, buddy—" he said, all the time thinking, the damn gun's upstairs in the drawer next to the bed. He could picture it now, lying there next to his reading glasses, the copy of Tom Robbins's *Even Cowgirls Get the Blues*, the Excedrin. "Drink, Giff? Beer or something?"

Gifford S. Devane shook his head. He was still smiling that hollow crocodile smile as he surveyed the kitchen. "Made some changes, eh, Charlie? Fixed it up some. New cabinets, parquet floor. Nice."

Charlie struggled with his facial muscles, trying to paste on a smile of his own. But he felt it hanging askew on his face, like a painting knocked crooked. "What a memory, Giff. Yeah, me and Muriel had the place remodeled, what, two years ago, I think. Raised the house's value by a tidy sum, I can tell you. Still, you know how many braces I had to wire to pay for it? Don't ask." Stop babbling, he told himself. But he was thinking about his daughter upstairs. He could barely hear her shower running.

"Where's Muriel?" Devane asked.

"Where else? The mall. Took the girls over for some basic training in credit-card combat." He chuckled dryly. It sounded like sand being ground in a garbage disposal. Silently he begged his daughter upstairs not to make a sound, to stay in the shower.

A tense silence fell between them as Devane lifted a hip half onto the high stool next to the wall phone.

"Cute outfit, Charlie," Devane said, pointing at Charlie's sport shirt with the number eight on the back, and the matching blue shorts and knee socks.

"This? Yeah, I coach Barbara's soccer team. We got stomped this morning. I was just about to step into the shower. Left it running upstairs."

"Little Barbara playing soccer? How old is she now?"

He choked out the word. "Fifteen."

Devane nodded. "Yeah, I guess it has been that long, huh? Ten years."

Charlie edged behind the kitchen counter, relaxing a little, now that there was at least some kind of barrier between them. The knives in the wood block near the sink reassured him.

"Ten years," Devane repeated for no apparent reason.

"They let you out, huh?"

"Time off for good behavior, pal. To tell you the truth, at least this is what my lawyer told me, the parole board took a look at the transcripts of my trial and thought that I got the shit end of the stick. Honest to God, they told my lawyer they didn't understand how I got convicted in the first place. The testimony was so flimsy. You ask a bunch of kids if the doctor's touched their privates, they say yes. They don't know if it's medical or not. I'll tell you one thing, Charlie, making those kids testify like that, confusing them about sex that way, that did them more harm than they thought I'd done."

As Charlie listened to his old neighbor, he felt himself relaxing a bit. He'd always had trouble believing that Giff had actually done what they'd claimed. The child molestation, the wife beating. Gifford Devane had been one of the most highly regarded pediatricians in the state. Had even taken care of Charlie's two daughters, Danielle and Barbara. Charlie had even questioned them at the time, delicately probing to see if they'd been unnecessarily touched at all. Both had said no.

Now here Gifford was, released from prison. Okay, maybe it was awfully early, but the officials must have known what they were doing. He'd paid his debt, if indeed he was guilty, and he deserved a chance to start over. Maybe he even deserved a helping hand from an old neighbor. Still, in the back of his mind, Charlie hoped Barbara would stay quietly upstairs.

"You look fit, Giff." Fit, hell, he looked as if he could run a hundred miles without breaking a sweat. "Prison must have agreed with you. I mean, you know."

Devane kept smiling. "Sure, I know. Actually, you're right. Started working out, taking vitamins. I feel like a whole new man. Want to arm wrestle?'' He chuckled.

"No way. The most exercise these arms get is pulling an occasional tooth or crushing an empty beer can." Suddenly he felt a little self-conscious about their physical differences, sucking in his paunchy gut as he eyed Devane's veined forearms where he'd pushed up the sleeves of his sweater. "My legs are strong, though. From soccer."

"Your daughter's team, huh? Better be careful, Charlie. One of those girls twists her ankle and you hold the ice on it too long, they'll claim you were trying to rape her. It can happen, believe me. You won't know what hit you."

Charlie nodded. He'd given some thought to that already. Devane's fate had made every male in town sensitive to the dangers. Aside from a hug of encouragement or comfort now and then, always in front of another team member, Charlie kept his distance out there, even from his own daughter. "What can I do for you, Giff?"

"Money," Devane said, turning his smile up a few degrees.

"Sure. How much? Couple hundred get you settled?"

"Well, I've got a little business opportunity, a chance to start my own service. Guaranteed to be a money-maker. Just need a little seed money."

Charlie stiffened. He didn't mind loaning the guy a few hundred, forget even paying it back. But this was sounding expensive. "How much?"

"A couple thousand should do it. I remember you telling me you kept that much around the house. I kept trying to get you to invest it, but you claimed you couldn't. Some promise to your grandfather. Remember?''

Charlie remembered. His grandfather, Max, had been a wealthy merchant in Germany before the war. When the Nazis seized power, they came to his furniture store one day, took the keys and told him to get out. Fortunately he kept going, all the way to the United States. Some of his relatives had not been so fortunate. Max had lived long enough to see Charlie's successful dental practice, the big house, the cars. But he'd made his grandson promise to keep some cash handy. ''A Jew has to be prepared to leave quickly. No matter what country.'' Charlie had kept that promise.

He looked over at Devane's smiling face. ''What kind of business?''

''Like I said, personal service.''

''That's a little vague, Giff, if you're asking me to invest.''

''Oh, I'm not asking you to invest, Charlie,'' he said, rising. ''I'm just going to take it.'' Then he was across the kitchen faster than Charlie had ever seen anyone move. His left hand snapped straight out and grabbed Charlie's windpipe.

Even as he closed his fist, Devane could picture each detail from the texts from medical school, the colored diagrams labeling each body part, the plastic overlays. The tips of his fingers dug into the flesh around Charlie's trachea, separating the 4.5 inch tube from the esophagus directly behind it. Devane's fingers and thumb punctured the flesh.

Charlie hadn't even had time to beg. His scream of protest had been strangled off by Devane's pincer grip. He clawed and pounded at Devane's head, wrist, arm, but the man didn't seem to feel anything. He just grinned at Charlie, his grip tightening by notches as if his hand were operated by levers and gears. Charlie felt his lungs burn, his chest convulsing as it demanded air. But none came. His fists fell limply on the counter. He had a foggy awareness that Devane, still using only one hand, was lifting him in the air, dragging him over the mosaic Mexican tile of the counter. The blood from his throat dripped to the white tile. Charlie didn't even know his feet were twittering in a death dance, scuffing the new cabinets. His eyes rolled crazily in his head.

Devane let the body thud indifferently to the parquet floor. His smile disappeared for the first time as he regarded the mess on his hands. He walked to the sink, squeezed some Joy onto them and washed the blood from under his nails. He dried his hands on a paper towel, wondering where to start looking for the money. The bastard probably hid it someplace tricky. No matter, he'd find it.

The shower upstairs suddenly stopped.

Devane looked up, as if he could actually see through the ceiling. His smile returned.

"Daddy," the young voice chided from upstairs. "You'd better hurry up and change, or Mom'll kill us. We're supposed to meet them in half an hour. Daddy?"

Devane remained silent, sipping the last swallow of beer from Charlie's Coors.

"Daddy?" The voice was closer now, probably the top of the stairs. Some tentative footsteps on the stairs now. A few more. "Daddy? You still in the kitchen?" No fear, just confusion. She was all the way down the stairs now, coming toward the kitchen.

Devane stepped through the swinging door and blocked her just as she was about to enter. He didn't want Charlie's condition to spoil the mood.

She pulled up, almost bumping into him. At first she looked surprised. Then she recognized him. "Dr. Devane."

"Hi, Barb. Where's your dad?"

"Uh, he was here just a minute ago." She pulled her terry-cloth bathrobe tighter around her body. Her black hair was pasted against her forehead in wet curls as sharp as scythes. She'd filled out nicely since Devane had last seen her, maybe even a couple pounds overweight. There was a fresh scrape on her knee.

"Soccer?" he asked, pointing at the wound.

"Yeah. How'd you know?"

"Your dad and I kept up. Letters. Didn't he tell you?"

She shook her head.

He reached out and stroked her cheek with the backs of his fingers. They smelled of Joy. She winced from his touch.

"Maybe you'd better let me take a look at that knee?" he said, smiling. "I'm still a doctor."

"It's okay. Just a scratch."

He grabbed hold of her hand and pulled her toward the stairs.

"No, Dr. Devane. Really." There was anger in her voice.

He tightened his grip and yanked. She stumbled forward as if towed by a truck.

"Owww." She rubbed her shoulder socket with her free hand. "Leave me alone!" There it was, the panic in the voice. He liked that.

He felt his body tingling as she tried to twist her hand free, her robe drooping open revealing a glimpse of girlish breasts and nipples, looking not fully formed, like doughy half-raised rolls. He'd killed Charlie without raising one drop of sweat. Now he was sweating all over, his heart thumping against the rib cage. He snatched her by the collar of the robe and shoved her toward the stairs. She tripped over the bottom step and sprawled onto the stairs, sobbing.

Devane prodded her buttocks with his foot. "Come on, Barbie. Up those stairs now like a good little girl."

As he pushed her up the stairs, he reminded himself how he'd made it a policy back then never to touch any of the daughters of his friends. Too risky. And how he'd had to be so very careful not to harm his tender victims, leave no marks or bruises. He smiled. Fortunately he no longer had to be so careful.

9

Two hours later, Gifford S. Devane was standing at the back door of another house, three large manicured lawns away from where the bodies of Charlie and his daughter lay dead. It had taken him only forty minutes to find the two-thousand-dollars cash, hidden amateurishly behind a wall socket in the bedroom. It had taken considerably longer to fully enjoy young Barbara.

Her smells were still on him. Her wet hair still piny from that herbal shampoo, her skin too sweet from deodorant soap, the pungence of her own musky aroma. He took a deep breath and enjoyed her all over again in his mind.

Devane glanced around the familiar yard. Nothing much had changed, except for the wooden fence that enclosed the yard. Over there by the garden hose was a fresh pile of dog droppings. So she got herself a dog, huh? He smiled.

He peeled back the corner of the rubber Welcome mat, but the spare key wasn't there. Damn, he hadn't counted on that. He ran his fingers along the sill of the doorframe. Nothing.

The clackety-clack of a large dog's nails prancing across kitchen linoleum came through the door. Followed by a low rumbling growl. Devane peered through the curtained window of the door. A German shepherd stared back at him, its black lips curled back to reveal long white teeth.

Devane quickly searched everywhere around the door for the spare key. Certainly she wouldn't have stopped keeping one, not after all he'd done to her when she'd forgotten to leave it under the mat that one time. He'd held her hand under the steaming hot water faucet until the back of her hand had puffed with clusters of white blisters. For every whimper of protest, he'd added five seconds more.

The dog's growling was becoming louder.

"Iago," her voice scolded from another room. "You just came in fifteen minutes ago."

Devane dropped to his knees, began overturning the rocks in the garden that circled the house.

The dog began to bark sporadically.

"*Iago!*" she hollered. "Let me finish what I'm doing first."

Iago's barking became more insistent, louder.

"Oh, all right. I'm coming."

Devane pawed through the rocks, flipping them over, finding nothing but slugs and worms. Busting the door down would be no problem, but he didn't want to take the chance of attracting attention. There was too much to do first. Then he would have everyone's attention. The world's.

He heard the slight creaking of a wheelchair. Then her voice. "Okay, I'm here. Now what's the fuss about?"

Devane hefted one of the last rocks, realized it wasn't a rock at all. Too light. He turned it over, saw the little trap door. Clever, he thought, shaking the key loose.

He jammed it into the lock, twisted, and was into the kitchen before his ex-wife had time to react. The dog crouched, snarling, looking confused at Devane's boldness, his utter lack of fear. The dog's teeth dripped with saliva, but still he waited for his mistress's command before attacking.

"Hi, honey," Devane said, smiling. "I'm home."

She looked surprised for a moment, then nothing. None of the fear he'd come to expect, to enjoy. He stopped smiling.

"Miss me, Karen?"

"I wouldn't move, Gifford. Iago's a trained guard dog. I wouldn't want him to hurt you."

"I bet you wouldn't."

She rolled her wheelchair forward a couple of feet. "I take it you've managed to escape, Gifford. I can't imagine them letting you out on purpose."

"What does it matter? I'm back, right?" He looked straight at her with his most menacing glare. She didn't flinch. He was getting mad. "You look kinda sexy in that wheelchair, Karen. Does it turn many guys on?"

She smiled at him. "God, I can't believe I ever married you and put you through medical school." She shook her head. "It started in med school, remember? The first time you hit me you cried and begged me to forgive you. Remember?"

"Barely."

She shrugged. "What do you want, Giff?"

"Christ, I love this bored act of yours. Let me guess, you've had your feminine consciousness raised? Am I right? Countless sessions with groups of repressed dykes bitching about oppressive men. I guess you had some stories to tell. All that crap in the newspapers about me being some kind of Dr. Jekyll and Mr. Hyde. Hell, you must've been queen of the group."

"What do you want?" she repeated. "Money?"

Devane laughed. "No, I managed to secure a loan."

"What then?"

The dog's growling lessened somewhat as he watched the verbal exchange, the dark eyes glancing back and forth between his mistress and the intruder.

"Nice dog," Devane said. "What do you do for fun around here?"

"I write, Gifford. Novels."

"You're still screwing around with the stupid typewriter, huh? How many times did I tell you to quit wasting your time?"

"Hundreds, maybe thousands. Fortunately I didn't listen. I've sold six novels while you've been gone, and I'm contracted for three more." It was her turn to smile now.

He forced a grin, but his face hardened. "I guess they'll publish anything nowadays."

"I guess so. Not that I do anything real literary, mostly romances now. But I enjoy writing them and I get lots of fan letters. And the money—"

"That's nice," he cut her off. "I just came to use your typewriter. I've got a few letters to write."

"You risked coming here just to write a few letters?"

"They won't be looking for me here. They'll be expecting me out in California, looking for some rock 'n' roll has-been named Price Calender. And I won't disappoint them. But first things first."

"What are you talking about? What do you have to do with Price Calender?"

"Just shut up and point me to the typewriter, okay?"

"No," she said. "I don't know how you got out of jail, but I'm not helping you in any way. Now get out, Gifford." She pointed at the door.

"You've got to be kidding. Who do you think you're talking to, Karen? Maybe you don't remember how you got in that wheelchair."

"Get out before I let Iago loose."

He saw the anger and fear in her eyes now. He smiled, his teeth like white shields lined across his mouth. He felt the rush of adrenaline mixed with the drug from the Masked Dog Project. He started toward his ex-wife.

"Iago," Karen commanded. "Attack!"

The German shepherd sprang at Devane with black claws outstretched and mouth open. His mottled brown-and-black fur bristled.

Devane didn't flinch. He caught the ninety-five-pound animal in midair, staggering back a step or two from the impact. But Iago never had a chance. Devane grabbed the snout in both hands, one hand on the top of the mouth, the other on the bottom. He held the dog against his chest and slowly began prying the mouth farther and farther apart. At first the dog began to yelp.

Devane winked at Karen. "I saw Steve Reeves do this in a movie they showed us in prison."

"Stop it!" she pleaded. "For God's sake, you're killing him."

Devane continued. The dog whimpered as his jaw-bones snapped, his mouth now a useless flap of burning pain. Devane dropped him on the linoleum, still alive, but unable or unwilling to move. A faint high-pitched whine came from inside the animal somewhere.

Devane grinned at Karen. "Better start thinking about a cat."

"Iago!" she cried. His front paws quivered as he tried vainly to move. Karen lunged the wheelchair toward one of the kitchen drawers, yanked the drawer open and pulled out a large serrated knife. "You bastard!"

Devane walked toward her, unconcerned about the knife. She slashed it at him, snagged it on the side of the maroon polo shirt he'd borrowed from Charlie's closet. The blade sliced the shirt, nipped a bit of his skin. Blood began leaking onto the shirt. He showed no sign of pain as he clamped his hand around her wrist, shook the knife free, then gave an extra twist that snapped the ulna and radius bones of her wrist. She screamed with pain.

"I always thought you liked the pain, Karen," he told her as he shoved her and the wheelchair through the house. "I mean, there was a point where I actually thought it was kind of an obligation to you, like sex."

Karen said nothing, sobbing as she held her broken wrist.

Devane pushed the wheelchair through the living room to the den, where Karen had set up a study. Novels lined one wall, bulletin boards another. Note cards were pinned to the bulletin board. There were two desks, one with an IBM Selectric II typewriter, another with an Apple computer. Devane whistled. "My, my. The computer revolution has even hit little Karen Devane."

"Reese," she corrected defiantly. "I went back to Karen Reese."

"Tsk, tsk. No loyalty in this cruel world." He pushed her over near the desk with the typewriter and spun her around so she was seated next to him. "I know you've had your consciousness raised, Karen, but they didn't raise you to your feet. So just sit there like my good little girl and I won't have to punish you. Okay?"

10

"Don't be such a dope," Jo said irritably.

"Huh?" Price asked, lifting one of the ear mufflers so he could hear.

"Nothing. Look, it's easy. You just stand like this, feet slightly apart but balanced, cup your left hand under the butt of the gun and *squeeze* the goddamn trigger."

"That's what I did."

"No, it isn't. What you did was *pull* the trigger, not squeeze it. What you did was shoot a full clip at a silhouette target of a man and hit him in the shoulder, elbow and wrist. If that had been Devane, you'd be dead."

Price lowered his gun and gave her a side glance. "What are you so angry about?"

"I'm not angry. That's just the way my weathered skin makes me look sometimes. The way my wrinkles catch the morning light."

"What are you talking about?"

She stared into his eyes to see if he was kidding her, but couldn't decide. He looked innocent enough. But there was a hard edge beneath his balmy good looks, a tough no-nonsense current that bubbled to the surface now and then. Like when that tiny web of blue veins at his temple swelled with blood. She'd seen a little of it when he was with Rawlings, watching the tapes of his wife. Sometimes it was frightening to see so much pent-up passion. Sometimes a little thrilling. "Let's get back to work, okay?" she said, a bit flustered.

Price lifted the gun into position, cupping his left hand under the butt. He closed his left eye and squinted along the barrel. The target was slightly fuzzy to him, but he could still make out the outline of the burly, stubble-cheeked cartoon villain. He took a deep breath, exhaled.

"Squeeze," she said, "not pull."

Price squeezed the trigger. And kept squeezing. Eight shots later they removed their ear mufflers and peered at the target. He couldn't make out the tiny holes. "How'd I do?" he asked her.

"Better," Jo said. "You placed two slugs in the chest area. That should slow him down."

Price hefted the 9 mm Walther P-5. "You sure this gun is big enough? Don't you guys have something bigger?"

"Sure, but nothing you'd have time to master."

"I don't have to master the damn thing. Just point it at his chest and pull—I mean, squeeze—the trigger."

"Maybe. The bullets are hollowpoints with aluminum jackets, so there's plenty of stopping power. Problem is, anything less than a head or heart shot won't stop Devane right away. The way his body has absorbed that drug, you could shoot him in the stomach or chest and he'd still come at you. Oh, he'd be hurt, maybe even dying, but he wouldn't feel the pain. What stops a lot of guys who've been wounded with a nonfatal shot is shock. Devane won't react that way. He might even have enough juice left to kill you."

Price thumbed eight more rounds into the clip, palmed it into the gun, adjusted his ear muffler and faced the target. He fired all eight shots.

"Better," Jo said, nodding. "But not good enough."

"YOU WON'T SEE ME," the big man in his underwear said, "but I'll be around."

"Great," Price said.

"Yeah," the big man said, smiling. He stood up. His boxer shorts had that pink tint Price recognized as coming from washing colors and whites together. That shade of pink ought to be on a flag, he thought. The official flag of bachelors. "Gotta get dressed now," the big man said, stubbing out a cigarette in the saucer of his coffee cup and padding barefoot to the bedroom.

"Fine," Price said.

"Hurry it up, will you, Crush?" Jo said. "We've got a schedule."

"Five minutes," he promised, closing the door behind him.

Price looked at his watch. In thirty minutes he was supposed to pick up Rebecca. He still hadn't decided how he would explain Jo. He'd never brought a woman by there before. It had always been just the two of them. He'd think of something.

He looked at Jo, who was nervously nibbling the lipstick off her lower lip. The same woman who, a few hours ago, had demonstrated the Walther, now holstered under his arm, by blasting eight rounds into the target's heart. The same woman who'd tricked him a couple nights ago in Westwood, standing half-naked in panty hose and pearls. The ex-wife of the astronaut, the ex-Secret Service bodyguard, now working for Rawlings. He pointed to his watch. "I don't want to be late."

She met his gaze. Their eyes stared unblinking. "We won't be." She broke off her stare first and began rummaging through her purse. "We had to stop by here and give Crush your itinerary for the day. Damn, I'm out of cigarettes. You have any?"

"I'm quitting." He reached toward her purse, and her hand lashed out and caught him by the wrist. He was surprised at the strength in those narrow fingers. "My lighter," he explained.

"Oh," she said. She released his wrist and he plucked his Bic from her purse. She stood up, went to the closed bedroom door and hollered, "Crush, you have a spare pack of cigarettes lying about?"

The husky voice echoed from the bathroom. "Sure, there's gotta be some in one of the drawers out there. Help yourself."

"Crush?" Price said, wincing. "That one of those cute Agency code names? I mean, I know he's big. What is he, maybe six feet four inches, two hundred and fifty pounds?"

"More like six feet five inches, two hundred and seventy pounds. And the nickname doesn't have anything to do with his size. Or the Agency."

"Football, huh? Used to crush 'em up in college?"

"Nope." Jo was pulling open kitchen drawers, pawing through their contents, but without luck.

"Well, then, what?"

She walked over to the refrigerator and tugged open the door. Aside from a scattering of Tupperware containers and aluminum-foil shapes, there was a whole shelf of Orange Crush sodas. "Drinks about a dozen of them a day. Has as long as I've known him."

"Oh," Price said. He got up and began helping her search the kitchen drawers. Most of them were unorganized messes, stuffed with utensils. Finally, under a cheese grater and the cord to a Crockpot, he found a pack of Salems. And something else. "Jesus Christ," he whistled. "Look at this." He held up a gold and a bronze medal by the ribbons. They clanked together.

Jo examined them. "They look like Olympic medals."

"They are. Where the hell did he get them?"

"I won 'em," Crush said. He was standing less than a foot behind them. Neither had heard him approach. "The gold's really only got six grams of gold. They stopped handing out solid gold back in 1912."

Price glanced up at him. He looked completely different, standing there in his tan sport jacket, Levi's and aviator sunglasses. His thin blond hair was slicked down. If it weren't for that huge square jaw dominating half his face and the ample gut straining against the jacket buttons, he would look almost handsome. As it was, he looked like a high-school football coach going slowly to seed.

"What year?" Price asked.

"I dunno." Crush shrugged. "Maybe '60 or '64, one of those. When was Tokyo?"

"In 1964," Jo said.

"Yeah, that's when. Butterfly. . . 100 meter and 200 meter both. I would have grabbed more gold, but they banned the flip somersault turn that year. Had to change my strategy."

Price looked at the giant man before him, about thirty-eight—only four years older than Price. "What happened to you?"

91

Crush grinned. "You mean how'd I turn from a shark into a whale?"

Jo looked at Price, expecting him to say something polite. All he said was, "Yeah."

"No great mystery, Mr. Calender. I like to eat. And I drink those sodas. After all those years of watching my diet and training like a maniac, I was relieved to be out of it." He looked Price in the eye. "Tell me something. After all those hit songs and tours and everything, all that pressure to produce. When it all came apart, weren't you just the teeniest bit relieved?"

Price tapped a cigarette from the pack of Salems and lit it. "Let's go," he said. "We'll be late."

"I DON'T SEE HIM ANYWHERE," Price said, searching the rearview mirror of his VW Rabbit.

"That's the point," Jo said. "Crush has got a dozen agents working you, all in different cars. As long as they have your schedule in advance, they can pretty much stay out of sight. We don't make any changes without phoning them in first, right?"

"Right." The Walther under his arm was uncomfortable and made him feel just a little bit silly. The woman at his side made him feel the same way. "You have a breath mint?"

"Why?" she asked. "My breath bad?"

"It's for me. I don't want Rebecca to know I've been smoking. I kinda promised her I'd quit."

Jo dug into her purse, found a roll of Velamints. Handed him one. "Here, they're sugar-free. At my age you have to be careful."

"Do you have an age hangup or something?"

"No, why?"

"You mention it a lot."

She looked at him but didn't say anything.

They drove in silence toward Pasadena, avoiding the freeway as Crush had suggested.

"Your daughter lives with your grandmother. How come?" Price didn't answer right away and Jo thought maybe he didn't hear her. She tried again. "Why does your daughter live with your grandmother?"

"I don't see where that information will help you do your job any better," Price snapped.

She turned, ready to snap back, saw the look in his eyes as he stared at the road and thought better of it. "Sorry," she said. "It's none of my business."

"Agreed."

Neither spoke for the rest of the trip.

When Price pulled up in front of the old well-tended house, the front door opened and a ten-year-old girl stood there, her arms open, her face split with the biggest smile Jo had ever seen. As they climbed out of the Rabbit, the little girl stepped out onto the porch, and Jo saw for the first time the shiny metal brace that encased the whole left leg.

"Daddy!" Rebecca cried, hurrying down the porch steps, dragging the heavy leg awkwardly behind her. "Oh, Daddy."

"A BULLET," Price said, "no bigger than the tip of your little finger. It shattered her three-year-old knee as efficiently as if someone had pounded it with a sledgehammer."

He and Jo were walking in the backyard while his grandmother and Rebecca fussed in the kitchen over lunch. The walk had been Grandma's idea, as if she could see the tension between them. "Get out of our hair for fifteen minutes while me and the kid fix this up right," she'd said.

Price nudged Rebecca's kickball with his toe while they walked. He didn't look at Jo as he spoke; that would have been too hard. "It's all in the files somewhere, though probably not displayed very prominently."

"It said she was wounded. I had no idea . . ."

Price shrugged. "Why should you? It had nothing to do with the case. You know about her mother, right? Liza R?"

"That she set you up with that narcotics bust, yeah. That she planned to break Devane out, either to sell him or go into business with him, no one's sure."

"Turns out my dear wife had done some dealing in international secrets before meeting me. We found all this out later, after she was killed. She married me in the first place as a cover, then somehow in the course of her spying, found out about the Masked Dog Project and Devane. Christ, I thought she was out shopping, or maybe having an affair. But espionage?" He laughed harshly. "God, I'm up there onstage singing 'Rock 'n' Roll Drive-In' while my wife is plotting against the United States government."

Jo wanted to say something to help, but couldn't think of anything. Finally she simply said, "Go on."

"Yeah, well, Rawlings approached me one day while we were playing Washington. Laid out the whole thing for me. Photographs, documents, everything. 'Your wife's a spy,' he told me. 'And we want your help in putting her away.' Hell, I'm from the sixties, man. Don't trust anyone over thirty, especially guys with narrow lapels, black ties and white shirts. We're talking Nixon in the White House. Why would I help these guys against my own wife, who, believe it or not, I still loved as much as when we'd first met.''

And maybe still do, Jo thought.

''Anyway, after they showed me how Liza R had been using Rebecca to stash microfilm and crap, I came around. They set her up with some phony plans to break Devane out of an isolated building in the woods. But things went wrong. There was shooting. Liza R used Rebecca as a shield while trying to escape. One of Rawlings's men accidentally shot Rebecca. Liza R dumped her in a ditch and ran.''

''And you got to her first?''

''Rebecca and I were both in the jeep, leaving. Liza R had been in custody. She'd tried to kill me then with a knife.'' He touched his right side where the scar was. ''I managed to fight her off, maybe even a little too zealously.'' He flexed his bad hand. ''Anyway, the kid and I were leaving, when she managed to escape from the two agents holding her. She killed one, disabled the other. She burst out of that barn, grabbed Rebecca before I could stop her and started shooting. After she ditched Rebecca, I went after her in the jeep.''

''She was still armed, wasn't she?''

''Yeah, only I wasn't thinking about that. I just wanted to kill her, the way you want to kill something you know is just plain evil. Sounds melodramatic now, but not then, not with her arm holding her three-year-old daughter in front of her while she shot over the kid's shoulder.''

''Does Rebecca remember what happened?''

''Not much. She remembers the pain, her mother running. I told her her mother was trying to protect her from the out-of-control jeep, that she died saving Rebecca's life." Price sighed. "What harm could that do?"

Jo looked back at the house as the screen door creaked open. Rebecca waved at them, at him, really. So far she'd managed to ignore Jo's presence completely.

"Come on, Daddy. Lunch is ready."

"Coming—" He waved back, smiling.

They started for the house.

"What about her leg?" Jo asked. "Any hope?"

"Sure. At least she's walking now without crutches. She just came back from the hospital yesterday from more tests. The doctors think another operation, her eighth, might get rid of the brace. Then again, might not." He stooped, looked at Jo. "You asked why she lives with my grandmother?"

"I'm sorry, it was none of my—"

"Because I'm on the road a lot. My bread-and-butter appearances are in the South and Midwest. Hell, California has more ex-rockers than it knows what to do with. But back there I'm still a minor curiosity. Rebecca needs stability now, school and a home. I stay here most of the time I'm in town so we can be together. My other apartment is for when I get in on those red-eye flights, or I'm playing backup until 2:00 A.M. in the studio for someone else. Or when I want some female companionship."

She looked away.

"My parents moved to Florida, and I don't want her that far away from me. Besides, I don't want them bringing her up, though God knows they've asked often enough."

"Too strict, huh?"

"No. They're good people and we get along just fine. But they're just not right for her. I don't think they really like kids—they like the *idea* of kids. It's hard to explain."

"Not really," Jo said. "I know exactly what you mean."

A phone rang inside, and Price heard his grandmother saying, "I'm coming, I'm coming." He held the screen door open for Jo. When they stepped into the kitchen, Grandma held the phone out to Jo. "It's for you. Someone named Dees. Seems awfully excited."

"YOU AND YOUR YOUNG FRIEND staying the night?" Tillie Calender asked her grandson once Rebecca had been sent upstairs to wash her hands.

"It's not like that, Grandma."

"Not like what?"

Price leaned back in his chair, peered down the hallway to where he'd directed Jo to answer the phone. She was talking animatedly into the receiver, her finger stabbing the air for emphasis. He couldn't hear everything she was saying, but the few words he caught were twanging with her Texan accent. She was upset. He looked at his grandmother, at her kinky black hair hanging down to her shoulder, hardly a gray hair to show for her seventy-four years. That's okay, he thought; he had enough for both of them. She was thin but not frail; her skin puckered, but otherwise smooth. Her eyes were steady, unflinching. Most people thought she looked fifteen years younger. The only betrayal of her true age was the constant quivering of her hands, the slightly stooped posture, the slowness of movement from Parkinson's disease.

"Well?" she said. "Not like what?"

He smiled and patted her shaking hand. "Not like what your dirty mind is thinking. No sex."

She raised a skeptical eyebrow. "Hell, Price, I'm seventy-four, but I haven't forgotten sex. I'm six years younger than Cary Grant and hardly a week goes by I don't think there's a chance that he and I might still get something going."

"God, the original 'Little Old Lady from Pasadena.'"

"I wasn't an old lady when that song came out, buster. Your granddad and I were still backpacking the Sierras then while you were home begging for a guitar."

"Which you bought for me."

"So, don't get prissy with me all of a sudden. This is the first time you've brought a woman over to this house. What do you expect me to think?"

Price shook his head. "Forget it. Jo and I are just doing some business together. Nothing more."

"Strictly business, huh?"

"Yup."

Tillie Calender shrugged her bony shoulders and stood up from the kitchen table. "Just remember, I don't mind her staying over and I don't mind you sharing the same bed."

"Give me a break, Grandma." Price laughed. "You know what it's like to have your grandmother less hung up about sex than you are?"

She laughed, too, a slight shakiness in the timbre, which he hadn't noticed before. "Somebody in this family's got to be open-minded. It sure isn't my son or your mother." She stirred something on the stove. Price thought she might be moving a little more slowly than usual. When she turned to face him again, there was a moistness in her eyes. "Listen, Price. Rebecca's going to be back here in a minute, so I have to make this fast. While Rebecca was up at that hospital last week, I had them run some tests on me. Didn't tell me anything I didn't already know. Namely, I'm getting worse. I'm having trouble keeping my balance lately, and the shaking's so bad I feel like I'm always sitting on one of those motel beds with the Magic Fingers. And no, there's nothing really that can be done. It'll just keep getting worse."

"I'll spend more time home then. Cut the gigs down."

"You will not," she said sternly. "At least, not for my sake. Right now, it's Rebecca we've got to think about. Her future." She paused, staring at her quivering hands with a mixture of betrayal and contempt. "I've been thinking of taking Rebecca and moving in with your parents. They've been begging me to for years."

"No," Price said, standing suddenly. He'd never expected to hear this from her. She was so fiercely proud of her independence. She'd been one of the first successful women lawyers in the state and had amassed enough savings independent of her husband's small legacy that she could afford to live quite comfortably alone. But more than that, she had a powerful, inquisitive mind that never got along with her son's and daughter-in-law's more docile predictability. The fact that she was willing to move in along with Rebecca was a sacrifice motivated solely by her desire to watch over her great-granddaughter.

"Calm down, Price. It's not my decision to make. It's yours. But there are some realities we've got to face. My body's been rebelling for the past few years now. I was hoping you might start thinking about marriage again, or at least some sign that you were able to spend more than three hours with a woman without running away.''

Price didn't bother denying what she was saying. He couldn't.

''Hell, Price, if you'd even have lived with a woman in the past seven years, I'd have been thrilled. At least then you'd be moving in the right direction.''

''Grandma, we've been through this before.''

''Yes, yes, we have. But before, we could afford to be patient. Can't anymore.'' She took a deep breath. ''I know you've been burned.'' She lowered her voice. ''You loved a woman who turned out to be rotten. It happens. Maybe not as dramatically as it did to you, but your feelings and fears aren't any stronger than the guy whose wife runs off with the piano tuner.''

''What do you want me to do? Marry the first woman I see?''

''I want you to *see* the first woman you see. Not as a possible Liza R, but for who she is herself.''

They heard the clomping of Rebecca's metal brace as she worked her way down the stairs.

Tillie Calender gave her grandson a stern look. ''There's no rush. No decisions have been made. Just think about it. You want to take Rebecca in with you, you're going to have to stick around more.''

''And do what?'' Price asked.

''All clean,'' Rebecca announced brightly, holding up her hands as she entered the kitchen. ''When do we eat? I'm starved.''

''Soon as you finish setting the table,'' Tillie said. ''Napkins on the left.''

''Okay.''

Price reached out and snagged his daughter as she headed for the napkin holder on the counter. ''Give me a hug first. Then maybe I'll give you your birthday gift.''

She did so with enthusiasm, burying her head in his chest, her tiny fingers digging into his arms. When he released her, she wrinkled her nose at him and made a sour face. "You've been smoking. I can smell it on your jacket. You promised me you'd quit."

"That was me," Jo said from the doorway, her voice even, accentless again. But her face was different. A little sad, Price thought. "I smoked in the car."

"It stinks," Rebecca said.

"Manners, Rebecca," Grandma Tillie said firmly.

"Sorry, Ms Montana," Rebecca said.

"Nothing to be sorry about," Jo said. "It does stink."

"It causes cancer, too," Rebecca added.

"And worse, wrinkles." Jo gave Price a look indicating she needed to see him alone.

He followed her back into the hallway. "What's up?"

"We're being pulled off you."

"What?"

"Crush and his men. Me. We've been called off."

Price was incredulous. "You're kidding?"

"I wish. Look, I argued with him. Apparently so did Crush. But it didn't do any good." She paused, looking him in the eye. "I'm not supposed to tell you this, but Devane's been busy since he got out. They found some bodies. His ex-wife, a neighbor, a fifteen-year-old girl. All murdered, the girl raped. Christ, 'rape' is a kind word for the sick things he did to her."

"Then why is Rawlings calling you off?"

"Because they now know exactly where he'll be."

"How?"

"He told them," she said. "Wrote them a letter."

Price laughed harshly. "And they believed him."

"Apparently." She looked embarrassed. "Psychological profile says he's telling the truth."

"Great," Price said. He patted the Walther P-5 under his jacket. "Do I get to keep the gun?"

"You'd better." Jo slung her purse over her shoulder and headed for the door.

11

Rawlings adjusted the Levolor blinds on his office door so that no one could see into his office. With surprising agility, he hefted his considerable bulk up on top of his desk and tried to stuff some crumpled paper into the air-conditioning vent in the ceiling. As usual, it was goddamn freezing in there. A couple of the women in the outside office even wore thick sweaters and made a show of warming their hands at their desks over steaming cups of coffee. All for his benefit. Not that there was anything he could do about it, for Christ's sake. Changing the thermostat in this building practically took an Act of Congress.

He climbed down from his desk and sank into his chair. The crumpled paper trick had never worked before, and it didn't work today. Within seconds, the paper was blown free from the vent and dropped from the ceiling onto Rawlings's desk with a defeated bounce. Rawlings smoothed out the paper, checked the information: 2,050 acres of soybeans were harvested in Alaska in 1981, down one hundred acres from 1979. Real nail-biting stuff. He shoved the wrinkled page back into one of the plastic trays on his desk.

He sighed heavily, leaning under his desk and flicking on the portable heater he didn't want anyone else to know he had hidden there. Soon his feet were toasty enough that he could smell the shoe polish on his Oxfords melting.

Aside from the usual garbage that cluttered his desk, three stacks of file folders were neatly arranged on the blotter, each about a foot high. "Masked Dog stuff," his secretary had said, plopping it onto his desk this morning, making sure he saw her sweater buttoned up to her throat. He thumbed through a few folders. Biographies of Devane's recent victims, autopsy reports, analysis of the letter, including fingerprints, brand of typewriter and paper. It had all been fed into Fat Boy, and the computer had reached the same conclusion Rawlings had three hours earlier. They were in deep shit.

Nevertheless, the operation was already steamrollering and decisions had to be made immediately. The direct phone line from Rawlings's desk to the director's desk had been blistering all morning. The director was angry about Devane's impossible escape, anxious about Devane's threatening letter and frightened about what the consequences would be if Devane made good on his outrageous threat. The director wanted Devane stopped. He wanted Rawlings to do it.

Actually, what he'd said was, "I want that bastard's balls bronzed and on my desk as paperweights in two days, Rawlings. His or yours."

Rawlings frowned at the three stacks on his desk. He unfastened the straps on his weather-beaten leather briefcase that Dees had once said looked like the kind the Gestapo was always carrying in old movies. Inside was the one thing that made Rawlings's day bearable: the sports section of *The Washington Post*. Unknown to most around the section, Rawlings was a rabid tennis fan. He followed the sport, devouring Jimmy Connors's first-serve percentages and Matts Wilander's baseline game with intense interest. Would cadaverous-looking Lendl ever stop beating himself on the big ones? What young female dynamo would emerge soon to finally wrestle the mantle of invulnerability away from Martina Navratilova? He missed the oldtimers sometimes, Rod Laver, Ken Rosewall and John Bromwich, with his two-handed shot on his right, left-handed forehand and right-handed serve and smash. The Spaniard Manuel Santana, who took Wimbledon in 1966. Maria Bueno from Brazil, ladies' Wimbledon champion in 1959, 1960 and 1964. The newer players were better, he conceded, but he missed actually *liking* the players.

Rawlings never discussed tennis with anyone around the section. They would see it as too ludicrous, this square man built like an ape, extolling the virtues of a sport that demanded such grace. Yet three times a week, he was out on the courts of his club, whacking the ball with more power than skill, dreaming of the perfect overhead smash, which always eluded him. On Sundays, he and his wife played doubles against Dave and Lori Ammes, friends for over twenty years. Every week they lost. It drove Rawlings mad.

Thinking about it made the wormlike scar on his wrist itch. The one he'd told Price Calender had been the result of the stray bullet Calender had fired seven years ago. Of course, it actually was the result of Rawlings's running into the chain-link fence surrounding the tennis court when he'd stretched too far for Dave's damn wide-angle serve. The gash had taken seven stitches. Worth it, he figured, if it helped keep Calender in line.

The sharp knock at the door startled him a moment. Recovering, he shoved the sports section under one of the stacks of file folders and said, "Come in."

Dees bounced into the room, smiling.

"What're you so happy about?" Rawlings asked.

"Are you kidding? Who'd be happy about leaving Washington when it's a balmy ninety-four degrees with a delightful ninety percent humidity. This isn't happy. I'm just putting on a brave face."

Rawlings grimaced, his huge slablike teeth lined up like gravestones. "Everything set?"

"Check. I've assigned agents to the San Diego office. I'll be flying out there tonight to coordinate the operation."

"Coach class, I hope."

"Yeah, yeah. If it were up to you, it would be stage-coach."

"Someone's got to guard the taxpayers' money."

"Sure you don't want to come along?"

"Director wants me here, within whipping range."

"Too bad," Dees said. "We could use you there."

"Quit cackling, Dees. You sound like a Broadway understudy telling the star how sorry she is to have to go on in her place. Besides, you know section chiefs don't go into the field. We delegate."

"Right. You mean take the credit if it succeeds, place the blame if there's a fuck-up."

"Cynicism is so unbecoming in the young."

"What are you doing with Godfrey?"

"Godfrey? He'll be here, uh, coordinating."

"Coordinating what?"

"Whatever will keep him out of the way." Rawlings smiled slyly. "He's hoping you'll fall flat on your face, you know? He's tired of feeling your hot breath on his ass."

"Tell him to relax. It's not his job I want. It's yours."

"Sure. Who wouldn't crave this kind of glamour?" He leaned back in his chair. The heater was a little too warm; the backs of his knees were beginning to sweat. "How's our boy doing?"

"Calender? Fine."

"Jo and Crush are in place?"

"Yeah. But I don't see the point. Now that we know where Devane's going to be, we could use them in San Diego. They know the area."

"No," Rawlings said, his hard gaze leaving no room for discussion. "I want Calender followed every day and tucked in every night. He's your responsibility. If this San Diego fiasco doesn't work, we're going to need him."

Dees nodded. "Okay."

"Have a nice flight." Rawlings bent over the stack of file folders and began studying them, ignoring Dees's presence.

Dees left, unable to account for the smell of burning shoe polish in his nose.

TWELVE HOURS LATER Dees stepped off the elevator onto the third floor of the Los Angeles office. He'd stuffed his tie into his jacket pocket as the plane was landing, opened his maroon shirt an extra button and arranged the collar on the outside of his gray linen jacket. In his wallet was the phone number of an entertainment reporter for the *Los Angeles Times*, who he'd met at an American Film Institute bash a couple years ago in Washington. They'd ended up in the sack together, and with any luck, he might wrap this whole thing up with time left over for her again. She did a little something with her tongue that raised goose bumps just thinking about it.

Dees was met at the elevator by two armed men in the uniforms of a nonexistent security company. They examined his ID, then proceeded to search him, both by hand and with a metal scanner. Proper procedure. They directed him to Conroy's office, down the hall past the photocopying room.

Conroy was the head of the Los Angeles office. Dees had never met him, only spoken with him over the phone, but he recognized the nasal voice now, as he neared the open office.

"How about when a cat's just finished taking a crap and he's, you know, scratching around in the litter. Set's my teeth on edge."

"Yeah," the second voice agreed. "Or like when Greenbaum down the hall sniffs real hard and you can hear the snot sucking into his throat. Most the time he does it at lunch, and I want to strangle him right then."

Dees entered the room. "Gentlemen."

Conroy was tall, with red hair and freckles scattershot all over his face. "Hey, Dees. My man pick you up at the airport okay?"

"Yeah." Dees was smiling.

"Me and Tom here were just compiling a list of obnoxious sounds, the kind that make your gonads jump, know what I mean?"

Tom looked a little embarrassed, but Conroy continued explaining, grinning like a schoolboy. "Like when a real hefty woman's walking around in panty hose and you can hear her fat thighs scraping together like sandpaper. Yeech, now that's a really obnoxious sound."

"Oh," Dees said, his face suddenly stony, "like the sound of you two jerks tearing open your pay envelopes every month?"

"Hey, come on now, Dees," Conroy started to protest. They both had the same level of authority, but Dees's being sent out here from Washington to head up the Masked Dog thing added a little extra weight to his position. Technically Dees was in charge, so Conroy kept his mouth shut.

"I want everybody gathered together in fifteen minutes for briefing," Dees said, all business.

Conroy nodded at Tom, who looked relieved as he raced out of the room to gather the troops.

"How long does it take to get to San Diego?" Dees asked.

"An hour and a half driving. Forty minutes flying."

"We'll fly. Have a plane standing by."

"Okay." Conroy picked up a phone, punched a few buttons, began making arrangements.

Dees wandered over to the window and spread the blinds with his hand so he could study the street below. Conroy was all right, no genius, but capable once he knew who was giving orders. Dees had established that right away. He looked out on Wilshire Boulevard, counted three Porsches and two Mercedes waiting at the same light. Some town, L.A.

Wilshire Boulevard. Same damn street where he'd followed those two phony FBI guys the other night. He hadn't stopped them. No need—he recognized them as KGB right away. Now he was back. He thought briefly of that night, Jo Montana, the astronaut's wife, who'd been in *People* magazine, standing almost naked, yelling at him because he was late. Calender standing there like a surprised teenager, fumbling with his fly, not saying a word, even after he'd figured out he'd been suckered. His cold silence all the way back to Washington had unnerved Dees a bit—eyes closed the whole flight, pretending to sleep. Calender gave off weird, what would you call them, vibrations? Dees almost envied him. Not his predicament. God, no. But his passion, his amazing resilience. Calender didn't have much savvy when it came to being tricked by women, but he had an old-fashioned view of right and wrong, and when he was cornered or protecting a loved one, he was dangerous. Ask his late wife.

Well, Calender was on his own now. Despite Rawlings's orders, Dees was field coordinator, and as such had the right to override certain orders, had already done so before he'd even spoken to Rawlings. Pulling Jo Montana and Crush off Calender was necessary, no matter what Rawlings thought. With only thirty-six hours left, Dees would need as many experienced agents as possible, especially ones familiar with the locale. They were shipping in agents from five nearby states, but none of them would know the freeways like Crush and his agents. Or Jo.

Dees permitted himself a small smile. Devane had screwed up this time. The drugs gave him a super memory, extraordinary strength, made him fearless. But also cocky and careless. He'd overestimated his abilities, underestimated the Agency's. This time he'd told them too much, and they'd be waiting for him with shotguns. There would be no trial this time, no prison. Those were his orders. In thirty-six hours Devane would be dead. And Dees would be up for promotion, at least to Godfrey's job. Maybe even higher.

"Plane's fueled and waiting," Conroy called from across the room as he hung up the phone. "Everyone's waiting in the conference room down the hall, hands folded, eyes bright.''

"Good.'' Dees started out the door, but Conroy stepped in front of him.

"You're in charge, Dees, so I gotta take your crap. That's okay with me—I've taken my share before. But I'm not eating shit and pretending it's ice cream. So you mind telling me just what the hell's going on?''

"Sure, Gary.'' Dees smiled. "It's simple. Devane sent us a letter, kind of an announcement of services available, like those flyers advertising the grand opening of a car wash you always find stuck under your windshield wiper. Only Devane's services are a little more specialized.'' Dees swept his hand across the air as if envisioning a Broadway marquee. "Assassin for hire. Neat, huh? Our informants tell us he's sent similar letters to a handful of governments who are always interested in such services, a few corporate heads who might be in the market for some easing of competition, and even letters to some Mafia families.''

"Jesus,'' Conroy muttered.

"But our boy Devane doesn't expect anyone to hire him sight unseen, a pig in a poke, so to speak. No way. So, like all good salespersons, he's set up a classy little demonstration. He's announced in his letters the date, the time, the place and the victim of his first assassination. His debut—which, by the way, he's doing gratis. Once he's proved his effectiveness, the bidding will be open for his services on a per body basis. Minimum bid, two hundred thousand dollars.''

"Who's the target?''

"Gee, Gary, who's going to be in San Diego in thirty-six hours?''

Conroy knew immediately. It was one of the most publicized visits in years. "Shit."

"Yup. Rupert Hesse."

Rupert Hesse was the East German longshoreman from Rostock who followed in Poland's Lech Walesa's footprints and organized many of his fellow workers to fight for better conditions. The struggle had resulted in bloody battles on the docks, with East German police attempting to beat the workers into submission. Unsuccessfully. Strikes continued, followed by more beatings, imprisonment and worse. Rupert Hesse lost his right eye during an overnight stay in prison. Officials blamed it on a prisoner who freely confessed, then miraculously escaped from prison a week later. Rupert Hesse, young, dynamic, handsome, had become a symbol for the struggle of all of Eastern Europe. There was even talk of his receiving the Nobel Peace Prize. Anxious to have him out of the country for a while, the East Germans had permitted him to come to the United States to speak. Apparently they hoped the foreign travel would lend itself to propaganda that would compromise his reputation by equating travel with contamination by the corrupt values of the West.

"If Devane's successful," Dees said, "if Rupert Hesse is killed in this country, the whole world's going to be on us. Violent society. Killer mentality. Blah, blah, blah. The publicity alone will certainly destroy any propaganda gains we've made in Eastern Europe in the past three decades. And even worse," Dees said, smiling, "Devane would have made you and me look like incompetent assholes."

"What about the Feebees?" Conroy asked, referring to the FBI. "Isn't Hesse's security their turf? They're not going to like us butting in."

Dees shrugged. "Fuck 'em if they can't take a joke."

Conroy shook his head. "Devane's nuts, man. Even without his stupid letter, the security around Hesse is tighter than the First Lady's twat. Now that we're on to him, there'll be more of us than there will be people to come and hear him. Devane knows we'll be there to stop him. He knows we'll be waiting to kill him."

"Yes, he does," Dees said, starting down the hall. "Intriguing, isn't it?"

12

She was running toward him now, her tight pink leotard soaked with sweat. Dark wet spots cupped each breast, drenching the nipples so that they appeared naked poking against the thin material. A wet patch clung to her hard flat stomach, disappearing into her white jogging shorts. The long muscled legs glistened in the midday sun as they pumped effortlessly up the hill. She wore no socks, no headband, no wristband, no Walkman. Her hair, as always, was wild. Even when she was standing still, it seemed to be windswept behind her, as if desperately trying to keep up with the rest of her. One of her more attractive features, he noted.

Like the sweat.

It seemed she was always soaked in the stuff. Slick and sticky and dripping. Personally, Alexei loathed sweat. One of the many things he liked about being assigned to this country was the many products they had to combat it, practically banish it from your body. Of course, on him sweat was more than a discomfort or a nuisance. It was an embarrassment. Maybe it was his body chemistry, his diet, his genetic disposition—he had no clue. All he knew for certain was that at the slightest outbreak of moisture on his body, he began to stink like a Moscow fish market. Like a peasant, he'd been told more than once back in Russia. Dreadful stuff, this sweat.

Except, of course, on her.

On Liza R it was as powerful an aphrodisiac as ever dreamed by lustful adolescents or waning old men. My God, look at her now, arms churning, legs scissoring up the steep incline. The drivers of passing cars, both men and women, cast admiring glances. By comparison, she made one feel so sedentary, so unhealthy.

She ran up to him, circled him playfully in a trot, then stopped. The drops of sweat streaking her body were thick and musky. Even now Alexei felt his desire stirring.

"So?" he said.

"I don't see how," she panted. "I ran through the whole place, checked everything." She continued pacing, hands on hips, gulping air. "Let's get back to the hotel. I gotta pee."

Alexei surveyed San Diego's dock area below. The old warehouses, the huge ships greasy from the dirty water rocking against the wooden docks. This was where the insolent troublemaker Rupert Hesse would speak tomorrow. This was where Devane had boasted he would kill Hesse. It looked impossible.

"Come on, Alexei," Liza R said.

"*Alex,*" he hissed, his face contorted into a menacing visage that had frightened many bigger men.

Liza R laughed. "I'm going to pee right here if you don't get your butt in gear."

Alexei climbed into the rented Chevrolet, unlocking the passenger's door for Liza R. He missed his own Mercedes, the rich smell of leather. Within seconds they were on their way to the Joffrey Hotel, less than two miles away. "What is your assessment?"

She shrugged. "Assassination would be difficult, but not impossible for a skilled marksman, say, with a Weatherby Mark V rifle. Of course, they'll be expecting that, which means they'll be staking out all potential sniper locations." She opened the window, stuck her head out. She giggled as the wind dried her face. She pulled her head back into the car. "God, that feels good!"

"Let us concentrate on business," Alexei said briskly.

"Don't lecture me, *Alex*," she said. "No one has been dissatisfied with my results yet."

Of course she was right. His impatience was the result of sexual jealousy, sitting next to her perspiring body, remembering that one night together, knowing there would never be another. He was misbehaving, acting unprofessionally. One did not treat Liza R as one might any other associate. First, because of who she was, her international reputation for ruthlessness and efficiency. Second, because she was a free-lance operative, and they were a particularly dangerous breed, perhaps because there were so few still alive. Naturally she was on retainer to the KGB, for which she received a handsome annual stipend. In return she gave priority to them in assignment choices, though certainly not exclusivity. Last year alone she had also worked for the Arabs, the Italians, the Cubans and even the Israelis. Not as Liza R, of course. Only the KGB knew her from her old name.

"I apologize," he told her.

"Accepted," she said, then smiled. "We all gotta do something that feels good sometimes, right?" She reached over and squeezed his crotch. The suddenness caused him to press the gas pedal, and the car jumped forward. She laughed. "See what I mean, *Alex*?"

Alexei said nothing. She had felt his stiff penis, knew why he'd been harsh with her. Now he was worse off than before. Before he had been frustrated and jealous; now he was humiliated.

When she continued, her voice was brusque and businesslike, as if nothing had happened. "But, of course, Devane is not a skilled marksman. He knows very little about guns. So unless he intends to attack the platform with a machine gun, I suspect he has another plan."

"A bomb, perhaps?"

"He's a pediatrician, for God's sake, not a physicist."

"But that memory of his makes him anything he wants to be."

Alexei thought about it for a moment, then nodded. "It's possible. He has the scientific background."

"They will be expecting that, too. I suspect they will utilize their electronic detectors and bomb-sniffing dogs and such."

"Count on it."

They arrived at the hotel and discontinued the conversation until they were back in her hotel room. Liza R hurried into the bathroom and, without closing the door, stepped out of her shorts, unfastened the snaps at the crotch of her leotard and sat on the toilet. She continued speaking over the trickling sound. "The only question left is whether we should try to find him and intercede—damn it, I don't want to shout."

Alexei appeared in the doorway, his anger great. She wanted him to watch; she was treating him not like a man, but like a sexless little boy.

"We can try to kidnap him before the assassination," she suggested, kicking off her blue running shoes while she sat.

"No." Alexei shook his head. He forced himself to meet her eyes, hide his anger. "Orders are to let him proceed. The propaganda value of Rupert Hesse's assassination in this country is immeasurable."

"Fine, but that will make it riskier. I wouldn't bet the farm on his succeeding, which means they'll kill him. Dead, he's no use to us."

"Orders," he repeated.

She tore toilet paper from the new roll. Alexei turned away from her until he heard the toilet flush. She was giggling. "Mommy's all done now, Alexei."

He turned back as she reached into the shower and started the water, testing it with her hand. Her leotard remained unsnapped and he noticed the blond pubic hairs as she leaned over the tub. He swallowed thickly.

She said, "Well, then, we have to hope Devane kills poor, one-eyed Rupert and manages somehow to escape. Then we wait for him to contact us, which he'll do immediately, the little show-off, and we make him an offer. Lots of money. All the little girls he can eat. And more money. Show him pictures of your Mercedes."

Alexei bit his lower lip. His excesses in spending had been a subject of some scrutiny with his KGB bosses over the years, but his superb record of achievement allowed him some concessions. Even the KGB understood that one could not hope to keep the loyalty of a specialist of Alexei's ability on the usual paltry salary. Especially when stationed in the United States. They permitted his luxuries and in turn he did not free-lance.

"Our orders are clear, Liza R," Alexei explained patiently. "We must get him back to the Soviet Union. Offer him whatever he wants. But if he refuses, we are to kill him."

"I dunno. He's very strong."

Alexei clenched his fists behind his back. She was goading him again, pushing him. Liza R was the small-weapons specialist. With a gun in her hands she was unbeatable. He had seen her demonstrate her skills before—in Cairo once and again in Rome—had seen the cold bodies, their hearts drilled through with small holes, their foreheads smashed with bullets. The Arabs called her the "Seamstress" because of the delicate stitching of bullets she sewed across her victims. But when it came to hand-to-hand, Alexei was thought to be one of the three best in the world. His speed was legendary, his athletic prowess undeniable. In his expensive clothing he looked like a trim businessman, mid-forties, maybe watched what he ate and played a little handball at the YMCA. That he could drop to the floor right now and do a hundred push-ups would not surprise any who knew him. Nor would the fact that he could enter a crowded room without any weapon, kill half a dozen people and be out again before anyone realized anything was wrong. Despite his small stature, he prided himself on his strength, so naturally that was what Liza R picked at.

"Yes," Alexei conceded, "Devane is strong. But between the two of us, we shall dominate. However, our main objective is to transport him back to the Soviet Union alive so our scientists can study him. After they are done, if he is still alive, the KGB will make proper use of his abilities."

"I don't give a shit about any of that. Just so we get him and I get paid." She peeled the leotard over her head, tossed it to Alexei, who caught it out of reflex. He could smell her on it. He glared at her, but she laughed and stepped into the shower. "We'll just have to convince ol' Devane, won't we? Give him something he wants."

"Yes, of course. Money."

"Oh, sure, money will help. But something else. Something he *really* wants."

"What?"

She pulled the curtain aside, soap foaming around her face, and smiled. "We'll give him Price Calender. My darling hubby."

SHE EASED THE RENTED MAZDA to the curb of the narrow residential street and waited. Stucco apartment houses with names like Manfred Arms or Seaside Woods hunched behind the palm trees like overgrown children, trying to hide. People, students mostly from UCLA, came and went. Students in cars with rough-sounding motors whipped around the winding street always above the speed limit, not in any particular hurry, but just to be doing something faster than studying. Someone's orange cat was almost hit twice crossing the street. Now he hid under a rusty yellow Datsun and licked himself.

Liza R noticed everything.

She stared at the empty parking space for apartment number seventeen across the street.

The drive from San Diego to Los Angeles had not taken long at all. A quick spurt up 5 to the 405, and right on into Westwood. Less than ninety minutes. Alexei was probably still in his hotel room, scheming on ways to go to bed with her again. She smiled to herself at the notion. Perhaps she would take pity on him. Probably not. He worked much better under pressure.

Out of boredom, Liza R checked her weapons. The 9 mm Star Model 28 was tucked into her clutch purse. The only other things in the purse were an extra clip of bullets, five one-hundred-dollar bills and a German switchblade. She reached under her seat and patted the butt of the 9 mm Detonics VI holstered there. Enough firepower, should it come to that. However, she didn't expect any trouble today. This was just a scouting mission. An amusing trip down memory lane.

She watched Price's apartment for almost an hour without spotting any signs of surveillance. No reflections from telescopes, binoculars, camera lenses. Nothing. No not-so-young "students" hanging around outside, pretending to read chemistry textbooks. Nobody. Surely Rawlings would have at least warned Price about Devane's escape. The danger he was in. Staked the poor bastard out as bait. But no, there was no one around. This would be easier than she'd expected.

She looked at her watch. Perhaps he'd gone to Pasadena today to spend time with his grandmother and Rebecca. Yes, she knew all about that, too. She knew everything. She leaned back into the seat, adjusted the rearview mirror so it reflected his empty parking stall. Give him time. Yesterday was Rebecca's birthday and he was between playing dates. She was sure they would celebrate in his apartment. Liza R sneered. That was the kind of sentimental man he had always been, even when they'd been married. The little gifts, the songs, the joking.

Liza R shifted in her seat, stared at herself in the mirror. It was not her face. At least, not the same face she'd had when she'd married Price Calender. Her hair had been blonder then, not this reddish tint, and it had been much shorter, resembling a too-tight helmet, a look favored by some radical feminists. It had fitted the part she'd been playing. The facial structure was slightly different now, too. The doctors had to reconstruct some of the shattered bones. The eyes were still the same pale blue, almost too pale. She refused to wear tinted contacts to change the color because they bothered her aim.

She'd been in that hospital in Virginia for a month, hidden there under a false identity provided by the Agency double agent who'd been at the scene when she'd tried her escape. He'd pronounced her dead to keep the others from examining her, switched her broken body with another corpse, doctored the records and sneaked her to a hospital. He was paid handsomely for his efforts—more than for the tidbits of useless information he'd been leaking to the KGB for the past year. When Liza R was finally released from the hospital, she terminated him within the week. The fewer people who knew her secret, the better.

She hadn't expected the ruse to last forever, just long enough for her to recover and start over again. Now that Devane was free, all that would start unraveling. But too late, she smiled. Too late.

"Lookin' for somebody?" the young man asked, grinning. He threw his schoolbooks into the back of his convertible VW bug and leaned against the fender in what he undoubtedly thought was a manly pose. "Maybe I can help."

Liza R smiled at him. "Maybe you can. I'm with Public Health. We're tracking down a nasty new strain of gonorrhea. Completely penicillin resistant. Have you ever had sexual contact with a Ms Sally Danridge? Goes to a lot of fraternity parties.''

The young man paled, glanced at the Alpha Sigma sticker on his car, shook his head furiously. ''Uh, never heard of her. Gotta run. Class.'' He hopped into his car and sped away.

When he was gone, she continued watching Price's empty parking stall. What was that line from *West Side Story*, when the old guy who runs the store where the Jets hang out is scolding one of the gang? ''When I was your age—'' he begins, and the street kid interrupts with something like, ''Man, you were never our age.'' That is how Liza R felt looking at these kids now, how she had always felt, even among people her own age. Always the outsider, too special to fit in.

Her mother had been a minor scientist working on minor early computer programs. Her father had been a writer of obscure articles about social injustice. Following the Korean War, they had become more and more politically active, marching with Ban the Bomb signs, decrying sexism, sitting in for racial equality. They were jailed, received hate mail and threatening phone calls, had their home stoned and a cross burned in their yard by neighbors who painted ''nigger lovers'' on their house. Frustrated and angry, they defected to the Soviet Union in 1963, taking their ten-year-old daughter, Liza R, with them. There was some publicity, but neither of them was important enough to cause an international fuss. They lived in Moscow for the next five years, and Liza R watched them wither under even harsher social injustices than those they'd left. Her father was arrested and jailed shortly thereafter for subversive writing. He never returned. Her mother took Liza R to a scientific conference in Helsinki, Finland, the next year, went to the hotel lobby for some cough drops and never returned. Liza R, sixteen, managed to scrape enough money together to go London. Her flawless Russian and English provided adequate income as a translator and interpreter. An impulsive marriage resulted in Rebecca, and her husband's shocking confession that the proper British banker she was married to was also selling information to the KGB. Men found it difficult to keep secrets from Liza R. Her husband proved not good at keeping secrets from anybody. He was arrested, convicted and jailed.

Following her husband's trial, Liza R was approached by a kindly elderly gentleman offering sympathy—and cash. He was her husband's KGB contact. He suggested that since she already knew many of her husband's contacts, and had an undeniable attractiveness and charm, she might continue in her husband's work. She accepted.

She began as a courier, using her daughter as a cover. The money was excellent, but she wanted more. Her ambitions elevated her into the more dangerous realms of espionage where the big money was to be made. She moved to the United States. That's where the action was. Naturally she brought Rebecca along, just as she brought the other tools of her trade, her wardrobe, her jewelry, her gun. But when Rebecca's growing needs became too demanding, began interfering with business, Liza R drove her to an orphanage, sat her down in a waiting room and drove off. It had been surprisingly simple. Unburdened, Liza R's reputation bloomed, as did her ambition, her desire for the risky, more lucrative top-secret assignments. To prove herself worthy, she pursued the Masked Dog Project, something only rumored about among other agents. She planned her attack carefully, as any person mapping out a career move: infiltrate the Agency as a lowly courier, slowly gather information, then make her move. To make this work she needed an unimpeachable cover. She went back to the orphanage, tricked her way into her daughter's files, found the address of the New Jersey couple who were her foster parents and kidnapped Rebecca from their home. Using her daughter as a cover, she sought a man whose traveling agenda fitted her needs and married him. Price Calender.

It had been easy.

But there had been complications. She had married several times during her career, never bothering to get a legal divorce from any of her husbands. The marriages had been strictly for business purposes, like the one to Price. Yet her personal and business relationships with men had so far always been predatory, on their part when she was young, on hers as she matured. But Price was not easily manipulated. He was tender, but very strong. And his love was strong, too. He doted on Rebecca, chided Liza R for neglecting her daughter. He didn't realize that *any* attention she paid to Rebecca was pure acting. She had no feelings for the child at all.

She'd gotten so close, had almost stolen Devane. But she hadn't counted on Price's passion, his terrible anger. He had destroyed everything, including, almost, her life. Afterward, having recuperated, she became a free-lance agent, expanding her expertise from merely courier to everything from international blackmail to assassination. She practiced with guns daily. She had missed Price as he'd come hurtling toward her in that jeep. Now was her second chance. She would not miss again.

Across the street, a shabby VW Rabbit squealed into the parking stall. She hunched over a Thomas Brothers map of Los Angeles, pretending to be lost.

Three of them emerged from the car. Trinidad, she remembered from the old days. Black, wisecracking bass player, always with an adoring young groupie on each arm, fiercely loyal to Price. For Price's sake Trinidad had tried hard to be friends with her, but it had been a strain. She'd always been pleasant with him, but he would stare at her as if he knew she was up to something. He hadn't changed much, gained weight, maybe twenty pounds. Cut his Afro shorter. His round face still had that disarming boyish look; his Negroid features were muted, washed out by some white genes.

Trinidad reached into the back seat and helped the little girl out. For a moment, Liza R abandoned her pretense with the map and stared directly into the mirror. Rebecca, ten years old. Of course Liza R knew about the brace—that had been reported along with all the other miscellaneous information regarding Price Calender. Still, she had wondered how she'd feel when she saw her own daughter again after seven years, saw the shiny metal brace clamped around her leg.

Liza R smiled with relief, for she felt nothing.

Price emerged from the driver's seat. Lanky, his hair longish and ruffled, but much shorter than it had been back then. Dark and naturally curly, the kind women always wished for but Price found a nuisance. No beard. She had never seen him without that beard, and it surprised her how handsome he was. Oh, he'd been plenty good-looking back then, but this was different. Age had tempered him, added a toughness she liked.

Yes. It would be a pleasure killing him.

13

Trinidad glanced around the cramped apartment and shook his head sadly. "I gotta tell you, Price. Looking at this place makes me have serious doubts about your manhood."

"Give me a break, Trin," Price said, flopping down on the sofa with the scraps of mail he'd unclogged from his mailbox on the way in. Rebecca immediately limped to the stereo system and began picking through the thousands of albums that lined the entire wall from floor to ceiling. The massive record collection dwarfed the expensive but well-worn furniture that echoed distant more successful days.

"No, man, I'm serious. Just look at this place." He swept his hands around to encompass the tiny living room, dining room and kitchen. The bedroom and bathroom were through the closed door.

"What's wrong with it?"

"What's wrong? I'll tell you what's wrong. It's too fucking *clean*. That's what's wrong."

"Hey, man," Price cautioned, nodding at Rebecca.

"Oh, yeah. Sorry 'bout that language, Buckeye."

Rebecca looked over her shoulder and giggled. "That's okay." She didn't allow anybody to call her "Becky," which she hated, but Trinidad refused to call her "Rebecca" because it reminded him of his mean aunt with the garlic breath, so they compromised with

128

"Buckeye." Sounded close and gave Rebecca a nickname, which made her feel special.

"Anyway. Like I was saying, you're a bachelor on the prowl, man. Hot to trot, loose as a goose, hatchin' for some action. You bring a woman up here, she's gonna expect to see some, you know, manly mess. Some underwear under the sofa. Dirty socks in the refrigerator."

Price let him go on without actually listening. Once Trin got started on something, he'd ramble for twenty minutes, elaborating, refining. Price liked the funny chatter even when he wasn't paying attention. That's the kind of friends they were; they enjoyed being in the same room without having to do anything about it.

"Like those albums. Whatta ya got there—a couple thousand records? You got them alphabetized, for Christ's sake. Or like the furniture. Where's the water rings from setting wet cans and glasses on the coffee table. Where's the dirty dishes stacked around the sink? Or like this refrigerator, man," Trinidad continued as he rummaged through the refrigerator for the Michelob that Price kept just for him. "Where the hell—sorry, Buckeye."

Rebecca was fitting a record onto the turntable. "'Hell' is okay," she said. "And 'damn.' But 'fuck' and 'shit' Daddy doesn't like."

Trinidad looked at Price and the two of them exchanged grins. Rebecca was always saying or doing things that made the two of them stop and just smile as if she'd just invented something amazing. She was just being a normal ten-year-old girl, but to them that was miraculous. Trinidad had twin eighteen-month-old baby girls of his own at home, but Rebecca had always been special to him. He didn't know the complete details of what had happened with Liza R; he just knew they'd been bad and that Price had never fully gotten over her.

Trinidad stuck his head back in the refrigerator. "Like this refrigerator. Where are the little crusted yellow stains from spilling God-knows-what six months ago. And where's the sour milk and yogurt with the expired date on it. Don't you have any respect for the institution of bachelorhood?" He twisted the cap off the beer and sipped.

Rebecca carefully lowered the turntable arm onto the record she'd selected. Immediately the speakers thumped out the deep mellow voices of the Drifters: "Oh, when the sun beats down and burns the tar up on the roof. And your shoes get so hot you wish your tired feet were fireproof . . ."

Price watched her sway with the music, do tiny dance steps that were amazingly graceful, considering the awkward metal anchoring her left leg. But she didn't try to fight the brace; she used it, incorporated it into her made-up dance as if it were a partner. Price's heart clenched with love at the sight. She'd sensed his down mood despite his hollow cheerfulness, and put the record on because she knew it was one of his favorites. Like most of his favorites, her friends at school never heard of them, never saw them on MTV, never heard them on the radio, except on an oldies station. But that didn't bother Rebecca. She and Trinidad and Price would sing "Up on the Roof" or "Woodstock" or "Lady Jane" or "Positively Fourth Street" in the car at the tops of their lungs.

Rebecca hummed along, adding her voice only for the refrain of "Under the Boardwalk." Her high sincere voice sounded funny bumping up against Rudy

Lewis's silky tones. Her earnestness made Price want to reach out and hug her up against him, bury his face in her sweet-smelling hair. But she was enjoying her singing and dancing, lost in a fantasy where she no longer had to drag the metal brace around, where she spun freely and outran horses.

Trinidad sat on one of the high wooden stools next to the kitchen counter, with Price's Fender guitar on his lap. Absently he plucked along with the song, never hitting a false note, giving the song a certain bluesy flavor it hadn't had before. He was still one of the best guitarists in the business with—Price knew, though Trinidad would never tell him—more offers for studio work and backup playing than Price ever got. Trinidad could have twice as much work if he left Price. For some reason he didn't.

Price had never been much more than a competent musician. His guitar playing was just okay, his fingers dexterous, but his mind was more tuned to singing, expressing the lyrics just right. His voice was limited, more scratchy than lilting, but it had a raw power that had excited the crowds. Still, it had been his songs that had made him popular, the songs about living and loving on the dangerous edge. Forbidden sex in a drive-in, the sinister allure of a tatooed beauty, a spurned lover forcing her man's car off the freeway at seventy mph. Explosive, violent passion. The very stuff Price had really known nothing about, only imagined for his songs. Until he'd met Liza R. And after her death, he'd stopped writing. They did only the old songs now.

When the Drifters song was finished, Rebecca said, "Bathroom," and went through the bedroom, closing the door behind her. Closing doors was a sign,

Grandma had said, that she was growing up. Somehow the thought of her growing up frightened him.

"Quick! Where's the cigarettes?" Trinidad whispered around the bottle.

"I don't smoke anymore," Price said.

"Yeah, right."

"I mean it. I quit."

"Come on, Price. Just a few puffs before she gets back."

"She'll know."

"I swear, I'll swallow the damn thing before she sees it."

Price pointed to the kitchen drawer. Trinidad hopped off the stool and had one lit within seconds.

"Ahhh," he said, sighing, puffing out perfect smoke rings. "This is all I have left since I settled down and got married. No more groupies—Lord love 'em, they never had headaches until *after* sex. No more grass. Just an occasional light beer and filtered cigarettes. Now Tina wants me to quit smoking so I'll set a good example for the twins. Shit, man, I'm a rock-'n'-roller. I'm not supposed to be a good example."

Price didn't answer. He was staring at the bedroom door, frowning. He wiggled his two fingers like scissors and Trinidad stuck the lit cigarette between them. Price took a deep puff and the cigarette flared. "Grandma's shakes are getting worse, Trin."

"Damn," Trinidad said. "That old lady's got a lot of spunk, man. Don't count her out yet."

"She's suggested moving in with my parents—her and Rebecca."

"Oh-oh. Buckeye and your folks just weren't meant to be. She's got too much of her old man in her. You remember what it was like for you growing up there."

Price took another puff and nodded. "The only other option is I bring her in here with me."

Trinidad lit up. "That's what I been telling you for the past three years. We line up some gigs closer to home, start getting our shit together to cut a new album."

"Oh, sure, just like that. And what do we put on that album? All the songs we're doing now we've already recorded."

Trinidad snatched the cigarette away from Price. He stared at the stub that was left. "Good thing you quit, huh?" He pinched the butt, took a final drag and carried it to the sink, where he flushed it down the garbage disposal. "You've heard this all before, Price, but maybe this is the time it sinks in." He wiped his wet fingers on his pants and stared at his partner. "You've got to start writing some new songs. Hell, they don't even have to be that good. Just get started and we'll work out the bugs later. But that's the only way we're going to scrape up a record deal in this town. Unless you want to borrow another five hundred dollars from your Grandma and we go back to making cheap demos."

Price grinned. "That was a time, wasn't it?"

"Yeah, but that was *that* time. This time is different. This time I got a wife and a couple howling daughters. You got a daughter with her own platoon of doctors. We ain't doing it just for ourselves this time."

Price looked at Trinidad. The kindly dark face frowned in that disapproving expression he got when he was scolding Price. "I just don't want to screw up, man."

"What do you mean? The music?"

"No, Rebecca. I'm afraid of messing up raising her. Like I messed up my career, like I messed up the marriage."

"Hey, you didn't mess anything up." He stalked across the room, stood directly in front of Price. "You never told me the whole story about Liza R's death, except she was killed in a car crash. Christ, Price, I know there's a hell of a lot more to it than that. That's your business. But I also know you. I know you're good—compulsively neat, a tidier, a clean freak—but basically decent. If I hear Tina say one more time, 'Why can't you be more like Price,' I'm going to throw one or both of you into a crowd of yelping music critics and may God have mercy on your souls."

Price took a deep breath and glanced around the apartment. Was this the kind of place to confine an energetic ten-year-old girl? He looked over his shoulder, out the window to the curvy street below. Another cheap used car driven by a sleepless student sped around the corner. Directly below the window a young man was trying to talk a reluctant coed up to his apartment. She kept pointing to her watch. And that Mazda on the curb, under the streetlight, the woman with the map open in her lap, looking up here now, looking directly at him. Their eyes locked and she quickly turned away.

"My God," Price gasped.

"What?" Trinidad asked, concerned. "What is it? You look terrible."

"Come here, quick! Look down there, the woman in the Mazda."

Trinidad knelt on the sofa and peered out the window. The Mazda had started up. The woman looked over her shoulder before pulling the car onto the street.

"What about her?" Trinidad asked.

"It's her, man. Liza R." His finger stabbed the window excitedly.

Trinidad stared out the window. "No way. Her hair's a different color. It's cut differently, too. I could see. Even the face looks different, the shape." The car roared around a corner and disappeared. "Besides, man, she's dead. Remember?"

Price nodded. Of course he remembered. And yes, those things had been different. But those eyes, those pale eyes that threatened to consume anything they saw. That vengeful look. She was staring right at him.

But Trinidad was right. She was dead. Killed seven years ago, the same year Paul Ackerman, editor of *Billboard* for thirty years, who coined the phrases "country and western" and "rhythm and blues," died of a heart attack. The same week Debby Boone's "You Light Up My Life" bumped Mecco's "Star Wars Theme" as the number one pop 45.

Price rubbed his eyes, reminded himself that he needed glasses. The pressures caused by Devane's escape, his grandmother's illness, his daughter's needs, had caused him to see things that weren't there. Yet, at that moment of recognition, when he'd thought he knew her, what had he felt? What emotion had electrified his body so forcefully? Hate? Vengeance? No, that's what he'd expected. Adrenaline had flooded through his stomach; blood had gushed through his veins like the swollen gutters after a storm. But what had he felt? To his own horror, he identified the feeling.

He had seen her as he had first seen her that evening after the concert. And he had *wanted* her again.

"Caught you," Rebecca scolded as she returned from the bathroom. "Okay, who's been smoking?"

14

Jo had never seen so many cops before.

"Hey, Jo," Crush called as he hurried down the hotel corridor, adjusting the plastic ID badge on his jacket. He jostled a few people clogging the hall, but no one said anything. They were all waiting for orders.

"Where's my coffee?" she asked.

"Gimme a break, Jo. The fucking machine ran out half an hour ago. I'm standing in line like some jerk, turns out to be the line to bathroom. I finally get in the right line and word comes down that the machine is empty. No coffee, no tea, no hot chocolate. One of the Secret Service guys told me the soft-drink machine was empty, too. Hell, they're even running low on toilet paper."

"Damn. I had my heart set on a caffeine fix." She gestured at the dozens of plainclothes and uniformed people milling about. "Look at all of them. FBI, Secret Service, SDPD. They got everybody out here but the Green Berets."

"Did Dees tell them yet? About Devane?"

Jo shrugged. "He went into that room half an hour ago with Bedlow from Secret Service, Chapin from FBI and Chief Gravis, SDPD. There's been yelling ever since."

"Seen the mystery man, yet?"

"Hesse?"

Crush nodded.

"Nope. You?"

"Hang on to your heart. He's a looker."

Jo smiled, and for no reason she could fathom, an image of Price Calender popped into her mind and wouldn't go away. She didn't know what to make of it. She just knew that she wished she were with him now, instead of hanging around the Castilian Hotel with half the law-enforcement agents in the country. But why Price? Guilt? Or something else?

"What do you think of him?" she asked Crush.

"Hesse? He's okay, I guess, if—"

"No, no. Calender. What do you think about him?"

Crush squinted at her, ran his big hand over his blond head. "I guess I like him. It seems to me he's down to earth. Doesn't give a rat's ass about people who aren't worth it and is willing to knock himself out for those who are. Why?"

"I don't know. Guess I'm feeling guilty about the way we set him up, then left him hanging there alone."

"It's not personal."

"No," she answered quickly. She looked up into Crush's kindly eyes and sighed. "I don't know. Maybe. Too early to tell."

Crush slipped a thick arm around her shoulder. "Don't worry, pumpkin. I been around guys like that before. Kinda quiet on the outside because they're afraid of what they might do if they lose their temper. My guess is that he can take care of himself when he has to."

"Thanks, Miss Lonelyhearts, but I'm not talking about lovesick or anything. I'm just interested, that's all. Hell, I get interested in somebody at least twice a day."

also knew he was engaged to a young woman back in East Germany, the daughter of a fellow longshoreman.

Somewhere in the middle of the shouting, Rupert Hesse stood up and spoke in German. His voice was soft but commanding. He was a natural leader of men. He spoke for several uninterrupted minutes.

They all stared at him as he spoke, though none understood German. His eyes twinkled and he smiled frequently, with humor. When he was finished, he sat down and the translator spoke. "Mr. Hesse assures you that he is quite aware of the dangers that await him, whether they be on a dockside in East Germany or a dockside in San Diego. He also appreciates the difficulty, indeed, the impossibility of your job, and regrets the imposition. However, he has no intention of canceling his speaking engagement. It is important that the workers in the United States realize that he did not come here to speak against the German Democratic Republic, of which he is a patriot, but against tyranny possible in every government. Therefore, regardless of the risk, he will speak today, and suggests that we will have to hurry if we are to be on time."

Rupert Hesse tapped his watch with the stem of his pipe and smiled charmingly. "We go," he said. Then he turned and disappeared into the bedroom, closing the door behind him.

There was a full minute of silence as everyone stared at one another. Finally Dees said, "Crush and Jo will stay with Hesse, along with whoever else you want. But I want them up there on the dais."

No one disagreed.

"Good." Dees checked his watch. "We've got forty minutes to get him there. As the great man himself so aptly put it, 'We go.'"

Out in the hall he herded Crush and Jo into a corner and pressed his face close to theirs. "Okay, we've got the chicken in the house. Now let's kill the fucking fox."

"Dog," Crush said. "Masked dog."

"Whatever," Dees said, shrugging. "As long as he's dead."

15

Devane leaned against the second-story balcony railing and watched the big ugly Mexican with the gold earring lug his duffel bag around the motel pool, looking for Devane's room number. Devane could have called out to him, but he didn't. If the jerk was too dumb to figure it out on his own, the hell with him. He looked at his watch and shrugged. There were still forty minutes before Rupert Hesse would arrive. Plenty of time.

He smiled to himself and continued to stare into the small swimming pool below. A dark crack zigzagged across the bottom of the pool, up one side and along the poolside concrete all the way to the ice machine next to the manager's office. A couple of young kids ran out of room twelve, skipping across the parking lot and jumping into the shallow end of the pool, splashing each other in a frenzy of giggles. The boy was about thirteen, the little girl about twelve.

Devane leaned farther over the rail to watch, studying the little girl. She was pale and scrawny, her hair a mousy brown, dirty and home cut. With some child's instinct, she suddenly glanced up over her shoulder at Devane. He flashed his toothy movie-star smile at her. She whispered something to her brother, and they both laughed and went back to splashing each other.

"Hey, kids," the big ugly Mexican called to the kids. "Where's number twenty-three?"

The boy shrugged, dived underwater, popped up spitting a mouthful of water into his sister's face. She laughed.

"Fuckin' kids," the Mexican said, and spit into the pool.

"Hey, Diaz," Devane hollered down. "Up here."

Diaz looked up, his gold earring sparkling in the sun. "The fuck you say so before, man." He hefted the duffel bag onto his broad shoulders and ambled toward the stairs.

Devane waited, shirtless, letting the hot San Diego sun slap against his pasty jailhouse skin. This was his first trip to San Diego, his second to California. He'd been in San Francisco twelve years ago for a pediatrics convention at the Mark Hopkins. He liked it here. Even in this cheap motel, the sun was cheerful, seemed to energize him.

He felt the balcony quiver a little with each step Diaz took up the stairs. He'd first met this man in prison. Devane gripped the metal railing with both hands, flecks of old green paint sticking to his skin. He studied his arms and chest while he waited for Diaz, fascinated with his own body. He'd always been average height, slightly built, with neither the speed nor strength to compete in school athletics. Instead he'd used his charm, his good looks to get what he wanted. He'd been in two fights in his life, both of which he'd tried to avoid, both of which he'd lost miserably. He'd give anything to have both those guys in front of him now. They'd made him ashamed of his body. But now he was proud of it, wanted to show it off. His hands tightened around the railing and he watched the muscles along his forearm flex and bunch like small hills. He tightened his grip more, and the metal railing groaned and bent, leaving indentations where his hands had been.

"You got the money?" Diaz said, walking toward him, each heavy step shaking the balcony.

Devane smiled. "Inside."

Diaz followed Devane into the small room. "Sleeze-bag motel, man. Smells like shit in here," Diaz said, taking deep sniffs and making a face.

"Probably a more accurate assessment than you realize."

Diaz snorted, tossed the duffel bag onto the bed. "It's all there, man. You owe me a grand." He gave Devane a menacing look that showed he was fully prepared to break a bone for every dollar short of the thousand.

Devane leaned against the wall, still smiling. "Show and tell first."

Diaz tugged on his gold earring and grinned. "Sure, man. What the fuck. You're the customer, right?"

"Right."

Diaz unzipped the canvas bag and pulled out a small black box with four toggle switches next to four red lights. He telescoped the antenna from the box. "You just flip this switch here, man, to turn the thing on. Then, when you're close enough, say, quarter of a mile, you just jack these other switches on, and bam, bam, bam. Like you asked for." He pushed the antenna back into the box and dropped the box on the bed.

"Any way they can detect the charges?"

"Hell, no. They can use trained dogs or pigs or whatever they want, but there ain't enough explosive there to blow your nose. Nobody get hurt from this shit, man."

"Okay, good. Any problem setting it up?"

Diaz snorted. "No way. I know my shit, man. Worked eight years as a stuntman on some of the biggest fucking movies you ever saw. *The Wild Bunch*, man, I was the cowboy that goes through that plate-glass window. Fuckin' slow-motion shot. Everybody says Peckinpah was a fuckin' genius, man, but I'm the one pickin' glass out of my ass for a week. Sure, it's nothin' but fake toffee glass, but that stuff ain't cotton candy, either. Then the little bastard fires me. Peckinpah's an asshole, man. Same with George Roy Hill. Fucker made *Butch Cassidy and the Sundance Kid*. Got me playing some Mexican gets shot off a wall—I gotta do a somersault into a wagon. Hill ends up going to parties in Beverly Hills, probably feeling up Katharine Ross's ass, and I get fired by some script girl. Biggest thing in her life is waitin' for her period to start. Fuckin' show business, man." Diaz spit on the carpet. "Busted my leg for the fifth time flipping a car for *Charlie's Angels*. Figured it's time to get out of that business. Got a cousin with big tits and tight ass, always wanting to visit me on sets, hoping Robert Redford gonna leave his wife to take up with her. Hell, I wouldn't leave my *dog* for her. Best she can do is shack up with this special effects guy named Dutch, happy to get laid by someone he don't have to pay first. The bastard hires me on to work with him. I can do all that shit now. I went in, planted the stuff, got out again, no sweat. Even got paid five hours' overtime."

Devane smiled, but didn't move.

Diaz was still breathing hard, angered by his own story. But then his expression changed as he directed some of that anger toward Devane. "So where's my money, man."

"How much was that again? A thousand?" Devane still didn't move.

"Hey, man," Diaz warned, shaking his meaty fist at Devane. "Don't fuck with me. You may think you're hot shit around the gym, pumping iron, pussying around with Nautilus crap, getting all hard for the faggot magazines. But that don't mean shit out here on the street, man. So gimme my bread now."

Devane studied Diaz a moment, felt the surge of adrenaline icing through his stomach. Diaz was big, about six foot two, two hundred fifty pounds. The gut sagged a bit, but there was power in that body. He was younger, early thirties. But that wouldn't be enough. He pushed himself off the wall and walked up to Diaz, his eyes level with Diaz's whiskered chin. He glanced up into the Mexican's eyes and smiled. "Would you settle for five hundred dollars?"

Diaz looked incredulous, his mouth wide, his eyes fiery. He tried to speak, but anger choked off the words. Instead he punched Devane in the jaw. Devane was surprised by the force of the punch as he staggered all the way back to the wall, his head thumping against the plaster. The swag lamp dangling from the ceiling shook from the impact. Devane's jaw felt awkward, but didn't hurt. The inside of his mouth was raw from where his teeth had chomped onto the membrane. He tasted blood, but still there was no pain.

"The fuck's the *money*, man," Diaz shouted at him, both fists raised, ready to lunge.

Devane shook his head groggily. His heightened strength had made him forget that even though he didn't feel the pain, the damage was still done. He was hurt. He had been childish, insulting the man to his face. Better to have struck first. Now he would have to make a fight of it, risk injury, jeopardize his whole plan.

"The money!" Diaz screamed.

Devane raised his hands in surrender. "Okay, man, okay. Take it easy. In the drawer."

Diaz knocked the desk chair out of the way and pulled open the drawer. "Better be a full thousand in here, man, or they'll be fishing bits of you out of the bathroom drain." His big hands swept the drawer, found some postcards, a Bible. "It ain't here, you fuck." He spun toward Devane, who was already moving. Devane grabbed Diaz's shirt with both hands and jerked hard, expecting to fling the big man to the floor. But because of his enormous strength, instead he ripped the dirty blue workshirt from Diaz's body, leaving the Mexican standing. Had Diaz thought about what had just happened, he might have been frightened, he might have run out that door and kept going. But anger had always guided Diaz's actions, and now was no different. First the gringo tried to screw him out of his one thousand dollars. Then he ripped his fucking shirt. Diaz would make him pay for both insults. Pay with his life.

Devane threw the shirt to the floor and leaped at Diaz's throat. But Diaz had been in enough real and studio fights to know what to do. He caught the smaller man in midair and catapulted him into the wall behind the bed. Devane crashed into the wall; the plaster caved in where Devane's shoulder hit. Devane flopped onto the bed. He felt no pain in the shoulder, though he could tell from the scraping feeling that the bone was probably cracked. He glanced up in time to see Diaz tearing the swag lamp from the ceiling and twirling it over his head like a lasso.

Devane scrambled to the edge of the bed and dived to the floor just as Diaz let the Tiffany lamp fly at his head. The lamp bounded harmlessly off the mattress, but Diaz was already swinging the chain, bringing it around toward Devane as he rolled across the floor. The lamp whipped through the air and crashed a full foot from Devane's head. The dirty glass shattered and two of the three light bulbs popped. The metal edge of the lamp dug into the stained carpet.

Though Devane was able to roll free of the blow, Diaz still managed to loop the chain and lamp cord around Devane's neck and jerk him to his knees. Diaz braced his body against Devane's back and yanked hard on the chain, snapping Devane's head back as the chain pinched deeper into his flesh. Devane tried to reach over his shoulder and grab Diaz, but he couldn't quite get a hold of anything. It was one thing to have great strength in a fight, but another to have actual experience. Devane was realizing now just how serious a mistake he'd made goading the big Mexican.

"Fuckin' asshole," Diaz was saying, spitting the words, spraying saliva over Devane's head. "Cut your fuckin' throat in half."

Devane felt no pain at his throat, though he could not breathe. He clamped his fingers around the cheap lamp chain at this throat and pulled. Nothing. Lack of oxygen had weakened him considerably. He pulled again, his teeth gritting, his neck muscles swelling. Then the chain snapped, and he gulped air greedily into his body.

Diaz was stunned for a few seconds, uncomprehending. He stared at the broken chain and cord in his hand, then at Devane. Then he got angrier. "Motherfucker!'' he hollered, diving onto Devane's prone body, smothering the smaller man with his great weight. His huge hands encircled Devane's throat, the thumbs big as hummingbirds and pressed against the windpipe.

Devane's arms were pinned under Diaz, making it impossible to get leverage to use his strength. It was like being buried up to you neck in sand. He bucked, using his legs and hips, bouncing Diaz up enough to free one hand, and with that free hand reaching up and grabbing the first thing his hand touched. Diaz's ear. He yanked, and the ear tore partially away from the face, blood surging out of the tear, Diaz yelping, his grip loosening. Devane released the ear, and it sagged uselessly like a rubber flap. He used his advantage now to heft Diaz off him, shoving him up against the wall. Before Diaz could recover, Devane grabbed the Mexican's arm and twisted it almost a full three hundred and sixty degrees. Diaz screamed as his arm unscrewed out of the socket with a grating pop.

''How about five hundred dollars now,'' Devane sneered, straddling the moaning Diaz. ''That sound okay now?''

Diaz, flat on his back, nodded through the pain. ''Sure, man. Five hundred's fine.''

''Yeah? How about three hundred dollars, then. That okay, too?''

''Whatever you say, man, okay. Just let me get to a doctor. My fuckin' arm's busted.''

''Okay, sure, man. Better get to a doctor.'' He stood up, pulled Diaz to his feet. Diaz leaned against the wall, trying to catch his breath, his face contorted with pain. Devane smiled at him, those perfect white teeth right from a commercial. "You wouldn't tell anyone what happened, would you? I mean, about our deal."

"No, man," Diaz promised, fear starting to edge out his pain. "I'd be just as guilty."

"Guilty of what?"

"I dunno, man. Of whatever you're planning."

Devane stared at him a long minute, then gestured toward the door. "Get to that doctor."

Diaz felt a warm wave of relief wash through his insides as he hobbled painfully toward the door. First, get down to the clinic and get fixed up. Plenty of time to take care of this dude later. Him and a couple buddies come down here and crack that fucker's head open and fry his brains in a skillet. Son of a bi—

Sound of splintering wood behind him.

Diaz turned, saw everything at once. Devane's fist crashing down through the wooden desk, breaking the thing in half, Devane ripping one jagged piece of wood free, Devane running at him, shoving the hunk of splintered wood right into Diaz's chest, wedging apart ribs until they cracked, piercing his heart and tunneling on through, poking right out his back. The roar of blood filled his ears, and at first he thought it was the sound of the surf, until he realized they were about four miles from the beach. He died confused.

Devane stepped over the body, opened the door a crack. Nobody seemed to have noticed anything. The two kids were still screaming and splashing in the pool.

He closed the door and checked his watch. Still plenty of time, he thought, smiling.

JO SAT IN THE BACK SEAT of the limo with her gun lying loosely in her lap. Next to her, Rupert Hesse was chatting away in German with Wanda Hertz, the thick-waisted translator from the State Department. Wanda sat in the front seat next to Crush, who drove the limo slowly through traffic, stopping at all yellow lights so as not to lose Dees and the others in the limo behind them.

Crush chuckled. "What would you give to have a bug in Dees's car right now, listen to him and Bedlow and Chaplin and that Chief Gravis bitching at each other, trying to prove which is the supercop among them?"

"I wish Rawlings were handling this personally," Jo said, scanning the streets and sidewalks as she spoke. "He's a bastard sometimes, but at least he knows what the hell he's doing."

"Yeah," Crush agreed. "Rawlings isn't so bad."

The rest of the drive was eventless. Jo was certain that no one was following them other than Dees and company, and the route they took was so roundabout that even Jo was lost a couple times. No chance of sniper stakeout on this route.

With all the room in the wide-body limo, she thought Rupert Hesse managed to sit pretty close to her. His thigh brushed hers occasionally, sometimes with him apologizing, sometimes with him pretending nothing had happened. Wanda was half turned in the front seat so she could easily glance back and point out certain features of San Diego as they passed them. Each time Wanda faced Rupert, Jo thought she caught a disapproving grimace directed at her.

"Okay, gang," Crush announced, wheeling near the wooden platform from which Rupert would speak. "This train don't carry no sinners. Get ready to deboard."

"Quite a crowd," Jo said. They sat with the engine idling, watching the crowd of at least a thousand scatter about for seats in the newly constructed grand-stand. About a hundred of the gathered were media people, pointing cameras and microphones. Uniformed cops with bomb-sniffing dogs still patrolled the aisles.

Dees's limo sailed up behind them. Bedlow hopped out first, calling to a couple of his Secret Service men. Jo recognized one of them, whom she'd been partnered with once while guarding Nadia Comaneci during the Romanian gymnastic team's U.S. tour. Chapin was next out of the limo, waving his neatly combed FBI agents into place. Chief Gravis climbed out slowly, like a patient father enduring the childish antics of his children. He lit a cigar and disappeared into the crowd. Dees was last. They could see him stepping out of the limo, the car phone still pressed to his ear as he shouted final orders at someone. He tossed the phone back into the car and marched over to Rupert Hesse's limo, tapping impatiently on the glass with his finger. Jo opened her window, studying his clenched face through the descending tinted glass. Dees had changed during the past few days. The slick self-confidence had eroded slightly, and his calm veneer was now marred by flaring nostrils and involuntary twitches around the eyes and mouth.

"Okay, guys," Dees said. "This is it. In about three minutes, the mayor and some local cronies will be climbing onto that platform. Introductions will be made, bullshit tossed around about free speech and our brothers behind the iron curtain, applause, applause. Hesse will make his little speech. Then you guys whisk his German butt the hell out of here, not to the same hotel. Just pick one and phone in the name. That should take care of any security breech and waiting ambush. Questions?"

"Nope," Crush said.

Jo shook her head.

"Fine," Dees said. "Half that crowd out there are undercover cops or agents of some kind. If Devane shows, his ass is mine." Dees walked off into the crowd.

"Whew," Jo said. "You think Ahab had it bad for Moby Dick. Dees is so hepped up he wants to pull the trigger himself."

Crush shrugged. "As long as they get Devane."

"Hello, hello," someone said into the microphone. It was Councilwoman Debra Tyne, who'd ridden into office as an outspoken mother opposed to school busing. *"Today we are honored . . ."*

Jo felt Rupert's hand on her arm. Instinctively her fingers flexed around her gun.

"Bitte, Fräulein," he said softly to her, his face creased with sincerity. *"Vielen Dank für ihre Bewachung. Ich Wünche wir hättenen uns nicht unter solchen gefärlichen Umstände kennen gelernt."*

Jo glanced at Wanda, who translated grudgingly. "Mr. Hesse thanks you for your help and wishes that you'd met under better circumstances."

"Whoa." Crush grinned into the rearview mirror. "I think that boy is hitting on you, Jo."

"He's just being polite," Jo said, but she knew from the pressure of Hesse's hand and the press of his knee against hers that there was more to it. He was handsome enough—maybe a little too handsome with that studied casualness, the long bangs hanging over his forehead. He reminded Jo of her ex-husband, Steve, the same intensity and commitment, but with a secret eye on the future, a certain what's-in-it-for-me look. And then there was Price Calender, ex-rock star, ex-Agency mule. Why was it all the men she knew were ex-somethings? Ex-astronaut running for the Senate. Ex-longshoreman leading disgruntled workers. At least Price was still a musician, still playing. And he was a father, a damned good father from what she'd observed, even though Rebecca wasn't biologically his. All things considered, he was pretty stable. Jo couldn't help but think back to that night they'd met, standing next to the bed, stripping, stalling for time waiting for Dees to arrive. And all the time almost hoping he wouldn't show.

"Time to go," Crush said. One of the Secret Service guys with an earphone in one ear was signaling to them.

"Es ist Zeit," Wanda told Rupert.

He nodded, leaned over and kissed Jo on the cheek just above her neck. His tongue flicked against her skin and she felt a tingle along her jaw. He winked at her, nodded at Crush and slid out the car, waving to the cheering crowd as he mounted the platform steps.

"Hell of a polite guy," Crush said, grinning at her.

"C'mon," Jo said, wiping her cheek. "Let's work the crowd."

"QUITE A TURNOUT," Liza R said, impressed.

Alexei shrugged. "Typical Americans. They have such bland personalities of their own, they worship anyone who has any charisma. If Hitler were living here, he'd be on the *Phil Donahue Show*."

"My God, Alexei," Liza R said, laughing. "You made a joke."

"Alex," he reminded her, brushing a wrinkle from his expensive jacket.

Liza R and Alexei stood at the back of the crowd, among the latecomers, the curious, the wailing children, the stocky dockworkers who'd been encouraged to attend by their local union in exchange for some free tickets to the Clippers basketball game. There were a couple of hecklers, but they lacked enthusiasm, jeering out of habit rather than passion. A few burly men swigged from bottles wrapped in brown paper bags. Some eyed Liza R, grinning broadly or winking at her. She smiled back to each, more to annoy Alexei than anything else.

"We must be inconspicuous," he chided her. "Not be noticed."

"Why? No one can recognize me anymore. Liza R is dead and my ID describes one Sandra Levy, accountant, slightly overdrawn at the bank, with credit cards that are nudging their limit. Your average working woman." She jabbed a finger against Alexei's natty twelve-hundred-dollar sport jacket. "It's you they might recognize. And if anything happens, it's you they might just drag in for questioning."

Alexei bristled. "They have no reason to suspect me of anything. I am, to them, nothing more than a Hungarian immigrant with a successful import business. Even my accent is almost gone."

Liza R laughed. "You practically sound like a native. It's almost eerie, Alex."

"Why do you persist on goading me like this, Liza R? We are working this assignment together and it is to our mutual benefit to get along."

"I don't know Alexei," she answered with a sigh. "I guess it's because you're such a boring turd."

Silently they continued to scan the crowd for Devane.

DEVANE RETIED the Windsor knot of his tie for the fourth time. The point of the tie had to just barely tip the top of his belt. Any shorter and it made him look like some yokel Bible salesman from Oklahoma. Any longer and he looked like a geeky computer programmer dressed by his mother every day before work. "Goddamn it!" He frowned, yanked the tie apart and started it again.

Everything else was ready and packed in the car. All laid out for easy access. He'd have to move fast down there. They'll all be waiting for him, itchy for a shot. Elsewhere around the country, around the whole world, there were powerful men with sour expressions waiting to see what would happen in the next thirty minutes. Right now they were just curious, intrigued by the oddity of someone so reckless as to announce his victim. Someone so amateurish. No doubt they all thought he'd be killed in his attempt and that would end it.

Devane smiled into the motel mirror. At the bottom of the mirror he could catch a glimpse of Diaz's hunched body. Someone else who'd underestimated him. Well, within the hour, they would all have heard about his success. Then they'd be reaching for their checkbooks.

He slid the knot under his chin, flipped the collar down. The tip of the tie hovered barely an eighth of an inch above his belt. Perfect.

He stepped over Diaz, picked up his jacket from the bed and hurried out the door. Rupert Hesse had only minutes to live.

"ANYTHING?"

Crush shook his head. "Not yet."

Jo picked through her purse for a cigarette. "Shit. Got a cigarette?"

"Sorry. I never smoke on the job."

"Fine, I'll recommend you for a citation."

Crush chuckled.

"Okay," Jo said, sighing, "back to work. I'll sweep through this half, you take that half. We'll meet back down at the dais and keep watch there."

"And if I spot Devane, you want me to wiggle my ears or wave a white handkerchief or something like that?"

"Too subtle. How about a couple of handsprings down the center aisle, ending with a rendition of 'Mammy.'"

"Gotchya."

They split up and Jo began pressing through the thick crowd, excusing herself, apologizing for constantly bumping into people. Still the best way to check someone out for weapons. She didn't find any. Except once. Tall guy with sunglasses, wearing a Nike jogging suit. About twenty-two. Didn't look anything like Devane, but who's to say Devane didn't hire a partner, or that some other nut wanted to kill Hesse.

"Excuse me," she mumbled, her hand brushing over the hard metal stuck in his waistband under his jogging jacket. The man's hand clamped around her wrist and she started for her own gun in her purse.

"Uncle Bedlow mentions you often, ma'am," he said, smiling.

Jo relaxed and moved on. One of Bedlow's Secret Service agents. Gawd, he looked so young. Bad sign, girl, when they start calling you "ma'am."

She wormed through the last crush of bodies bursting into the aisle. She saw some men's heads turn and she smiled to herself, thinking, yeah, you still got it,

kid. Then she turned around and saw they were looking at another woman, kind of blond, her nose a little
crooked. Bright turquoise minidress with wide red
belt. Not a real beauty, but athletic-looking, with gorgeous legs. Snooty expression, like she didn't give a shit
who you were, you'd still have to prove yourself to her.
The kind men would line up to impress. Hair a little
wild, windswept, giving the feeling nature was her
hairdresser.

Jo wanted to rip her lungs out.

But that passed. She smiled at herself as she negoti-
ated the steep wooden steps to meet Crush at the foot
of the dais. He shrugged to indicate he hadn't seen
anything suspicious.

After waiting for four speakers to take turns heaping
praise on him in a language he didn't understand,
Rupert Hesse finally was ushered to the podium. He
nodded politely at each of the speakers and smiled at
the anxious crowd, giving a little extra wattage, Jo
thought, to the media people and their cameras. He
tapped the microphone, put his mouth next to it and
said with his thick accent, "Hi, Mom."

The crowd loved it, applauding and laughing.
Whooping for more.

"A hero for our time," Jo said to Crush.

Crush nodded. "He's all right. No worse than some,
better than most."

"Sorry, forgot I was talking to Captain Free-
dom . . . doesn't smoke, drink, or have sex on the job."

"Who said anything about sex?"

Jo punched him playfully on the arm. "Look at Dees
over there. Looks like he's using his eyes to x-ray
everyone in the crowd."

"Hallo, my friends from America," Rupert Hesse said, his broken English echoing through the loud-speakers with confidence. Then he switched to German, and thick-waisted Wanda from the State Department translated from a microphone at the far end of the stage.

"'I speak from my heart,'" she translated with much emotion, "'though what is in my heart is shared by many in my country, in your country, in countries around the world. For in our hearts there are no countries. Only people.'"

"Fuck you, Kraut," someone shouted from the back. A couple of cronies laughed, but when there was no support from the rest of the crowd, they shut up.

Rupert Hesse continued speaking.

Jo whispered to Crush, "Sure knows how to hold a crowd, even in another language. Boy, he sure likes the attention, doesn't he?"

Crush smiled. "Didn't you?"

DEVANE HEARD the throaty German words amplified as he drove along Ocean Boulevard. He pulled into the parking lot of Henri's Fish Grotto across the street from the festivities.

"'In our hearts, there are no countries. Only people...'" Wanda's amplified translation sifted through the busy boulevard traffic to the parking lot.

Devane picked up Diaz's transmitter from the floor, extended the antenna and looked across the street at Rupert Hesse, hands slicing the air to punctuate his impassioned speech. "Let the games begin." Devane smiled and flipped the first switch.

16

Jo leaned against the side of the speaker's platform and studied the large crowd, hoping to recognize Devane under some nutty disguise. Did they show *Tootsie* in his prison? Maybe he'd shaved his legs, plucked his eyebrows, was out there right now, prancing around in Leggs panty hose and high heels, maneuvering closer and closer, reaching into his bulky purse for a gun.

But no. Jo didn't see anyone like that. The crowd kept their seats and listened attentively, applauding occasionally or laughing when Wanda translated a joke. Overhead an occasional helicopter would drone by on its way to Camp Pendleton, the Marine base. On the water behind them, ships and boats drifted by, sails arced with wind.

Behind her dark sunglasses, Jo's eyes raked over each person, checking for wigs, false beards, anything. She remembered in the Sherlock Holmes stories how he was able to identify people by the shapes of their ears. She tried to do that now, match Devane's square little ears with someone out there. No luck. They were all starting to look alike, big ugly flaps of skin. She decided ears were unnatural appendages, best ignored.

"Anything?" she asked an equally watchful Crush.

He shook his head. "Not yet."

She continued her vigil, not really listening to Rupert Hesse's impassioned speech, humming Price's

"Tattooed Tina," trying to remember the lyrics—
something about "she had a heart like a subway tun-
nel/Her mistakes scratched in blue on each slender
arm/So much bitter graffiti that—" something, something "—meant no harm." She was trying to remember the missing words, when the first shots cracked the
air.

The podium where Rupert Hesse was standing suddenly shook with a series of explosions. Chips of wood
flew out, leaving a zigzag pattern of smoking craters like
bullet holes. People screamed. Rupert dived to the
platform floor, toppling the podium. Immediately another rat-a-tat barked like a semiautomatic weapon, and
bullet holes were stitched across the front of the dais.

Jo snatched her gun from her purse and dropped to
one knee, pivoting around, looking for a gunman to aim
at. *"Where?"* she shouted at Crush.

"Don't know," he yelled back, and hopped up onto
the stage. He hoisted Rupert Hesse under one arm,
snagged Wanda with the other and herded them toward the limo.

Another burst of explosions sounded, and the side
of the dais away from Jo exploded with bullet holes.
The different angle meant that there had to be at least
two gunmen, she figured. But where were they? Where
was the muzzle flash from their weapons?

The crowd had panicked at the first shots, shouting
and running, trampling one another as they clawed
their way down the grandstand. One teenage boy
tripped and tumbled down the wooden seats, smacking his head hard on each bench level. A couple of
young girls helped him to his feet, then ran off.

Jo saw Dees frantically directing his agents. Bedlow,
Chapin and Chief Gravis were shouting orders to their

confused people. But all they could do was stand there with their weapons drawn, looking over their shoulders for a target and jumping every time another series of invisible bullets pounded into the dais in an explosion of wood splinters.

Jo followed Crush's lead. She ran after him as he pulled Hesse and Wanda toward the front limo. Unable to keep up, Wanda stumbled and sprawled to her knees. Jo hooked a hand under Wanda's arm and dragged her back to her feet. The momentum propelled them the rest of the way to the limo.

Crush yanked open the back door and shoved the dazed Rupert Hesse across the seat. Jo nudged Wanda on top of him. "Stay down!" Crush ordered. They did. Crush ran around the car and jumped behind the wheel. Jo started to climb in next to him. "No," Crush said, starting the engine with a roar. "Take the follow-up car. I'll need you to cover my back."

"Okay. Where to?"

"Hotel Flora on Tony Street."

"Right," Jo said, and ran back to the second limo. As per emergency procedure, an extra key was in the ashtray. She dug it out and started the motor. As she shifted into drive, the passenger door flew open and a frazzled-looking Dees slid in beside her, a .45 clutched uselessly in his hand.

"Let's go, Montana," he said. "Don't lose them."

Jo stomped the gas pedal and the tires squealed after Crush's limo, already thirty yards ahead of them. In the rearview mirror she could see the frustrated uniformed and plainclothes cops, randomly grabbing people as they fled and searching them. Fistfights between police and civilians were rampant as people struggled desperately to escape to safety. The scene reminded Jo of those old campus riots of the sixties.

"The shooting's stopped," Jo told Dees.

"Damn right." Dees nodded, sweat slicking his face, his teeth clenched in an uneasy smile. "Maybe we haven't caught him yet, but at least we stopped him from blowing away Hesse. We beat him." Dees straightened his tie, patted back his mussed hair. "So much for the fucking Masked Dog."

DEVANE TOSSED the transmitter on the seat next to him and eased his rented Pinto out of the parking lot into busy Ocean Boulevard traffic. The two black limos rocketed ahead of him, bullying smaller cars out of their way, but thick afternoon traffic and indifferent traffic signals slowed them down enough for him to easily stay on their tail. In his rearview mirror he could see the confusion and violence back at the docks. All according to plan.

God, he felt good. He snorted in a lungful of tangy salt air and smiled as he coaxed the gas pedal just enough to keep the limos in sight. No rush. His hard lean body was practically vibrating, his skin burning as if he'd ingested a bottle of niacin tablets. He couldn't remember feeling this good before. But, then, he'd never had this much power before and been free to use it as he wanted.

His body performed smoothly, wheeling the car through traffic with patience and control as if it could sense each dip in the street, feel the tires spinning over the rough macadam, scraping away thin layers of rubber. It felt like his own skin being painlessly peeled off. His muscles seemed like some thick black liquid as they performed their tasks without hesitation or doubt, independent of thought, like an Olympic athlete at the supreme moment of achievement.

And his mind felt even better. There was no fear, no anxiety that anything would go wrong—nothing had so far. But even if there was some unplanned problem, Devane knew he would overcome it. Staring at the road ahead, he imagined his brain as some huge stainless-steel computer, the microcircuits clicking away, sending pulses of electricity across near-invisible wires. The perfect human specimen.

A tan Audi changed lanes in front of him. It had a red-and-white bumper sticker that read I'd Rather Be Crushing Imperialism. Devane looked at his watch. Not yet, not just yet.

The first problem had been how to get close enough to his target, Rupert Hesse. With cops from every local and federal agency surrounding the guy, it would have been a suicide mission. So he'd had to separate Hesse from his protectors, at least from some of them. Enter Diaz.

Devane could have installed the charges himself. He knew how. Thinking about it, he could see the pages of electronic and demolition information that he had read now scroll before his eyes. Formulas, diagrams, instructions. It was all locked permanently in his mind, just like everything else that he'd read or heard or seen since he'd been in the Masked Dog Project.

But they were looking for him, and there was no way he would ever have gotten close enough to place the charges himself. That's where Diaz and his special effects know-how came in. The Mexican also had the contacts to get himself hired to help construct the dais and grandstand. Then all Devane had to do was sit across the street and flip switches. The charges detonated in a staggered series to resemble gunfire, just like in the movies. Only there was no gunman around.

Devane edged the Pinto into the left lane, the better to watch the limos. He knew they'd rush Hesse right to the car and hustle him out of there. He'd hoped for a chance to plant an explosive on the car, but there'd been too many people around. He'd have to stick with this plan. Riskier, but effective.

Without using their turn signals, both limos took a sharp right onto Flower. Devane followed, allowing two cars between him and the limos. He looked at his watch.

It was time.

He grabbed the Padres baseball cap from the dashboard and jammed it onto his head, the bill pulled low, almost covering his eyes. He stuck a pair of sunglasses on and clamped an unlit cigar between his teeth. Not much of a disguise, but enough for the few seconds it would take for them to figure it out. By then, of course, it would be too late.

Slowly, without drawing any attention, he waited for an opportunity, then pulled into the left lane, passing a blue Omni. The driver, a young woman, slowed so she could slap the hands of her son, who was playing with the radio. They stopped at the next light: a white Cadillac, the two black limos, a red Mazda RX-7 and Devane's Pinto. He studied his digital watch, made a notation on the pad in his lap. When the light changed, they all pulled out like a parade.

Traffic was still too heavy for the limos to try any dangerous driving like running lights, so Devane just bided his time. He was about to pull ahead of the Mazda RX-7, when it made an illegal left turn into a Kentucky Fried Chicken lot.

Devane was directly behind the second limo now. He saw the woman driving; the man next to her was pointing animatedly, as if he were afraid she'd lose the limo in front. Despite her companion's hysterics, she seemed cool and professional. Devane smiled. He would know how to rattle her.

He swerved his car into the right lane, cutting off a lumbering LTD. Then he punched the gas pedal and his car pulled alongside the rear limo. He could see the man on the passenger's side, his face fixed on the limo ahead, his eyes frantic. The woman was calm, her attractive features frozen with concentration. They both glanced over at him, the man with annoyance, but the woman was studying him, trying hard to recognize him under the hat and sunglasses and cigar.

Devane rolled down his window and shook his fist at them. "Get the fuck out of the way, assholes," he shouted, honking his horn like a maniac.

The man on the passenger's side looked panicked for a moment and Devane thought the guy might start shooting at him. But no, he'd just startled him.

They would expect anyone following them to maintain a low profile, keep a few cars back, try to find out where they were going without being spotted. They wouldn't expect him to honk his horn and call attention to himself. And it worked.

The man on the passenger's side mouthed, "Fuck off!" through his closed bulletproof window and flipped Devane the finger. The woman returned her gaze to the road ahead, though Devane thought he saw a doubtful expression on her face. He swore at them both again, honked his horn and rocketed past them to pull up with the first limo.

He saw only the driver, a huge broad-shouldered man who clutched the wheel with intensity. He drove well, Devane noted, squeezing the maximum amount of speed out of the situation, yet without creating a hazard to the other drivers. The guy knew what he was doing.

Devane nosed slightly ahead as they crossed an intersection, just catching a green light. Now he would have to concentrate, start his countdown. His research all began to scroll before him, everything he'd read on the subject in the past couple days, each page flashing just as he'd last seen it. *Digital computers have made possible more complete and more extensive forms of traffic control... Information derived from various traffic detectors in the street system that measure presence of vehicles, traffic flow rates, stopped time, speeds and turning movements... Microprocessor activated by loops buried in street send message to equipment housed in metal control box on corner.* He saw the diagrams, the interlocked boxes with arrows. Figure 1: Relationship of Elements in a Road-traffic Area-control System. It was all so clear to him, the detectors, the signal controller, the out-stations with data links to the data channeler. More and more information began to jam into his head, facts and figures, much more than he needed. *... 77 intersections with 26 primary sensor points at which traffic is... signal control patterns stored in computer... 16% reduction in number of stops... 30% reduction in average delay... average peak hour speed increases from 20 mph to 30 mph... 8% decrease in accidents... saving motorists 19,500 hours of traffic time in one city alone... advanced systems in Munich and Toronto...*

Devane shook his head, dispersing the rushing images of book and magazine pages from the library. He had the knowledge; he knew what to do with it.

The cars all slowed for a dip at the next intersection, with Devane still half a car length ahead of the front limo. He didn't make any attempt to look into the car. He knew that Hesse would be hugging the floor as ordered, feeling relieved and grateful that the Americans had saved his life.

They zipped through two more intersections, almost parallel to each other, before Devane's calculations told him the time was right. Immediately he honked his horn at the front limo, scowled at the driver and pulled in front of him, narrowly missing the front bumper. Once in the lane he slowed down and put on his left blinker to indicate he was going to make a left turn at the intersection. He watched as the limo driver checked the right lane as if to pull over, but a line of cars had already pulled up to fill the vacant slot.

Devane counted aloud, pacing himself and the car as they moved toward the next busy intersection. The green light glared ahead. That wouldn't do. It was important that they stop up there, with the cars in this exact position. Everything had been calculated just right. He pumped the brake slightly and the limo behind him blared the horn. Devane shook his fist into the rearview mirror.

When they reached the intersection, the light turned yellow. Several cars in the right lane slid through on the yellow, but Devane stood on the brakes and brought the left lane to a halt.

Immediately he went to work. He had ninety seconds.

For the benefit of the limo driver, he made a big show of dropping his cigar onto his lap. When he bent over to retrieve it, he reached down and peeled the carpeting on the floor back, revealing the bare metal. A circle had already been partially cut into the floor. Devane used his fingers to tear the metal flap out the rest of the way. He reached under the passenger's seat and brought out his little homemade device.

He was proud of this baby. He had never been the best med student around, barely passing chemistry, in fact, barely graduating from med school at all. But now he was able to remember the most complicated formulas, the most elaborate instructions. The university library had provided him with the knowledge; the money he'd taken from Charlie's home had provided the equipment.

The first step had been making the nitroglycerin. He'd stood in the kitchenette of his beachfront motel room, filling the 75 ml beaker to the 13 ml level with fuming red nitric acid, 98% concentration, which he had purchased through Diaz. Immediately he'd plunged the beaker into the bathtub, which was filled with ice. Once it had cooled below room temperature, he'd added 39 mls of fuming sulfuric acid, acquired from the same source. And so he'd worked all afternoon, knowing that the slightest cough and the highly volatile and unstable explosive could blow off his face. But he'd never been scared or worried. He could barely remember what fear was like, what it felt like to be terrified. Physically. He'd even begun to wonder if it really was the drug that had made him like this, or just some heretofore untapped inner strength he'd had all along. One that just needed to be released.

That same afternoon he'd combined 35.5% nitro-glycerin with 45.5% potassium nitrate, 6% woodmeal, 2.5% guncotton, 5.5% Vaseline and 6% powdered charcoal. That formed a more stable version of straight dynamite, easier to use. Then he mixed 5 grams of pure mercury with 35 mls of nitric acid, dabbling with the concoction until he finally had mercury fulminate, necessary to detonate the dynamite.

Devane hunched over in the front seat and checked his watch. Only twenty-seven seconds before the light would change. He opened the lid of the blue Dutch Delights shortbread cookie tin, adjusted the cheap digital clock from Radio Shack, adding the few extra seconds he'd calculated were necessary for the limo to be in position, closed the lid and reached it through the hole of his floorboard.

The live bomb sat under his car. Devane straightened up in his seat, tapping his hand on the steering wheel, staring at the traffic light. Despite the fact that this was the first and only bomb he'd ever made and that the slightest miscalculation would send his car flip-flopping through the intersection, he was not worried. He tugged the bill of his Padres hat and smiled.

"I DON'T KNOW," Jo said, peering out the windshield.

Dees turned to her. "What? What don't you know?"

"Huh?" Jo hadn't known she'd spoken her thoughts aloud. There was no reason to. She had nothing to go on, just a nagging anxiety rumbling through her stomach.

"What don't you know?" Dees repeated, letting his exasperation show.

"That guy in the Pinto . . ."

"That asshole."

"The way he smiled when he passed us . . ."

"I'd like to send a couple guys from section D to wipe that smile off him."

Jo shook her head. "No, I mean his teeth. So many goddamn white teeth. Like Devane's."

"Teeth?" Dees gave her a sad look. "Teeth, huh? What are you a dentist?"

Jo looked through her windshield, through Crush's limo, and saw the driver of the Pinto duck down in the front seat. She tensed, reached for the gun in her lap, as if she expected him to pop up with an Uzi or something.

"We're going to have start checking everybody's teeth now," Dees was saying, smoothing back his ruffled hair.

Maybe Dees was right, Jo thought. She was reaching. Sherlock Holmes identifying people by their ears; now Jo Dixon Montana was inspecting bicuspids. She saw the Pinto driver's head pop back up, saw him adjust his baseball cap. She couldn't shake that image from the videotapes in Washington: Devane curling those iron weights, his muscles lumping under tight skin like crawling reptiles. And that smug smile of big white teeth.

"Something's wrong," Jo said, grabbing her gun and popping open her door. "All that shooting back there and no gunmen?"

"Montana!" Dees yelled as she jumped out of the car.

People in cars behind her honked, until they saw the gun. A couple of students on motorcylces U-turned and sped away.

Jo had barely cleared her door, when the light changed. The Pinto drove calmly through the intersection, and Jo saw the flat blue can in the middle of the street. Suddenly she knew.

"Crush! No!" she screamed.

Crush turned around in his seat to see what Jo wanted at the same time he pressed his foot to the gas pedal. He'd been watching the light, anxious to get to the hotel, where they could get some backup. He hadn't noticed the blue cookie can as the limo rolled over it like a dark cloud. He saw Jo's pretty face contorted with horror, and wondered what was the matter. At that very moment, the expensive black limo filled with fire.

Jo watched helplessly as the car was lifted up off the street in a roar of flames. It was as if they'd passed over a hole that led straight to hell. The flames gathered around the car in a fiery shroud. Bits of flesh clung to the windshield like fat leeches, and blood sizzled against the glass. Suddenly the windows exploded and triangles of sharp glass flew far enough to reach Jo. One of them carved a furrow along Jo's cheek. She didn't flinch or duck or dab her hand to the open wound. She just stood there and watched, numbly aware that the Pinto had already escaped.

17

"Deep shit," Rawlings said.

There was no answer. Just three thousand miles of faint telephone static.

Rawlings made a clicking noise with his tongue. "That's what you're up to your neck in, Dees. Deep shit."

"Don't sound so broken up," Dees said.

"Well, what can I do, Dees? You blew it. First, you went against my orders and pulled our people off Price Calender—"

Christ, Dees thought, mopping the sweat from his forehead with a Burger King napkin somebody'd left on their desk. How did Rawlings know about him pulling those people off Calender? Full reports hadn't been filed yet, and he certainly didn't volunteer the specific names of the agents involved in the bombing. How did he know?

"Then you allowed an international humanitarian to be assassinated less than thirty feet away from you. And third, you permitted the assassin, a vicious killer we've been hunting, to escape."

"That's not how it happened."

"That's how it looks. Now Devane is even more dangerous than before. He's proven he can outsmart us, outmaneuver us. Before the week's over, he'll have half a dozen representatives of governments and private organizations offering him money to kill selected targets.''

"I'll find him," Dees said hollowly.

"Oh, sure ... eventually. But we need to find him before he kills the President or the Pope or whoever they're paying for these days.''

Dees felt the sweat gushing from his pores so freely he was afraid Rawlings could hear it over the phone. He dabbed his cheek with the wet napkin. "We've still got Price Calender.''

"Yes. Yes, we do.''

"So we've still got a good chance of nabbing Devane before he contracts for any other removals.''

Rawlings's long pause made Dees nervous. Come on, you old bastard, answer.

Finally Rawlings sighed. "There's an extra player on the field now. Someone we hadn't counted on.''

"Who?''

"Liza R. I have reason to believe she's still alive.''

"How reliable is the intelligence?''

"C plus. An aide to an aide in the Soviet Embassy. One who knows Alexei.''

An involuntary groan escaped from Dees's throat. He wadded up the sopping napkin and lobbed it at the waste can in the corner. It missed. Gathering his frayed wits, he took a deep breath and decided to bluff things through. "That doesn't change the situation. Even if it's true, which is doubtful.''

"You'd better hope so, Dees. Just remember, in case anything happens to Price Calender, I was the one who ordered you not to remove Crush and Jo Montana from him in the first place. I just want that clear. For the record.''

"Record?" Dees snapped. "There is no fucking record."

A loud click echoed over the line. A tape recorder knob being shut off. "There is now, Dees," Rawlings said, his voice flat, menacing. "There is now."

18

Bob Hope wiggled three fingers. "Three against a thousand," he told the horrified guests. Lucille Ball shook her head disgustedly.

"This is my favorite part," Trinidad said, staring at the small black-and-white TV.

"I've seen it." Rebecca sighed. "What else is on?"

"I've seen it, too," Trinidad said, "but I want to see it again. It's funny. Don't kids today know funny?"

"I don't think it's that funny. I think *Paleface* was funnier."

Price was in the kitchen, scuffing the Jiffy Pop popcorn over the burner, watching the aluminum top balloon up until it looked like some kind of nuclear power plant. This was the third batch he'd made since the movie had started. He'd burned half of the first two, but Trinidad and Rebecca had eaten them anyway.

"How's it coming in there, chef?" Trinidad shouted. "I'm hungry."

"You can't be hungry," Rebecca chided. "You ate most of the last bowl. And look at all that beer." Five empty Michelob bottles stood guard around the empty popcorn bowl.

"Snitch," Trinidad growled, nuzzling her neck as he went into his wild tiger act. He snarled and roared, and Rebecca giggled, pretending to fight him off. He tickled her until tears came to her eyes.

"Stop!" she begged, laughing so hard her legs flew out, the metal brace clomping against the table and knocking over a couple of empty bottles. The brace dug into the edge of the table, notching out a fresh white scar.

Price had been half stirring the pan, half watching them, grinning as she'd squealed with happiness. When her leg smacked the table, something like a fiery nail went through his heart and he had to stop himself from running over to see how she was. Be cool, daddy. "What's the damage, guys?"

"Table's wounded," Trinidad said, making a big show of checking the edge of the table out, as if that were the most important thing.

"Hey, what about me?" Rebecca said.

"You?" Price said, peeling open the aluminum dome. "What about you?"

She gave him a look and smiled. "A girl could starve to death around you two. Where's the popcorn?"

"Coming, coming. Christ, if they ever remake *The Exorcist*, I think we've got the perfect little girl."

"What's *The Exorcist*?" Rebecca said.

"It's a movie that Bob Hope wasn't in," Trinidad explained. "Therefore it isn't worth talking about."

Rebecca scooted off the sofa and brought her empty glass into the kitchenette. Price was dumping the popcorn into a green Tupperware bowl, sorting out the burned kernels from the good ones. The batch was about fifty-fifty.

"Burned it again, huh, Daddy?"

Price shrugged. "Making Jiffy Pop is a lot trickier than it looks."

She pulled open the refrigerator and lifted out a liter-sized bottle of 7-Up.

"Forget it, kid," Price said. "You've had two glasses today. That's enough."

"Pleeease, Daddy. Just one more glass."

"Nope."

"Half a glass?"

"Milk or apple juice."

She sighed, put the 7-Up back and dragged out the bottle of unfiltered apple juice. "It looks muddy," she complained.

"Then don't drink it."

Price watched her pour the glass full and wondered if it ever got any easier saying no to your kid.

"Hey, Buckeye," Trinidad called from the living room. He had his thumb and forefinger each stuck in an empty Michelob bottle and was clinking them together. "How about bringing me another one."

"You've had enough, too," Price said.

"Come on, man. It's only beer."

"Milk or apple juice."

Trinidad laughed. "Apple juice."

Rebecca poured him a glass, carefully carrying both glasses back to the sofa, spilling only a little down the sides. Price followed her into the living room and dropped the bowl of popcorn on top of the table. All of them dug out a handful.

Bob Hope was in a saloon, drinking whiskey, puffing a cigar. He gagged and began to reel in a circle, though his feet remained planted. Price had seen that scene a dozen times, but he still laughed.

Then the screen went blank for a second. The words SPECIAL NEWS BULLETIN appeared.

"Damn it!" Trinidad said. "Notice how they never interrupt a commercial for a bulletin, only the damn show."

"Jim Harris here for KVLA Newswatch." Jim Harris's tie was askew, as if he'd had to knot it hastily. *"A bomb exploded less than two hours ago in downtown San Diego, killing famed East German longshoreman and labor leader Rupert Hesse. Also killed in the explosion were an unidentified man and woman. Their car was blown up only minutes after leaving the scene of a gunman's attack at the dockside rally where Mr. Hesse was speaking. No arrests have been made. More details as they come in. Jim Harris, KVLA Newswatch."*

"Jesus," Trinidad said, stunned.

"Who's Ruby Hesser?" Rebecca asked as if he were no more than a character in the Bob Hope movie she'd been watching.

"A man," Price said softly. "A good man."

"A dead man," Trinidad said.

Bob Hope was pumping a handcart on the railroad tracks. Lucille Ball was riding after him, twirling her lasso.

Price stood up and shut off the TV. "Time to go back to Grandma's, honey," he told Rebecca.

"Already?" she protested, looking to Trinidad for support. He was always good at squeezing another couple of hours out of Price. But this time Trinidad didn't say anything, and she knew this was not a good time to argue.

"Gotta go first," she said, and trooped off to the bathroom.

Price glanced over to the kitchen cupboard above the sink, where he'd stashed the gun Jo had given him. He couldn't walk around the house with it strapped on while Rebecca was here. But now that he'd seen the news bulletin, he was able to put a few things together. He didn't need to be clairvoyant to understand that he was in danger and had to get Rebecca the hell out of here. The gun might just come in handy.

Price opened the cupboard, unwrapped the shoulder holster and slipped into it. He shoved the gun into the holster. When he turned around, Trinidad was standing next to the counter, staring at him.

"What the hell you doing, man?"

Price sighed. "Can't explain it all now, man. Toss me my jacket."

Trinidad snagged Price's sport jacket from the counter chair and chucked it to him. Price shrugged into it, making sure the gun was well hidden.

"Hey, Price, don't shut me out. We go back."

Price didn't respond.

"I'm talking to you man. What's this macho bullshit. You don't even like guns."

"I'm not shutting you out, Trin. Honestly. It's just . . ." He hesitated, tempted to tell his friend everything but realizing the danger it might bring Trinidad to know too much. The people that were involved didn't like people who knew too much. "It's just that I've gotten some weird threats lately. You know, some ex-fan who's suddenly decided my lyrics played backward are really Christ's bar mitzvah. That kind of shit. There could be some trouble and I don't want you or Rebecca around. Okay?"

Trinidad stared at him, his mocha skin intense in the dim kitchenette light. "Let's get Buckeye out of here. Then talk."

"Nothing to say, man." Price reached into a drawer, shook a cigarette out of the pack and stuck it in his mouth. He flipped on the front burner of the gas range and stooped down, lighting the cigarette on the hissing blue flame. He dropped the pack back into the drawer and slammed it shut. Gray smoke curled around his face.

He was tired. Damned insomnia nibbled away at his strength a tiny bite at a time. His eyes burned, his mouth tasted sour, metallic. But this tiredness was worse than usual. It was a dull numbness, an apprehension that he realized had nothing to do with his fear for Rebecca's safety. Or Trinidad's. Or his own. It had to do with that news bulletin. And the unidentified woman who was killed in the crash. Jo?

That Devane had been responsible, Price had no doubt. That Jo had been there, he also had no doubt. Nothing mystical there; he knew those things for a certainty. But had she been in that car? He tried not to picture her body, ragged and bloody among the twisted metal hull of the car.

He wrung those thoughts out of his mind. He'd deal with that later. For now he had to worry about Rebecca and getting her away from him, to safety.

Rebecca came out of the bedroom, her hands pink from washing. She saw her father leaning against the refrigerator, puffing a cigarette, not trying to hide it. She didn't say anything. She walked up to him, threw her arms around his waist and hugged.

"Come on, sweetheart," he said, glancing nervously at his watch.

19

Devane watched the three of them climb into Price's VW Rabbit. The black guy he recognized from old photographs in *Rolling Stone* as Trinidad Jordan, lead guitarist. He'd never seen any photos of the little girl, but he knew from various articles that she was Price's daughter. Her leg brace supposedly was the result of the same tragic automobile accident that had killed her mother.

Price stopped to look around at the streets and buildings as they entered the car, searching. Devane had never met Price, but he recognized him immediately, even without his trademark beard. Calender gave one last icy scan of the streets and rooftops, dropped his cigarette to the ground, stomped it out and ducked into the car. Devane smiled and let the musty curtain fall closed. There was still enough of a crack to continue watching them.

The occupant of the apartment Devane was scouting from was lying behind him, his head twisted at some Picasso angle that on canvas would be art but in this dingy Westwood apartment was merely death.

Devane had driven up from San Diego immediately after watching Hesse's car flip and boil within that dervish of swirling flame. During the freeway drive north, he'd listened to the all-news station on his car radio that had confirmed Rupert Hesse's death. Certainly by now every person, government and intelligence agency he'd sent his letters to knew of Hesse's death—and Devane's potential. By now the only question left to them was, How much? Devane had an answer to that too: Plenty!

But first, Price Calender. His reward. It was important to get Price Calender now, before they swaddled him in agents. Maybe it was already too late. He'd need an observation post to make sure. Getting Calender's address had been easy—a convincing lie to a confused receptionist at Calender's old record company. Then Devane had driven up and down the street a couple of times to scout the place, make sure Price was home. He'd selected the best building from which to spy, knocked on a few doors. The first two apartments had someone home, so he asked them about some mythical street address and left. No one answered at the third apartment.

Picking the lock had been more difficult than he'd anticipated. He'd read everything possible about lock picking from books he'd bought in those survivalist stores. The diagrams and instructions scrolled in front of him as he worked the lock: *First, try to dislodge the spanner screws holding the escutcheon in place . . . insert hooked pick into keyway, probing for tumbler . . . insert along warding grooves . . . align . . .*

But knowing how and actually having the practiced skill were very different. Incredibly, picking a lock was harder than making a bomb. He fumbled with the lock, breaking off once or twice when someone passed by pretending he was jotting a note for the occupant. Finally, frustrated with the lock, he used his brute strength, applying increasing pressure along the edge of the door until the dead bolt ripped the entire latch assembly out of the molding. Once inside, he closed the door and began his watch of Price Calender's apartment from one of the unkempt bedrooms. The smell of marijuana was strong in the room's curtains.

But Devane's luck turned bad. Within fifteen minutes, a scrawny young boy about nineteen pushed open the door and yelled, "Fuck, Roy, you forget your goddamn key again? You're paying for the door, man...." Devane had leaped out of the bedroom, whipped his arm around the boy's head and yanked it around as if he were unscrewing some large jar. The boy's neck bones crackled like kindling wood and he let the body flop into a pile of dirty laundry next to the unmade bed. The killing hadn't been part of the plan, but it didn't bother Devane that it had happened. Actually, he was proud of himself for being able to handle the unexpected so efficiently. It almost made up for his failing to pick the lock.

Devane continued to stare across the street at them entering the car—the black guy helping the little girl into the back seat. Then the Rabbit was puttering down the street. The three of them were gone. Devane grabbed his paper bag and left the apartment.

Entering Calender's apartment was much easier. The lock was cheaper than the one across the street, much more like the one at the motel where Devane had practiced what he'd read. It took him only ten minutes to get in.

He walked around the apartment first, not touching anything, just looking. Getting the feel. Except for a few beer bottles and some popcorn, everything was neat and clean, not unlike the prison cells he'd been in. Tidiness somehow made the cells seem larger. Devane dragged his fingers across a ten-foot-long shelf of record jackets, tempted to topple the whole wall of records, smash every last one. He swallowed the urge, gritting his teeth against the rage welling inside him. No, it was more important that Calender not suspect anyone had been here. That was the only way the scheme would work. Afterward, when he was dying, writhing with unbearable pain, he would know.

Devane took a deep breath, let his mind empty. His head felt as if a warm black river were washing through his brain, carrying away all unimportant thoughts, soothing and cleansing the soft pulpy gray matter. There on the distant horizon of the black river a raft of information floated into sight. His mind began to fill with facts and photographs, details and interviews. Tiny words scrolled by. Page after page from the dozens of magazine and newspaper articles he'd read about Price Calender over the years. Everything from *People* to *Us* to *Sixteen* to *Teen Beat* to *Newsweek* to *Time*. All the reviews of his concerts, records, the gossipy bits about him and Stevie Nicks and Linda Rondstadt. The in-depth pseudoscholarly analysis of his lyrics in *The Journal of Popular Culture*. Though the articles had all but disappeared over the past few years, he still recalled every detail of the old ones, word for word. Like a devoted fan, Devane knew everything about Price Calender. Enough to know the best way to kill him.

It was only a matter of time before they staked out Calender, used him as bait. Devane was surprised they hadn't already. Not that it would have stopped him; their protection certainly hadn't helped Rupert Hesse.

He carried his paper bag throughout the house as he began his search. He pulled open drawers, patted down clothing in the closet. So far no luck.

The photographs and articles had all made one thing clear about Price Calender; he smoked to excess. Every story commented on the ever-present cigarette hanging from his lips, screwed into his mouth, protruding from his beard, pinched between fingers. Writers with delusions of being meaningful described the swirling smoke as "ghosts of his past pain haunting him," *(Rolling Stone)*; "a gray curtain as thin as luck, but also like a thick wall to keep others out," *(Crawdaddy)*; and "tendrils of smoke wrapping around him like a whip, driving him toward the Top Ten," *(Time)*.

Finally, Devane discovered the pack of Winstons in the kitchen drawer. He opened the paper bag and removed the jar and syringe, placing both on the tiny kitchenette counter. Carefully he shook out each cigarette from the pack and lined them neatly along the counter. There were twelve left. He unscrewed the lid to the jar, dipped the needle in and eased the plunger back, slurping up the liquid like a hungry mosquito. The poison was a form of strychnine mixed with a tiny dose of PCP and a few other goodies he'd concocted in his motel laboratory, which consisted of a hobby store chemistry set. The strychnine he'd extracted from Rid-Rat rodent poison.

There were other poisons he could have used, perhaps even more efficient ones. But Devane had chosen strychnine for its painful effects. Within fifteen minutes of ingestion, the victim begins to convulse with such violence that he lifts off the floor. The spasms are severe enough to actually break bones. Yet he remains conscious throughout, experiencing every nuance of pain. Even the slightest stimulation—light or a gentle nudge—will start the convulsions all over again. Ultimately he will die from suffocation or even exhaustion.

The single drawback is strychnine's exceptionally bitter taste. Discovered in 1818 in Saint Ignatius's beans, strychnine is an alkaloid compound. Most of it now comes from India. Devane knew all that and counted on the PCP, along with a pinch of this and dab of that, to neutralize the bitterness. The other additives amplified the poisonous effects, making the chemical act even faster when heated by the burning tobacco. There would be a trace of bitterness, but by then it wouldn't matter. After two puffs the convulsions would start.

When he'd finished injecting each cigarette through the filter, he stuffed them back into the wrapper, dropping the pack back into the kitchen drawer. He gave one final glance around, smiled at his own ingenuity, and left, confident that by tonight, the once-famous Price Calender would be convulsing and screaming his life away on the clean carpets of his tidy apartment. Devane hummed one of Price's old songs as he hurried to his rented car.

"QUARTERS," DEVANE SAID, sliding a five-dollar bill under the glass partition.

The fat woman behind the glass didn't look at him. She just dragged the bill toward her as if it were a dead rabbit she was deciding how to cook. With her free hand she pushed a roll of twenty quarters back at him. By the time Devane had picked up the roll, she was back to reading her science-fiction novel.

The arcade was two rooms crammed to bursting with video games. Electronic beeps and whirls and buzzes provided background music to the excited shouting of the kids in their early and mid-teens who were manning each video machine. Despite the open doors at either end of the arcade, the air was sour with sweat, cigarettes, candy and the scent of popcorn, drifting in from the movie theater next door.

Devane prowled the room, squeezing through the shifting crowds that gathered around various machines and cheered high scorers on. He felt funny. Giddy and hungry and restless all at once. At first he thought it might be some kind of delayed stress reaction after the excitement of today. But he knew it was something more, an intensity he'd not felt before. He felt jittery, explosive. He hadn't eaten all day except for coffee and toast, yet he wasn't just hungry for food. He wanted something else.

"Looks hard," he said to the young girl playing Ms. Pac-Man.

She shrugged. "Kinda."

She was no more than thirteen, with stringy brown hair. Her thinness was exaggerated by the grillwork of her braces bulging under her lips and her oversized glasses. She was homely even without the braces and glasses. Her morose expression said that she knew that.

"How do you play?" Devane asked her.

She gave him a look. "You never played Pac-Man before?"

He smiled "I've been away. Can you show me?"

She hesitated, her parents' warnings echoing in her head. She looked Devane over. He was dressed nicely, in a Polo shirt like her dad's. He was pretty old—in his thirties, probably—but handsome like a movie star. Maybe he was one, had his own series or something. Stars were pretty common in Westwood. "Okay," she said. "But only for a couple minutes. I gotta get home."

Devane smiled.

MASKED DOG

Debbie Harris's parents didn't begin to worry for another two hours. After four hours they began calling all her friends. After five hours they called the police. It would be another sixteen hours before Officer Timothy Yee, chasing a couple of high-school kids trying to buy cocaine through an alley, would accidentally find Debbie Harris's body at the bottom of a garbage dumpster. That night Officer Yee's wife asked him if the girl had been sexually assaulted. Officer Yee had stared at his young wife and said in Chinese, "That was the least of her problems."

20

Price inhaled a final drag on the cigarette before tapping it out in the overflowing ashtray. Immediately he reached across the coffee table for the pack, remembered that that had been the last cigarette and crushed the empty pack into a tiny ball. He shifted his gun to his left hand, holding the paper ball in his right. He eyed the trash bag against the kitchenette wall, measuring the distance. "Magic Johnson dribbles down court with only three seconds left in the ball game. The Lakers are behind by one point. One basket here will win the championship. Magic looks to Kareem, but the big man is covered. But wait. Over in the corner, shaking free from his man, it's Price the 'Marksman' Calender, newest player for the team. Magic rifles a pass to Calender. Calender shoots." Price lobbed the wadded cigarette pack over the counter. It banked off the wall, clipped the edge of the bag and dropped to the floor. "Heartbreak," Price said with a sigh. "The crowd is disappointed, yet they cheer the rookie's valiant effort. Wait a minute, ladies and gentlemen. Some of the fans are getting ugly...they're coming after the kid. My God, Calender's pulled out a gun." Price held his gun in both hands, making blasting noises as he pretended to shoot. "He drops half a dozen charging fans, and the rest of the crowd cheers. The refs decide to award him one point for each dead fan and the Lakers win it! Hooray!''

Price stood up and stretched. "You're going nuts, Calender," he said. He knuckled his red eyes and wondered how long it had been since he'd slept a whole night through. He needed another smoke. Then he remembered the pack of cigarettes in the kitchen drawer. The pack he'd just lost the game with he'd bought at Thrifty's on the way back from his grandmother's after he'd dropped Rebecca off. He hadn't even looked at a brand, just plucked a pack out of the dispenser, grabbed an armful of pretzels, potato chips, corn chips, Oreos, chocolate-chip cookies and 7-Up and rushed it all home. He'd been munching and smoking ever since.

The apartment was dark except for the pulsing blue light of the black-and-white TV. The sound was turned off, though, and his stereo played a stack of records he'd pulled randomly from the Ks: John Klemmer, the Kingston Trio, Gladys Knight, Carole King. Price snatched a handful of Fritos corn chips, packed them into his mouth and started for the kitchen for that last half-pack of cigarettes. It was either keep smoking or finish another bag of chips.

He stuck the gun into his waistband. At first it had felt silly walking all alone around the apartment carrying a gun—almost melodramatic. But then he'd gotten used to it—no, dependent—and he was never without it. The weight alone seemed deadly and made him feel formidable. Part of him almost hoped Devane would try something, would bust down his door and make a run for him. One way or the other, that would end it.

Price pulled open the kitchen drawer, scooped up the pack of Winstons and carried them back to the sofa.

tensed, shivered, then forced her breast harder against his mouth.

Since Liza R's death, Price had been with many women. He had always been a gentle and patient lover, performing and coaxing his lovers with dutiful perfection. He enjoyed the intimacy, but experienced none of the passion he had felt before. Yet now, with Jo, he was rougher, impatient, lapping her up like a thirsty animal. She responded in kind. She pulled at his clothes, her fingernails sometimes raking skin with her insistence. For the sake of efficiency, each disrobed themselves, watching the other as they did. Price stepped out of his pants and underpants with one movement. Jo kicked off her loafers first, then tugged at her zipper. It stuck for a second, but then opened, and she slowly pushed pants and panties over her hips as Price stood naked in front of her. The blue light from the TV made her skin look as cold as the pearls around her neck. But when she stepped into Price's arms she was warm. Very warm.

They fell back onto the sofa, a tangle of legs and arms and mouths. She started giggling, and Price sat up. "What?" he said, smiling.

She lifted her hips and brushed the sofa under her, then the skin of her butt. "Potato chips," she said, laughing. "They hurt." She put her hands behind his neck and pulled him back down on top of her. He kissed her mouth, then her neck, then used his tongue to make a trail to her breast. He closed his lips over it, teasing the nipple with his tongue. The nipple was hard as he took it between his teeth and bit lightly. She gasped, but obviously liked it. He bit a little harder and her body jumped against his, but still she held his head against her breast, urging him on.

The movie on TV had changed. This one had Errol Flynn and Alan Hale dressed as cowboys. He'd seen it before one night in some insomniac haze, but couldn't remember the title. He shook a cigarette loose and stuck it in his mouth. He pawed through the food debris on the table, looking for the matches.

The rapping at his door was light, but insistent.

Price jumped, biting the cigarette in two. He spit out the filter tip, dropping to his knees behind the sofa with a two-hand grip on his gun. He aimed at the door. For a moment, the idea of just firing through the door flickered in his mind. Blast the fucking door off its hinges and whoever was behind it. But then he realized that if it were Devane out there, he probably wouldn't be knocking politely.

"It's me," the voice on the other side said, as if it knew what Price had been thinking.

Price scrambled to his feet and lunged for the door. He twisted open the dead bolt and unhooked the chain, then stood back, his heart thumping, his gun still leveled at the door. "Come in," he said.

The door opened slowly. "Look," she said, "no gun, no weapon. No threat." She stepped through the doorway, her hands half raised. Her smile was weary. "Say, didn't you used to be someone?"

Price lowered his gun and kicked the door closed behind her, immediately snapping the bolt. His stomach rumbled loudly and a warm tingle climbed up his neck and clawed across his scalp. He looked at her and nodded, his voice flat. "You're alive."

"The way I feel, you might get an argument." Jo glanced at the gun. "Good idea. He's still loose. Devane."

"I figured."

Jo's hair was pulled back into a severe ponytail. She was dressed in baggy jeans and a maroon UCLA sweatshirt. The pearl necklace was still around her neck. A Band-Aid slanted across her right cheek where the flying glass from Crush's exploding limo had nicked her. She flopped onto the sofa with a sigh. "Well, we're back in your life again. Dees ordered twenty-four-hour surveillance of you, phone tapping, night scopes, the works. VIP treatment."

"Crush?"

She glanced up, her eyes steady, her voice firm. "Dead. Blown up in the car with Hesse." She paused, then smiled. "He liked you, you know. I asked him."

"Why?"

"Why'd he like you?"

"Why'd you ask him."

Jo shrugged. "I forget. Seems like a long time ago."

Price watched her dig her gun out of her purse and place it next to her right hip, the butt arranged for quick access. He had to smile, the two of them facing each other armed, almost as if they were more afraid of each other than what was out there.

Neither spoke for the next couple of minutes. The only sound was Gladys Knight and the Pips singing "Midnight Train to Georgia."

"Aw, hell," Jo said suddenly as she stood up and marched around the coffee table. When she was directly in front of Price, she took his face in both hands and kissed him hard on the mouth.

Price was surprised, but that didn't stop him from responding. He ground his lips hungrily against hers and their bodies pressed together, shifting as they tried to match curves and angles. She ran her tongue along his teeth, then withdrew, and Price had the odd sen-

sation that without her tongue his mouth felt suddenly empty, as if his own tongue and all his teeth had been removed. Her breasts flattened against his ribs, rubbing. His thigh was clamped between her legs and he could feel the pressure of her crotch straining against him. He pulled back far enough to look into her eyes, feel her warm breath puffing against his neck.

"Listen," he said, pulling back, "this isn't—"

"Don't," she said, her Texas twang coming back. "Don't say this isn't the right time, the right place, the right thing to do, the right way to do it. That you should be sure, I should be sure. That you don't love me, or like me, or want to have my children. That we should think first. Just don't, okay?"

Price kissed her again, pulling her close. Their tongues swam back and forth, each of them gaining more passion as if they were plugged into each other's secret source, tapping each other's deepest energy.

His lips gently brushed the Band-Aid on her right cheek. If he'd have seen the gesture in a movie he'd have scoffed, called it cornball, but here with her it felt good. His arms encircled her ribs and he hugged her tight, finally able to express his great relief that she was alive. Until she'd walked through that door, he hadn't known for sure. He was tempted to use words to tell her how he felt. He was good at words, or at least used to be. But words were somehow too permanent, too binding. He kissed her, instead.

She pulled her UCLA sweatshirt off. She wore no bra. A slight tan line arced above each breast, making the white skin all the more delicious looking. Price set his gun on the coffee table and leaned over and took a nipple in his mouth, rolling it between his teeth. Jo

But he was moving south again, his lips tracing her flat stomach as it dipped toward the plateau between the peaks of hipbones. He could smell her pungent yet sweet scent long before his mouth touched her pubic hairs. The odor excited him even more and he felt his penis bobbing anxiously between his legs. There wasn't enough room on the small sofa, so he knelt next to the sofa. She hooked one leg over the sofa back and one over his shoulder. He lowered his head between her legs. The taste was like some exotic broth that Marco Polo might have experienced and decided it was too wonderful to share with the rest of the world. Price plunged his tongue deeper and Jo pushed her pelvis to meet him. Gone was the hazy cottony feeling he'd had from lack of sleep. He was rejuvenated, feeling almost boyish as he explored her body. He felt almost cannibalistic, drinking at her body. But he didn't stop and she grabbed his head, began to buck and squirm and moan, the noise and movement whipping faster and faster until they blended together. His tongue was deep inside her. Then it was flicking against her clitoris as she pumped her hips. She reached down and peeled apart her vaginal lips, staring into his eyes, sweat streaking her face. His head was matching her accelerated pace, moving up and down like a jackhammer, until she tensed, her thigh muscles clamping against his ears, her butt lifting off the sofa, her head bent back. Neither moved. Then she relaxed with a long sigh. "Gawd, that was nice."

Price sat back on the sofa and took a deep breath. Her scent seemed to fill the room and he couldn't get enough of it.

Jo leaned over and licked his lips. Slowly she dragged her tongue across his chin and around his mouth, tasting herself. Then she was kissing him and he kissed back with all his might. While they kissed her hand scooped between his legs and gently squeezed his penis. She broke off their kiss and looked at it, tracing the heavy blue vein the length of his penis with her fingernail in the light from the TV. "Gawd," she said, "it's like a map of the Manhattan subway system."

"That's so romantic," he said with a grin.

She laughed and climbed on top of him, her wet warmth sliding over him like a heavy tropical rainfall. He was engulfed. Her movements were economical, flexing muscles here and there until she felt like a strong surf tugging him out to sea, then washing him back onto shore, then tugging him out again. Each time taking him farther and farther out. He had his hands around her buttocks, but she needed no encouragement. They stared into each other's eyes, watching the pupils shift, the lids flicker, the eyes swoon. Then she was rocking faster, and his eyes closed, the ocean waves tossing him roughly from wave to wave. He caught a glimpse of her face, her teeth clenched, the muscles in her slender neck pulsing out. They were both slippery with sweat and he was afraid she might slide off. But then he felt the aching start, the wonderful agony welling inside of him, rushing like a moth flying fullspeed at a distant fire, wings beating, heart bursting until it flies straight into the flame and is soundlessly consumed.

"Almost as good as rock 'n' roll, huh?" she said, easing off him.

"And doesn't hurt the ears," he said.

They lay next to each other, both facing out. His arms were wrapped protectively around her and she hugged them to her chest.

"Hold me," she said.

Though he already was, he knew what she meant, and kissed her lightly on the back of the head. They didn't move or talk. Both fell asleep as Carole King sang "Smackwater Jack."

PRICE WOKE AT THE SOUND of something snapping. He opened his eyes and saw Jo sitting naked on the edge of the sofa munching a handful of potato chips and sipping a flat 7-Up.

"I thought you had insomnia?" she said.

Price yawned. "Insomnia doesn't mean you never sleep, just not as much or as regularly as most people."

"Oh." She finished the 7-Up.

"What time is it?"

She picked up her jeans and dug into the pocket for her watch. "Quarter after five."

Price squinted out the window. Light was beginning to seep over the horizon. The TV had Dick Powell and a very young Debbie Reynolds playing cards. Price didn't recognize the movie.

"What's that?" Jo traced the four-inch scar on Price's right side. Her finger left a few potato chip crumbs. She brushed them off. Her touch sent a charge through Price that aroused him.

"A scar."

She frowned.

"Okay, nosy. A going-away gift from my late wife. She tried to carve her initials in my trunk."

"Sweet girl." Jo shook an empty pretzel bag, digging out a couple of broken pretzel stems.

He studied her body in the dim light of morning. She wasn't just thin or shapely, her body was toned, the kind he saw leading aerobics classes at the sports club where he worked out three times a week. Her skin was smooth and taut. Only her face with its fine lines hinted at her true age.

"Checking out my wrinkles?" she said, munching a corn chip.

"Yeah."

She laughed. "Take your time. Don't miss any."

He pulled her backward on top of him and kissed her, tasting the salt from the chips. When they broke apart, he said, "You're kind of attractive in a way."

"Hey, thanks a hell of a lot."

"I'm trying to work my way up slowly."

"To what."

Price shrugged. "Things. I don't know. One of us is supposed to say something mature here, like, 'Let's not rush things.'"

"Oh, like, 'We hardly know each other.' Like that?"

"Yeah."

"Okay." Jo sat straight, looked him in the eyes. "We hardly know each other. Let's not rush things."

Price kissed her and she kissed back; their hands gripped each other.

"Well," she said softly, "we tried."

Price nodded. "Actually, considering all we've been through, we know each other pretty well. You taught me how to shoot a gun."

"Squeeze, don't pull."

"That's right. In some countries, that's as good as engaged."

She smiled at him. "Sometimes you're good with words, Price Calender."

"Words are my life."

"You're pretty good at sex, too."

"Sex is my life."

"But your taste in food stinks."

"Food is my life."

She stood up, pulled her UCLA sweatshirt on. The hem didn't quite cover her crotch. She padded over to the kitchenette and opened the refrigerator, leaning her head into it. The back of the sweatshirt rode up over her buttocks, and Price felt the shiver of desire tighten his skin. He reached for the pack of cigarettes.

"Gawd, man, there's nothing in here but cholesterol, calories and grease." She closed the refrigerator door and patted her stomach. "I didn't work my ass off exercising to Jane Fonda's smug videotape all this time to pig out now. Gimme one of those cigarettes."

Price shook one loose from the pack and tossed it to her as she walked toward him. He rooted through the empty bags, empty cans and loose clothing, looking for matches.

"I thought you quit," she said.

"I did." He continued searching for matches.

"I didn't start smoking until I married Steve Montana. I did it to spite him, I guess. Mr. Clean-cut. Didn't smoke, drink, flirt with other women. Cooked better than me and was even tidier than you. Expected me to be the same. Every time I lit one of these up, he'd smile indulgently. Christ, I used to go nuts." She paused. "Funny, you quitting for somebody, me starting because of somebody. Maybe it's time we did something for ourselves."

"I thought we just did."

She grinned. "Yeah."

"Here they are," Price said, brushing aside a couple of chocolate-chip cookies to reveal the book of matches. But they were lying in a sticky puddle of spilled 7-Up—

too damp to light. "The burner," he suggested, and got up.

Jo walked up to him and kissed him.

"Your Band-Aid's loose," he said.

She kissed him again. When she finished, she pushed away, flustered. "Let's talk about something. Anything."

"Why?"

"Because I'm tempted to say things to you, things neither of us may be ready to hear. You like my pearls?"

Price looked at her without answering.

"They were a gift," she babbled on, "from Kissinger. He gave them to me for guarding his wife while they made a lecture tour of universities. You went to college, didn't you?"

He could see she was trying to compose herself, fighting the same feelings he was fighting, for reasons neither understood. "A couple of years. I dropped out to do my music and make a few million. When the big bucks dried up I went back part-time and finished up. Got my degree the same month Hoagy Carmichael died." That was all in his records, which he knew she'd read, but she pretended it was new information. "What about you?"

"Started at Texas A & M, finished at Bennington."

"Fancy."

She shrugged. "Spent most of my time reading self-help books, taking quizzes in *Cosmopolitan*—'Are you having the right kind of orgasm?' That kind of stuff. You know the rest."

"Do I?"

She walked around him and sat on the sofa, the unlit cigarette still in her hand. "What about Derek?"

Price stiffened. He hadn't spoken to anyone about his brother in years. Suddenly he didn't feel comfortable naked. "He died. You read the file."

"Just that he was a draft resister. Came back from Canada when Carter pardoned them. That he died mountain climbing."

"That pretty much covers it. Except that he kept getting involved in thrill-seeking sports like hang gliding and motorcycle racing and skydiving. Like he was trying to prove something to everyone. That he wasn't a coward."

"Was he?" she asked softly.

"I don't know. I know he went to Canada not because he was afraid to die, but because he was afraid to kill. Is that a coward?"

"I don't think so." She stared at Price's face, the jaw firm, the eyes cold and threatening, the way he'd been with Rawlings back in Washington. "Why didn't you go with him?"

"I might have, but my draft number didn't come up until late in the lottery. I knew I was safe."

She patted the sofa for him to sit next to her, but he didn't move. She leaned back, and smiled ruefully. "First thought that came to my mind when I awakened and they told me I'd miscarried was, 'Thank God. Thank God it wasn't me.' So I know a little something about guilt, son."

"I'm over it," he said.

"Right. You've got your comeback to keep you warm."

"Damn right."

"Whoopee."

He paused and looked at her. "Are we fighting?"

She thought about it. "I guess, kinda."

205

"Why?"

"You tell me. You're the one good with words."

"I just write songs, lady. Nothing profound, just a little something to make a few bucks."

"Bullshit, Price," she said, her twang even more pronounced. "I listened to those songs in college. Hell, my English professor used to teach a couple in class. With Paul Simon, the Beatles and Bob Dylan."

Price laughed. "You wuz robbed."

"I didn't think so," she snapped. "Look, Calender, I'm not some eighteen-year-old groupie. I'm a full-grown woman. If you think you made a mistake here last night, you don't have to bully me. Let's just call it a pleasant fuck and forget it. I don't want anything from you."

Price sat down next to her. "But I want something from you. That's why I've been acting crazy."

She laughed. "I'm glad to hear that, because I lied. I want something from you, too." They kissed, only this kiss was different from the others. The same physical actions took place—the mashing of lips, swapping of tongues—but there was a sense of open caring mingled with the passion, as if each had revealed some of their darkest secrets to someone they could trust. When they finished, she leaned back, grinned and said, "Don't point that thing unless you intend to use it."

He started to lift her sweatshirt off, when the bedroom door opened behind them and a sleepy voice said, "Hey, guys, what's happening?"

"GAWD!" JO SAID, frantically tugging the hem of her sweatshirt down to cover as much as possible.

"I tried to warn you last night," Price reminded. He reached for his pants.

"You didn't try hard enough," Jo said, searching for her pants.

A big grin split Trinidad's sleepy face. "I get the funny feeling I'm not exactly wanted."

"Depends," Jo said, hastily climbing into her jeans. Her panties, an oversight, she scooped up from under a potato-chip bag and jammed into her pocket. "Depends on how long you've been awake."

Trinidad yawned, rubbed his eyes. "Is this the face of a Peeping Trin?"

"Yes!" Jo and Price chorused.

Trinidad laughed, rubbed his hands together and said, "So what's for breakfast? Or have you two eaten already?"

Price tossed him half a bag of cheese puffs.

Trinidad caught the bag awkwardly, some of them spilling out. He stooped down, picked them up and gobbled them down. He made a sour face and tossed the bag back. "Yuck." He wore only a pair of wrinkled khaki pants that looked as if he'd slept in them. His slightly swollen stomach sagged over the waistband. "Hmmm," he said, peering into the ravaged refrigerator, absently rubbing his protruding stomach. "Doesn't look too promising." He grabbed a bottle of Michelob and twisted the cap. It hissed and he hissed back. After swigging a mouthful, he turned and smiled at Jo and Price. "So what's new?"

Price sighed. "Jo Dixon Montana, this is Trinidad something or other. Trin, this is Jo."

"Jo?"

"Without an 'e,'" Jo said.

Trinidad nodded, then burst into a huge smile. "Shit, yeah. The astronaut's wife."

"Ex-wife," Jo and Price chorused again.

207

"Right, ex-wife." Trinidad brought his beer to the sofa and sat next to Jo, who was sandwiched between the two men. "I read about you a couple times. How'd you hook up with my buddy here?"

"She's teaching me to shoot," Price said, his flat tone suggesting they end the discussion.

"Right, shooting. Okay." He noticed the unlit cigarettes Jo and Price were holding. "Hey, that looks like fun. Can I play?" He took a cigarette from the pack and stuck it in his mouth. "Now what?"

Jo laughed. "Now we find a book of matches."

"My favorite books." Trinidad walked back into the kitchen, climbed up on the counter and opened the cupboard above the refrigerator. "Even Mr. Clean there never used this cupboard." Kneeling on the countertop, Trinidad pulled out a carton of Marlboro cigarettes and a box of wooden matches. He hummed the Marlboro theme as he jumped down from the counter. "My stash."

"Son of a bitch." Price grinned. "How long have you been keeping stuff there?"

"Gotta have a few secrets of my own, man." He opened the carton of Marlboros and tossed a pack to Jo. "These are better than this shit from Price."

"This is okay," Jo said, holding her original cigarette.

Trinidad shrugged. "Suit yourself, Jo Dixon Montana." He tossed her the box of matches.

"Thanks," Jo said. She opened the box and dug out a match.

Trinidad twisted the knob to the gas burner and lowered his cigarette toward the flame, puffing it to life. "How do you always do this, man? Christ, I think I singed my eyebrows." He straightened up and plucked the cigarette from his mouth, staring at it with a bitter expression. "What the hell did you do to these, man. Taste like you scraped it from the bottom of your shoe."

Jo laughed, struck the wooden match against the box, held it out for Price. "Sire."

"I mean it, man," Trinidad said, taking another drag. "This is terrible." He turned on the faucet and drowned the cigarette under the water. Then he tore open the carton of Marlboros. "Cancer's one thing," he complained, "but tasting bad, that's unforgivable."

Price stuck the tip of his Marlboro into the flame that Jo held for him.

Then came the crash.

Trinidad staggered, jerked stiffly upright, his back arching like some contorted mime. He toppled to the floor, hitting his head hard against the stove as he fell.

At first Price thought Trinidad might be mugging, having some fun at their expense. Or maybe some smoke went down the wrong pipe. Then he saw Trinidad's arms and legs flailing, his friend's body curling up into a fetal ball as he convulsed on the kitchen floor. Price jumped up, throwing aside the cigarette as he ran to the kitchenette. Jo shook the match out and followed.

"J-Jesus help," Trinidad choked, his eyes rolling wildly as his body flung itself around. His leg clanged into the refrigerator; his head smashed into a cupboard.

Price tried to wrestle Trinidad to the center of the floor, away from the sharp corners and edges, but the power of the convulsions was too great. Trinidad's body bucked and twisted and flayed as if a charge of electricity were passing through his spine. Jo tried to force the corner of a kitchen towel into Trinidad's mouth to prevent him from biting off his tongue.

"Call an ambulance," Price shouted, and Jo sprinted to the phone and began dialing the number Price had taped to the phone.

A mighty buck flung Price off Trinidad and into the stove. His friend's head was whipping back and forth with such velocity the towel shook loose. Trinidad's mouth clamped hard and the tip of his tongue flew off. He continued shaking his head, spraying blood into Price's face.

"On the way," Jo said as she rushed back to help Price hold Trinidad down.

Tears of pain and fear filled Trinidad's face as he tried to talk between convulsions. "C-c-can't stop," he panted, grimacing. Blood leaked through his teeth, spilled over his chin. Then another series of convulsions sent limbs flying.

By the time they heard the ambulance screaming down the street, Trinidad's convulsions had lessened. He was lying still now, so familiar with the pain, it didn't seem to bother him anymore. Suddenly Price knew his friend was about to die.

"Tell…" Trinidad began, then grit his teeth against a sharp stab of pain. Price waited for the name, certain it would be Tina, his wife. At least he would be able to tell her Trinidad had spoken her name at the end. It wouldn't be much, but it would be something. The pain eased a moment and Trinidad tried again. "Tell…*Rawlings*!" He stared at Price, his lips slightly parted as if he would say more. He didn't. He was dead.

"Rawlings!" Jo said, the professional agent taking over from the compassionate human being. "How the hell does he know Rawlings?"

Price stood up, staring at the blood-splattered face of his best friend. The red splotches against the dark skin looked like painted freckles on a clown.

"How'd he know Rawlings?" Jo repeated.

Price walked out the front door and kept going.

21

They were waiting for him when he got back, three men with oakish tans and unsmiling faces. "Dees wants to see you," one of them said. Someone's beefy hand wrapped around Price's upper arm, guiding him toward their car.

Price shook the hand off with a jerk of his elbow. "I'll follow in my car."

The three men with tans exchanged bland expressions. "We're supposed to bring you in. For your own safety."

"I'll follow," Price repeated, and headed back to his Rabbit without waiting for an answer.

The three men climbed into their Camaro and waited for the Rabbit to fall in behind them. The man in the back seat stared at Price through the back window of the Camaro during the entire drive.

"Where the fuck you been?" Dees snarled when Price was ushered into the office. Dees was sitting stiffly behind Conroy's messy desk, shifting uncomfortably like a condemned man waiting to get strapped in. Conroy was sitting on a chair against the wall chewing on an enormous wad of gum; Jo was leaning against a gray filing cabinet.

"You okay?" Jo asked.

Price nodded at her, but was aware of a funny look in her eyes, as if she'd found out something awful. Something she didn't want to tell him.

"Sit," Dees said to Price, gesturing abruptly at Conroy, who vacated his chair. Price stood. Dees sighed. "Give me a break." It was a plea.

Price sat.

Dees fidgeted with a paper clip on the desk, bending it out of shape as he talked. "We were worried about you, Calender. Disappearing like that, shaking your bodyguards."

"Went to see Trinidad's wife."

"I told you it was something like that," Jo said to Dees. Then to Price, "He thought you'd run."

"I thought about it," Price admitted. "But where to?"

Dees nodded, concentrating intently on straightening the paper clip. He tried to iron the metal with Conroy's stapler. "I've got a call into Rawlings. He should be calling back any minute now. Straighten this whole thing out."

"Finally," Conroy said gruffly, as if to remind everyone that this was *his* office. He pulled a pack of cigarettes from his jacket and offered one around.

"For Christ's sake, Conroy," Jo said, making a face.

"Oh, yeah. Sorry." He stuffed the pack back into his pocket without taking one. "Forgot."

"Since we're on the subject," Dees said. "It was strychnine. Traces of PCP. A couple other goodies. Your friend didn't have a chance. Nothing you could have done for him."

"Except maybe put up a bigger fight when he insisted on spending the night with me," Price said.

"He was your friend," Dees said. "He wanted to help."

"How did he know Rawlings?"

Dees tapped at the paper clip with the edge of the stapler, pounding out a crook in the metal. "I don't know. That's what Rawlings is supposed to tell us." He nodded angrily at the phone as if it were Rawlings.

"What else?" Price asked.

"What do you mean?"

Price stared at him, waiting.

"Tell him," Jo said. "He's got to know."

Dees looked up from his paper clip and sighed. "This fuckin' job isn't all it's cracked up to be, you know?" He bent the paper clip in half and tossed it into the wastebasket. "Your wife. She isn't dead."

Price nodded.

The three of them stared at Price, waiting for some kind of reaction. A sudden outburst. Incredulity. Denial. Ranting. But there was nothing, just a weary nodding.

"What else?" Price asked.

Dees stared, open-mouthed. "That's not enough?"

Price didn't say anything. He didn't know what to say. He wasn't about to put on a show for them—that much he knew. But even more he wasn't sure how he felt. Somehow he wasn't surprised. Ever since he'd seen those eyes staring up at him from that car he'd known. Maybe he'd known all along, without ever seeing her. His emotions felt raw, scraped and bleeding from colliding with one another. What exactly was he feeling? Relief that he hadn't killed her? Despite all the rationalizations, he'd always been a little appalled, a little afraid of the part of him that was capable of killing someone he'd loved.

And there was still some undeniable desire for her. Something sexual and emotional. He didn't feel it in his brain or heart or genitals, but somewhere else, somewhere dark and hard, like the base of his spine. It was cold and impulsive. Primitive. Something left over from ancestors millions of years ago, the feeling they got the first time they saw fire then reached for it, tried to grasp a flame in their fists, their skin growing hotter as they neared, but still reaching, still plunging ahead. That's what it was like with Liza R. You had to keep reaching.

"Price?" Jo asked, as if she knew what he was thinking, asking him to choose.

He looked at her. "I'm fine." He turned to Dees. "Where does that put us? With Devane."

"Somewhere over the rainbow. Christ, I wish I knew. She's involved—that's all I know." Dees smacked the silent telephone. "Ring, damn it."

And it did.

The suddenness of the ring right after his command, startled Dees. It took him a moment to recover. He punched the speaker button and said, "You son of a bitch, Rawlings. That's how you knew I'd pulled Montana and Crush off Calender. This guy Trinidad was in your pocket."

Rawlings sighed, though through the speaker it sounded tinny and hollow, like a wind tunnel. "He wasn't in my pocket. He was a volunteer." He paused. "You there, Price?"

"I'm here."

"I want you to know, your friend wasn't spying on you or betraying you. I approached him seven years ago when we kicked you loose. One of the provisions of your staying alive was that we keep a casual eye on you.

I asked Trinidad to help and he told me to shove it where the buffalo roam."

Price smiled. Yeah, that was Trin.

"I convinced him you were in danger. You know I could do that."

"Yeah," Price said. He remembered the photographs, the reports, graphs and charts, everything Rawlings had shown him to get him to help nab Liza R.

"It wasn't a scam," Rawlings continued, "at least, not all of it. You were in danger as long as Devane was alive. Anyway, Trinidad agreed to keep us updated on you. We offered him money, but he wouldn't take it."

Price wished he had. The poor bastard was always short. "He told you about Liza R."

"Said you thought you saw her outside your apartment."

"Maybe, maybe not. Different hair, different facial structure. Could have been my imagination."

"Yeah, that's what I figured," Rawlings said. "But I did some checking, some very expensive checking. Had Liza R's body exhumed."

Jo frowned. "It wasn't hers."

"Right," Rawlings said. "Just some college coed reported missing from Georgetown seven years ago. Disappeared after her psychology class. Her car was still in the campus lot, her backpack on the driver's seat. Her parents received a telegram from her that she had taken off for Europe with some other student. They even got postcards for six months afterward, so no police were involved until the cards stopped coming."

"Liza R was always thorough," Price said.

Rawlings continued. "She had some help that time. Probably KGB. Which means they might be helping her now. Remember Zinov and Denisovitch, our phony FBI agents in the Mustang?''

"What next?'' Price asked.

"Don't ask me, ask Dees. He's still in charge. I'm just giving you some deep background. In fact, there's no record of this call even taking place. According to witnesses, I'm at my tennis club in Virginia, playing doubles with a couple of hustlers from Justice.''

Dees leaned his face right next to the speaker. "Rawlings, you're a bastard.''

Rawlings chuckled. "Yeah, so?''

Dees stabbed a button disconnecting the line. "All right, our first concern is to capture Devane as quickly as possible. I don't want to hear of any more teenage girls killed by him.'' Dees began counting off on his fingers. "First thing we do is lift the lid on Trinidad's death. Let the press know Calender is still alive. That way Devane will know. Second, take Calender back to his apartment so Devane knows where to find him.''

"He'll know we'll be waiting this time,'' Jo said.

"He knew we were waiting with Rupert Hesse. That didn't stop him. Hell, he likes the challenge. The guy's not exactly firing on all his cylinders, you know what I mean? All right, once we've got Calender nestled in, we wait, leaving only a minimum crew visible to meet Devane's expectations. He'll try again and he'll try soon. Questions?''

"How many people you want on this?'' Conroy asked.

"Everybody,'' Dees said.

"You're talking serious overtime now.''

Dees squinted at Conroy. "Is your résumé in order, Conroy?''

Conroy stopped chewing his gum. "I'll start calling now."

"You do that."

Conroy hurried out of the office.

"What about me?" Jo said. She expected some snide, leering comment, but Dees stared at her with a flat, professional expression.

"You stay on the inside with Calender. I want Conroy outside the place. He's kind of a surfer, but he's good."

"Okay."

Price listened to them discuss his safety for a few more minutes, then stood up and walked to the phone in front of Dees. He spoke to Dees as he dialed. "I want two tickets to Hawaii on the next flight out in the names of Tillie and Rebecca Calender. I also want one thousand dollars waiting for them at the ticket counter."

Dees reached out and hit the phone's plunger, disconnecting the call. "I can't promise that. Allocating money, sending civilians on planes—that opens us up to a lot of civil litigation. I can't authorize that."

"Who can?"

Dees sighed. "Rawlings."

Price handed the receiver to Dees. "Call him."

"Christ, I'd rather lunch with Devane."

Price continued to hold out the receiver until Dees took it and began dialing. "All right, get out of here. I hate for people to see me beg."

Price and Jo left the room and found another phone down the hall. He called his grandmother and told her to get Rebecca and herself packed for a week's vacation. Tillie Calender didn't protest. She knew the tone in his voice. "I'll have to go pick her up at school."

"Call me when you're ready," he told her. "I'll be home."

The drive back to Price's apartment seemed to take forever. Jo drove her yellow Ferrari while Price sat silently next to her. Conroy was behind them, driving Price's Rabbit. Two carloads of agents drove in front of them. At least there wouldn't be another bombing like the one in San Diego.

"You notice anything different about Dees," she said suddenly, cracking the silence.

"Like what?"

"I dunno. He just seems," she hesitated, "different. Changed."

Price shrugged.

"It's like he's not so snotty."

"Yeah, he's not as snotty or devious as he was in Washington. For the first time since he's been in charge I got the feeling he really cared about you staying alive, and even protecting any future victims of Devane. Not just because of his own career. I don't know, he's tougher somehow, but more compassionate, more like, uh . . ."

"Like Gandhi?"

Jo laughed. "I was thinking more like Rawlings."

"Rawlings?" Price said. "Must be a different Rawlings than I'm thinking of."

The silence closed around them again.

Jo stared at the road. "You want to see her again, don't you?"

"No," he lied.

She merely nodded. They drove past the Veterans Cemetery and she watched the breeze ruffle the shaggy grass. It looked to her like thousands of tiny dogs' tails wagging in the wind.

"That apartment the night we met. Remember?"

"Yes."

"That was mine. Those stuffed animals are mine. I didn't want you to know before. I mean, Jesus, a grown woman and all collecting stuffed animals. It's embarrassing. But I thought you should know."

Price smiled. "I knew."

"I figured. That's why I told you."

Price reached out and touched her arm. She didn't take her eyes from the road. "Liza R doesn't have anything to do with us."

Jo turned on the radio. "We're almost there," she said.

22

Devane stabbed his fork into the thick steak and began sawing a piece off with his knife.

"How's everything?" the blond waitress asked.

"Fine," he said, looking her over with the same hungry expression he'd used on his steak. Early twenties, sturdy legs, a little wide at the hips. He flashed his toothy movie-star grin at her. "Another glass of burgundy when you get a chance."

"Yes, sir." She hurried off.

He stopped smiling, continued sawing. Behind him the smoky windows revealed the calm display of the marina. Boats drifted lazily by, sea gulls swooped back and forth. The restaurant's popularity among the Marina del Rey set was due more to its view and classy atmosphere rather than its mediocre food. Sitting at a booth by himself, dressed in casual but flattering sport clothes, Devane looked like a successful young corporate executive on vacation. A couple of women in business suits eating chef salads eyed him openly while continuing their discussion of newly released actuarial charts.

Devane was barely aware of what was going on around him. He chewed his steak methodically, but without delight. Not to say it was tough, or tasted bad. It had no taste at all. Neither did the clam chowder, the asparagus, the baked potato. The burgundy might as well have been water. It wasn't that he wasn't hungry, either. He was ravenous. But the tasteless food offered no satisfaction. He dumped salt and pepper on the potato until it looked as if it had been rolled in ashes, but he tasted nothing. It was like chewing Styrofoam.

"Here you are, sir," the blond waitress said, bringing his second glass of burgundy.

"I wonder if you'd do me a favor," Devane said, opening his wallet, "and bring me some change."

She frowned for a moment as if she thought the proffered dollar bill was to be broken down for her tip. "Certainly, sir," she said, striding away with the bill.

This wasn't the first time food had been tasteless to him, but it was the first time *all* the food had been that way. Before it had been only certain foods, certain vegetables and meats. True, the list had been growing in the past months, but he hadn't expected this. He tried to determine the medical reasons, what might have been in the Masked Dog formula to cause this and what he might do to counteract this side effect. But he couldn't think straight. He kept imagining King Midas—fat, gluttonous, greedy, the way he looked in the Golden Treasury storybook he used to keep around his office for his patients—and how everything he touched, even his food, turned to gold. He felt an annoying twitching just under the skin at his temples. It wasn't fear or panic—he was incapable of those emotions now—but it was something. Rage, perhaps. He'd been feeling that more and more lately. He fought to control it, picking absently at his food.

"Your change, sir," the waitress said, funneling the coins into Devane's hand.

"Thank you." His smile was less dazzling now, almost impatient. She gave him a puzzled look and left. Careful, Devane, he told himself. Hold on.

He took his handful of coins into the foyer. The two public telephones were mounted on the wall between the rest rooms. One of the phones had a yellow Out of Order sticker pasted over the coin slot. Devane spread his change on the shelf, pulled out his list of phone numbers, deposited some of the money and began dialing. It took a while to finally get through to the people with power, but once he did the calls were brief and to the point. Money was the only topic of discussion.

Halfway through his third call, a man came from the dining room and stood behind Devane, waiting to use the phone. Devane ignored him, continuing to phone the people on his list, the same ones who'd gotten his letter a few days ago. After the fourth call, the man stood next to Devane and stared angrily at his watch. It was a gold Concord, thin as a communion wafer. The man's clothing was equally as expensive as the watch. He was barely thirty, Devane guessed, with a gold chain around his throat and several ostentatious gold rings. People who knew him probably considered him flashy. His silk shirt was unbuttoned far enough to reveal a hairless muscular chest. Probably played tennis or volleyball. He wore mirrored aviator sunglasses, even though the restaurant was fairly dark to begin with.

Devane thumbed a dime into the slot and started dialing again. The man stuck his fingers into the remaining group of dimes and stirred them.

"A lot of dimes, man," he said in a tone that indicated he was used to ordering people. "This isn't an office."

Devane kept punching the buttons, listening to the other electronic tones as the circuits searched out another Washington D.C. embassy. "Collect," he told the operator.

"Hey, pal. You hear me?" The young man angled closer, standing a full three inches taller than Devane.

Devane felt the ticking at his temples, like an insect trying to scratch its way out from under his skin. The thought gave him shivers. Control, he told himself. He was too close to winning to fuck up now.

"I'll be done in a minute," he told the man, waiting for the operator to connect him. A man's accented voice accepted the charges and asked Devane to wait while he sought out Colonel Nan.

"There are other people who want to use the phone, you know?" the young man persisted, fingering his gold chain.

There was a time, Devane thought, when the threat of a confrontation like this would have had him scooping up his change, apologizing all the way back to the table. The fear would have stayed with him, eaten at him until later, when he might have taken it out on his wife, blackening an eye, cracking a rib. Now he felt no fear, only a sense of caution lest he create a disturbance. Better to give up the phone to this punk.

"I'll be done in a second," Devane said, his voice uncommonly quiet.

The guy straightened his sunglasses, bounced on his toes arrogantly as if he'd just won something and said, "Fucking better be."

Immediately he knew he'd said too much.

Devane turned to face him, staring with eyes as dark and flat as shale. He picked up one of the thick Los Angeles phone books stacked under the phones, hefted

224

it once, then grabbed it with both hands by the spine. He smiled coldly at the man and, without struggle, tore the huge phone book in half as easily as ripping one sheet of newspaper. "I always wanted to do that," Devane said, his smile spreading like fire.

The man swallowed, nervously adjusted his sunglasses. "I've seen that before," he said uncertainly. "Some kinda trick."

"Have you seen this?" Devane said, snatching the sunglasses from the man's face. He opened his mouth, pushed them in and began chewing them, the mirrored glass crunching with each bite. To Devane they tasted no different from his steak. He plucked the wire frames from his mouth as if they were a pesky chicken bone, and stuffed them into the man's jacket pocket. Then he swallowed the chewed glass. He picked up the receiver again and said to the man, "Now get out of here, or your fucking head's next."

The man thought about it a second or two, spun around and walked quickly away, using all of his self-control to keep from running.

Devane turned back to the phone, only to find that he'd unknowingly crushed the receiver in his hand. The green handle was cracked from speaker to earpiece. He'd have to be even more careful. He hung the splintered receiver back on the hook and went back to pay his check and find another phone.

23

"The soup is excellent, no?" Alexei said, slurping another spoonful down.

"No," Liza R said. "It's too salty. And where are the fucking clams?" She voiced her annoyance loudly enough that Alexei became embarrassed, smiling apologetically at the other diners around them.

"Shhh. This is the Polo Lounge. Very famous."

"Very overrated." She dropped her spoon in the bowl with a clang. "We'd have been better off at a drugstore counter."

Alexei broke a sourdough roll in half and dunked it in the soup. He wrestled his anger under control. He had picked the Beverly Hills Hotel as their base because it was close to Westwood, where Price Calender was, but mostly because it was famous as an expensive and elegant hangout of movie stars. He hoped to see at least one movie star before their business was concluded out here.

He gnawed on the soggy end of the bread and pointed at a table across the room. "Isn't that, you know, the one who was fired from *Charlie's Angels*? Shelley Hack?"

Liza R laughed. "Poor dumb Alexei. You spend all this money on clothes and cars and fancy hotels, but you still have no taste. You can only mimic what you see others with money do. You're like some jungle ape who's watched a film of Fred Astaire dancing, and now you're trying to imitate him with your big feet and squat body. Not likely, dear Alexei—a peasant is a peasant is a peasant, no matter how you dress him up.''

Alexei dunked his bread in his soup again, but left it there. He had lost his appetite. What bothered him most about Liza R was that she was right. He spent large sums of money, but without any knowledge of what he was buying. His New York apartment had many expensive paintings he neither understood nor appreciated. Their singular recommendation had been their exorbitant cost. Left to his own tastes, he would have stapled bullfight posters to the walls.

''You are a cruel woman, Liza R,'' he told her, shaking his head sadly. ''In Russia, we have crude names for a woman like you.''

''We've got one in America, too.'' She grinned. '' 'Snob.' And proud of it.''

An elderly waiter shuffled by them, carrying a phone. ''Phone call for Ms Sandra Levy. Ms Levy.''

''I'm Ms Levy,'' Liza R said, raising her hand.

The old guy gave her an appreciative leer and plugged the phone into a nearby jack. He took Alexei's five-dollar tip with a contemptuous nod and shuffled off again.

''Hello,'' Liza R said into the phone. Her voice was crisp and energetic, and Alexei could see the gleam in her eye. ''Of course . . . yes . . . that could be arranged.'' She smiled at Alexei and mouthed a single silent word—Devane.

Alexei nodded. The embassy had given Devane the number, just as they were supposed to, though efficiency is not one of the main qualities of embassy workers. Alexei leaned closer to the receiver to listen, but Liza R didn't offer to share it with him. In fact, she pulled slightly away. In Russia, Alexei thought angrily, even a peasant would know what to do with such a contrary woman.

The conversation was brief. When Liza R replaced the receiver, she was smiling. "He wants to meet us."

"Of course. You gave him the address?"

"You heard me."

"What else?"

She shrugged, stirring her half-finished soup with the spoon. "He likes what we've offered to pay him and is willing to discuss specifics now. He wants us to bring a good-faith payment. Ten thousand. He must be running low of cash."

"That can be arranged."

"Also, he wants us to come alone. Just you and me."

"Did you agree?"

"Of course."

"Good." Alexei started dialing the phone.

"Who are you calling?" she asked.

"Zinov and Denisovitch. I want them along."

"That's dumb, Alex. What if he spots them?"

"So? By then it will be too late. My orders are to bring him in or destroy him. If the Soviet Union can't use him, we certainly don't want anybody else to use him against us."

She placed her hand over his, gently urging the telephone back to the cradle. He tingled from her warm touch. "Bringing those two along is too risky. There are other ways to get what we want. Subtle ways."

"Subtle?" He smiled. "We have a saying in the Ukraine—Even a blind hog finds an acorn sometimes. So, Liza R, even a dumb peasant such as myself can occasionally manage to do something right and fulfill his assignment."

She didn't argue. There was no point. She knew men, and she knew she'd pushed this one too far. She'd been the dumb one this time, indulging in baiting Alexei. Now she would have to revise her plans. It would be more dangerous now, but the rewards would still be great. As long as Alexei didn't suspect what she was up to.

24

Devane was careful not to step on the snails. He had to hopscotch down the sidewalk to avoid the dozens of them oozing along the white concrete, leaving slimy drunken trails that snaked here and there with no particular goal. Some old snail trails glittered silver in the waning twilight. One squashed snail was being swarmed by four others as they nibbled at his remains. Devane made a face and stepped over them all. Nothing disgusted him more than the crackling sound their fragile shells made when being mashed by a shoe.

He was an hour early. More than enough time to hide and watch, make sure the Russians delivered on their word. The woman, Sandy Levy, had promised him she and her partner would be alone, but Devane didn't trust anybody's word, least of all a woman's.

Devane checked his watch. It would be dark soon.

Her directions had been perfect, but the drive along the Hollywood Freeway had proved annoying. Traffic had been heavy and the drivers cranky and aggressive. The ticking at Devane's temples had finally stopped, but his skin felt funny now, somehow too tight. He thought he could hear his own blood rushing through the vessels of his ears, as if he had a seashell cupped to each ear. His lips were dry and he had to keep licking them. He tried to reason out a medical explanation for all this, but couldn't. He mentally scrolled through the medical books and journals he'd read, but he couldn't put it all together. There were too many experimental elements of the Masked Dog Project, chemicals in the drugs unknown even to him. Besides, he had to admit he'd never much liked being a doctor. But, then, he hadn't entered the profession with any noble humanitarian motives. He'd merely wanted to make money. Unable to handle the more complex medical disciplines where the big money was, he'd gravitated to pediatrics, not out of love of children like many of his colleagues, but because it put him closer to his objects of lust. His insinuating good looks and polished charm with young mothers built his practice into a success despite the fact that his medical expertise was less than terrific. He had to smile at that, because now, with his new mental and physical abilities, he was capable of becoming one of the greatest doctors alive. Instead he would become the greatest assassin. The pay was better.

Suddenly the sprinklers hissed on over the freshly landscaped grounds. Some of the spray misted the edges of the sidewalks, wetting his pants. He hurried forward, accidentally stepping on a snail. The shell crackled like knuckles and he scraped his shoe on the edge of the sidewalk, leaving the jellied lump of snail behind. He continued scuffing his shoe along the sidewalk long after he'd removed any trace of snail.

Devane passed a large hand-carved sign planted in the lawn: Stonebridge Estates. A stone bridge was carved into the sign, but that was the only bridge, stone or otherwise, Devane could see around here, except maybe the freeway off-ramp a couple of miles away. The sales office was finished and lavishly decorated, as were the three model homes next to it. The rest of the hill was still under construction, with wooden skeletons surrounding the models. Several swimming pools were under construction, each with a nearby spa. "California," he sneered, as if that one word said it all.

He didn't know why the Levy woman had chosen this location for their meeting. A construction site twenty minutes outside Los Angeles in the San Fernando Valley, just past Woodland Hills. Perhaps this was one of those hills, though he didn't see any woods nearby, either. It didn't matter. She had picked the place and he had picked the time. At least it was remote.

And he was early. That was important. If he was going to make a living dealing with these devious people, he would have to become more devious, a trait that had always been natural with him.

He checked the parking lot near the sales office. It was empty. His own car was parked a mile away at a Winchell's Donut Shop so they wouldn't know he'd already arrived. There were lights on in the sales office and the models, but that was normal, to discourage thieves.

He patted the Colt .38 Super nestled in his waistband. He'd bought it under the counter in a downtown pawnshop with the last of his cash. The persistent ticking at his temples, the surges of irrational rage, the loss of taste, all suggested some chemical imbalances attacking his system. Until he had a chance to experiment on himself with what he could remember from the Masked Dog Project lab and Dr. Frank Elder, he couldn't rely totally on his physical prowess. A gun might come in handy.

Devane walked cautiously toward the sales office. She'd told him it would be unlocked, the alarm disconnected. He tried the doorknob. It turned easily in his hand. He entered. The room smelled clean and fresh, like new carpeting. In the middle of the sales office was a wooden table model of the housing tract, with tiny wooden houses curving around painted roads called Cherry Blossom Lane, Huckleberry Street and so forth. Half the houses had red Sold buttons on them. Fancy brochures were stacked on the table next to the painted lake that Devane had also not seen outside. Part of the Final Phase, the glossy brochure promised.

"In the market?" Liza R said, stepping out from the kitchen. "I might be able to get you in here with only five percent down. Low monthly payments."

Alexei was right behind her, looking dour and cautious. His twelve-hundred-dollar jacket was unbuttoned, and he moved slowly, as if he expected Devane to attack at any moment.

Then two men holding heavy black guns descended the staircase. Zinov and Denisovitch. They pointed their guns at Devane.

Devane nodded, realizing now that he'd made a mistake. An amateur's mistake of underestimating his opponent.

"You're early," Liza R said.

"Not early enough," Devane said.

She shrugged. "Still, it's a sign. There's hope for you."

He smiled a white flash of perfect teeth and rested his hands to his hips. He felt the pressure of the gun just inside his jacket flap. He considered going for it, wondering if his speed would be enough.

"You're dealing with professionals now, Mr. Devane," Liza R warned. She leaned against the mirrored wall, next to the placard that said Optional Item. She wore black denim pants and a silky red pirate blouse. Her eyes and hair reflected the blouse's dark red.

He kept looking at her, aware that the others were slowly closing in. He wasn't afraid. He had his strength and speed and brain. The way he saw it, they were outmatched. The gun was merely a precaution. He certainly wasn't handy with one, but at this range, it would be hard to miss.

"Won't the owners mind?" he asked, waving a hand to encompass the entire construction site.

"We are the owners," Alexei said. "Not us, of course, but the people who employ us."

Devane looked surprised. "The KGB owns condos in Southern California?"

"We own many businesses in this country. Gas stations, clothing stores, even a few McDonald's franchises. One of the advantages of a free-enterprise system, Mr. Devane."

The four men formed an uneasy square, with Liza R remaining at a safe distance.

"Before we get down to business," she said coolly, "perhaps you'll permit Zinov and Denisovitch to remove that bulky gun you're carrying."

Devane looked at her. Her smile was almost as bright as his, but with a sly curl at the corners. He nodded. "Sure. Since we're all on the same side now. That is, if you brought the money."

Liza R opened her purse and removed two packets of fifty-dollar bills. "Ten thousand dollars, as agreed."

Devane plucked the gun from his waist and tossed it to Zinov, who caught the barrel with his left hand; his right hand was still wrapped around his own gun, leveled at Devane's chest.

Liza R walked across the carpet and slapped the two packets of money in Devane's hands, allowing her fingers to touch his hand a little longer than necessary. Devane smiled at her.

"Okay, folks," Devane said, thumbing happily through the money. "You just hired yourself an assassin. Now who do you want to die?"

"A couple of questions first," Alexei said.

"Who are you?" Devane asked him.

Liza R answered for him. "Alexei will be your contact, your control."

"My boss."

"Right." She said it in a mocking way that drew an angry glare from Alexei.

"What about you?" Devane said. "You must be Sandra Levy, but where do you fit in?"

"Don't you remember me?" she asked.

"No."

"Think back. About seven years ago."

"Seven years ago I was in a maximum-security laboratory and the only women around were Ph.D.s in chemistry with backsides like barrels and faces like toads."

She touched his arm. "Well, we never actually met. But we were in contact."

Devane stared at her face. The only woman he'd been in contact with back then was Calender's wife, who'd gotten word to him through a trustee when the break-out would occur. He'd seen her face in photographs in the magazines and this wasn't her. Besides, Liza R was dead.

"No, I didn't die," she said with a laugh, answering his thoughts. She framed her face with her hands and struck a flamboyant pose. "Reconstructive surgery, my dear. Certainly you better than most know the wonders of modern medicine."

Devane gave her a hard stare. "You fucked up, lady. Cost me another seven years."

"Almost cost me my life."

"That was your problem." He walked over to the table with the Stonebridge Estates model. He poked a finger at some of the tiny wooden houses. "At least I paid back your rock-star husband for both of us. Killed the bastard."

Liza R stood across the model from him and shook her head. "This time *you* fucked up, Devane. Price Calender is still alive. It was his friend, Trinidad, you poisoned."

Devane looked up quickly, the ticking suddenly back in his temples, his skin feeling too tight again. He licked his dry lips. "The cigarettes . . ."

"Amateurish," she told him, groaning. "You never leave something like that to chance. Besides, current intelligence information shows he's been trying to quit smoking for the past six months. A pro would have known that. You have a ways to go before you're ready to deal with the kind of tough pros you'll be up against."

Devane bristled. "Tell that to Rupert Hesse. What's left of him."

"Okay, that was a nice piece of work, though its success was partially due to the fact that you were an unknown factor to those guarding him. Now you aren't. They have an idea what you're capable of, how you think. Things will be a lot tougher for you from now on."

Devane plucked one of the little wooden houses from the model. "If that's all true, what are you guys doing out here talking to me?"

"You've got potential, that's why. With some training and a support system, you could do some real damage. And earn a lot more money than even you realize." She took the wooden house from his hand and placed it neatly back among the other homes.

"Yes," Alexei agreed. "The KGB will pay you well. Quite well. And we will help you eliminate this Price Calender."

"That's something I want to do myself." He pointed a finger at Liza R. "In fact, if you weren't part of this deal, I'd kill you, too, for not getting me out seven years ago."

She smiled. "Ambitious man, aren't you?"

"Yeah. Ambitious and capable."

"You have a lot to learn."

"I learn fast."

Alexei stepped between them. "We are aware of your extraordinary memory, Dr. Devane. Do you remember many details about the Masked Dog Project?"

"Enough."

Alexei looked very pleased. "Excellent. Such information will help us in providing you with all you need in the way of medication." He scratched his chin, trying unsuccessfully to hide his excitement. "I suppose, with the proper equipment and with your powers of recall, you would be able to duplicate the drug that gave you your remarkable abilities?"

"Sure," Devane said. "In time."

"Yes, yes, of course. In time, in due time." Alexei drummed his fingers on the edge of the table. "Then it is important that we accomplish two objectives as soon as possible. First, to provide a medical support system for your unique needs. And second, that we provide a certain amount of training and briefing to make you more effective in the field."

"Forget it. I like working alone."

"Yes, certainly," Alexei quickly agreed. "But you will need to learn certain procedures, uh, methods...."

"Just write them all down. I'll memorize them."

Alexei sensed he was handling this clumsily, but for some reason Liza R was not helping him, so he blundered ahead. "Even so, my superiors will want to meet you, discuss your, uh, assignments with you, determine which ones you are most suited for."

Devane stared at Alexei. "What are you saying? That you want me to go back to Washington with you? To your embassy?"

"Yes, the embassy. Then, later..." He hesitated. "Moscow."

Devane laughed.

Alexei hurried on. "A brief visit only. A formality After all, we are willing to invest a great deal of money—"

"Shove it!" Devane said. "I'm willing to kill for you people because you offered the most money. But this is strictly a business arrangement, not an exchange of ideologies. I don't give a fuck about you or your bosses. If you want to pay for my services, fine. If not, I'll take them elsewhere. There are other customers."

Alexei gestured wearily at Zinov and Denisovitch, who approached, guns in hand. "I'm afraid it's not that simple."

"What he means," Liza R explained, "is that you either go with him or you don't go anywhere."

Devane smiled wolfishly. He hunched over slightly as he felt the rush of adrenaline washing through his system, activating the drug. It was brisk and energizing, like an icy river winding down from a snow-covered mountain. Every muscle in his body seemed to harden with strength. "Fuck all of you," he said.

Zinov and Denisovitch approached cautiously, their guns level. Zinov, who'd played the flirting FBI agent when trying to kidnap Jo and Price, spoke now with a hollow bravado, his Dixie accent a little tattered. "Easy, pal. We don't want to get rough."

Then two loud pops echoed liked someone opening champagne bottles and Zinov was swatting at the fat black fly on his neck, only it wasn't a fly and it wasn't black. It was a red hole, the flesh around the hole burned from the heat of the bullet. Blood pumped freely as Zinov pressed his fingers against the hole and looked surprised as his legs went limp under him and he flopped to the floor, dead. Denisovitch felt nothing. The bullet punched a hole through his heart and lodged in his spine, killing his brain before his body got the message. He was already dead as his legs staggered a couple steps backward, then toppled.

Devane spun to see where the bullets had come from.

Liza R perched on the model table, her 9 mm Star Model 28 clutched in both hands. "And then there were three."

Alexei whirled, his face crimson with outrage. "Have you gone insane, woman?"

"Of course not, Alexei." She laughed. "I'm just taking care of business. The way I see it, gentlemen, is that there's a great deal of potential here for a lucrative partnership. The good doctor here has raw abilities, but no technique, no finesse and certainly no knowledge of the already overcrowded international espionage business. I have all three. So together we could be quite an effective team. And a very expensive team."

"I don't need a partner," Devane said. "Like you said, I've got the raw abilities."

"Ability is not enough. I would have thought you'd have learned that already tonight. Obviously a good memory doesn't necessarily mean you can analyze the data you retain. In other words, without me, you'd already be on your way to Moscow, where you'd be back in a prison until you succeeded in duplicating the Masked Dog drug."

Alexei shook his head. "This was stupid, Liza R. You realize the consequences."

"Don't be melodramatic, Alexei. The KGB is like any other business. If they can't own the product, they'll settle for renting it. Whatever turns a profit, right?"

"To allow betrayal is bad business, too. It encourages others."

"How would they know? There are many possible explanations for your deaths. Devane killed you all. That will only raise him up in the KGB's estimation. Bring us a better price."

Alexei was silent. She was right. He relaxed, allowed the fear and anger to drain from his body. They would do no good now. He knew what Liza R had planned for him and he prepared calmly like the professional he was.

"Sweet plan, lady," Devane said, his head tilted at a cocky angle. "Only problem is, I don't want to be your partner. If my business gets going and I need to take on some hired help, I might consider throwing a few crumbs your way. But otherwise, you're on your own."

Liza R smiled broadly. "I wonder if you were so arrogant before the Masked Dog Project, Dr. Devane. Or perhaps that arrogance comes from your experience with women being limited to little girls."

Devane smiled back.

"But back to the business at hand. I'm afraid words aren't going to convince you of your lack of experience. You'll need a demonstration. Free, of course, like the one you gave us."

"Oh?" Devane looked amused.

"A little unarmed combat."

"Against you?"

"That would be interesting, wouldn't it? But, no, against Alexei there."

Devane laughed. "Be serious. I'll kill him."

"That's the point. Unless he kills you. Which I'd hate to see, since it would cost me money. But it's obvious you need some convincing."

"What's the catch?"

"No catch. Alexei is unarmed. But you'll see there's quite a difference between an amateur and a professional. And in this business, the price for making that mistake is your life." She kept her gun pointed between the two men, able to swing it on either should they make a move toward her. "Alexei, teach this bore some manners before you die."

Alexei nodded. It would do no good to rush Liza R. With a gun in her hand she was invincible. Perhaps there would be an unguarded moment later, but he didn't want to think about that now. He had to concentrate on the American. Oddly, he felt exhilarated, almost glad for the opportunity. This would be his greatest challenge. He had never been beaten in unarmed combat, but, then, he'd never fought anyone with Devane's powers. If nothing else, it would be a glorious way to die. He felt no hate for Liza R. The KGB had known it was only a matter of time before she would seize some opportunity for her own. They had left it up to Alexei to prevent it. He had failed. If he survived his fight with Devane, she would be ready to negotiate a new deal and things would go on as they had before. Such was the nature of their business.

Alexei removed his jacket and folded it neatly on the sales-office desk. Then he strolled casually toward Devane as if they were two old friends meeting on a street.

Devane watched him approach, stripping off his own jacket and tossing it on the floor. There was no fear, just an anxiousness to get started, the way he imagined a hawk must feel just as it leaps off a thousand-foot cliff, knowing as it spreads its wings that it controls the air, not the other way around. As the little Russian got closer, Devane leaped at him, arms extended. But Alexei was gone.

Rolling across the floor, cursing the new carpet because it slowed his movement, Alexei whipped his legs around until the shins slammed into the backs of Devane's knees, unhinging them, bringing Devane crashing to his knees. Alexei rocked backward, his legs up in the air, keeping his body up so that his legs scissored around the startled American's neck, the hard bony knees clamping into the throat, squeezing, his ankles crossed for leverage, his knees pincering deep into Devane's throat.

Devane felt no pain, only the closing off of air, the dryness in his throat and chest. A spasm in his lungs. He grabbed Alexei's shins and began prying them apart. Alexei gritted his teeth, his whole body arcing as he fought to maintain pressure. But Devane's strength was too great. He forced the legs apart until they were unhooked from around his neck and then, to Alexei's horror, *kept pushing them apart*. Alexei felt his hip joints begin to strain as his legs spread farther and farther apart, the muscles tearing, the bones grinding, his genitals feeling exposed and vulnerable. Devane kept increasing the pressure. An inky darkness seemed to spill over Alexei's sight as he tried to wriggle free of Devane's grip. To no avail.

"So much for your lesson from a pro," Devane snarled, glancing over at Liza R, who merely shrugged in disappointment.

It was absurd, Alexei realized, but he felt as if he were letting Liza R down. He was one of the best in the world, and he was being beaten by an amateur. Combat was not merely a matter of strength; it was also a combination of knowledge and experience and character. Certainly Alexei had been around too long to be killed like this, his legs torn apart like a raped woman. Instead of drinking a toast in memory of his many fine victories, the others would gather and laugh at his degrading demise. That he would not allow.

He stiffened his hands, flat and hard as cutting boards, and sliced down at Devane's left shoulder, alternating blows like a lumberjack bringing down a stubborn pine. The first blow broke the collarbone, but that didn't seem to bother Devane. In fact, he increased pressure until Alexei felt his groin muscle pop. At this angle it was hard for Alexei to put enough body weight behind his blows, but he continued chopping at the broken collarbone, watching the sharp edge of bone poke through skin and shirt as blood sopped around the wound.

Devane noticed a weakening of strength in his left arm, and only then looked at the spot Alexei had been pounding and saw the tip of splintered bone and the dark blood staining his shirt. A sudden rush of rage gushed through him and he backhanded Alexei. The Russian's head slammed into the carpeted floor, the left side of his face caved in. His cheekbone was two inches lower than before and blood trickled from his ear and nose. The pain was great, like a herd of bulls trampling over his face, but Alexei did not stop to think about it. His mind focused only on survival. He rolled back with the force of the blow, swinging his sore legs over his head in a backward somersault. He used the sales desk to pull himself to his wobbly legs, standing now, looking at Zinov and Denisovitch's guns lying near their bleeding bodies.

"Don't," Liza R warned, shaking her gun.

Alexei quickly yanked his belt off and unfastened the buckle, which was a short dagger. He brandished the dagger in his left hand while twirling the leather belt in his right.

Devane was standing now, too, his left shoulder mashed and nasty, the tip of bone looking like a broken arrow sticking out. His face registered no pain, only anger.

"Amazing," Liza R said. "I've seen men go into immediate shock from Alexei's blows."

Why was she shouting? Devane wondered, then realized she wasn't shouting at all. His ears were suddenly sensitive to sound, any sound. Alexei's feet scraping against the carpet sounded like a rake dragged across gravel. His own breathing sounded like a harsh wind. He tried to ignore it. One thing was certain: the side effects to Masked Dog set up a chain reaction among his senses. He would need some time, some research to cure it. Time he'd never have if either the Russian or Liza R had their way.

Devane held his hands out awkwardly, the way he'd been taught in high-school gym class during wrestling, another sport he'd been abysmal at. Alexei slid slowly to the left, the sharp squat blade extended in one hand, the thin leather strap swinging lazily in the other. The leather strap flicked out unexpectedly and bit into Devane's forehead. A pock of skin was gone and blood rushed to fill the hole. Devane didn't feel the pain, but he knew the wound was bleeding, and knew it was very close to his eye. Alexei snapped the belt again, but this time Devane raised both arms to protect his eyes, realizing too late that that was what Alexei had wanted. The small blade plunged in under Devane's upraised arms straight for his chest. Devane quickly dropped his elbows on Alexei's hand, driving the blade downward. The tip pierced his skin and bounced along a couple ribs like a stick knocking along a picket fence. He hadn't expected the little man to be so fast, so cunning. Perhaps there was a greater difference than he had realized.

Alexei jumped back, still clutching his knife and belt. He flicked the belt again. The tip brushed Devane's eyelash, but missed the eye. Only this time Devane caught the belt in one hand and jerked it away from Alexei. Devane's handsome face was twisted into a visage of hate and rage, and Alexei was not surprised to see the American take the belt in both hands and snap it in half, tossing both ends over his shoulder. Devane stalked closer, conscious of the knife, but not fearing it. Alexei's legs were too weak to try any kicks—he was lucky to be able to walk. He could only wait and hope his next thrust would send the knife deep into Devane's heart.

"Is that all you boys got?" Liza R said. There was hint of mockery in her voice, and something else, sexual curiosity. It made Alexei angry.

And that was his mistake. Indulging in emotion was dangerous; it clouded and confused. It made him too anxious, and he lunged at Devane's chest too early. Devane snatched at Alexei's wrist, but Alexei recovered from the miss and angled in for another attack. Again Devane tried to catch the wrist, instead catching the knife full force through the palm of his hand. The stainless-steel blade gored the hand, jabbing all the way through to the other side of it. Devane's face remained calm as he flipped his hand, twisting the blade from Alexei's fingers. With that slow movie-star smile, he plucked the knife, slippery with blood, from his hand, dropped it to the floor and grabbed the stunned Alexei by the neck and crotch, hoisting him over his head and charging toward Liza R and the oak table with the model of Stonebridge Estates. Liza R skirted aside just as Devane brought Alexei crashing down on his back, smashing the tiny wooden houses into splinters.

Alexei felt his spine fuse into a lightning rod of flaming pain, but still he fought back, his arms and legs flailing weakly.

Devane clapped his hands together, raised them high over his head and brought them down with a hammering blow into Alexei's forehead that caved in the front of his skull. Bone mingled with brain. Blood pooled, drained into the closed eyes. Alexei didn't move.

Liza R said, "Nicely done. However, I think you can see from the damage he inflicted that this is no game for the uninitiated. You need me."

Devane looked up, Alexei's blood splashed across his face and shirt. He still showed no pain, but there was a weariness in his expression, a loss of confidence. Then he was moving again, suddenly lifting Alexei by the front of his shirt with one hand and flinging him at Liza R. Startled, she instinctively raised her gun up immediately and fired, but the bullets thudded into Alexei's body as it flopped into her. There was a crash of glass, and by the time Liza R had wriggled out from under the corpse, she saw the shattered window that Devane had dived through and heard his footsteps on the sidewalk clattering into the night.

Calmly she brushed herself off and punched some numbers into the phone. A crew of workmen would be here within the hour. By morning the bodies would be gone and everything would be repaired right down to the tiny wooden homes with their red Sold buttons.

Explaining Alexei's death would not be easy, but she was skilled enough to put the blame on Devane. They would be suspicious, but in the end they would have no choice but to believe. They still needed her. And since her plan had not worked, she needed them. They still were in the market for one Masked Dog, dead or alive.

She would find him—of that she was certain. And she knew right where to start. Price Calender.

25

"What's taking them so long?" Price complained, pacing about in front of the sofa.

"Channels," Jo said. She was sitting on the sofa, her legs curled under her, watching the black-and-white TV. The sound was turned down and the stereo played Roy Orbison's "Only the Lonely." The TV screen had a bunch of grubby guys in jeeps, flying over sand dunes and shooting at one another. She vaguely remembered the show from when she was a kid. *Rat Patrol* or something.

Price marched into the kitchen, poked his head into the refrigerator, didn't see anything he liked and came back to the sofa, empty-handed.

"Nothing for me, thanks," Jo said.

"Huh? Oh, sorry. Get you something?"

She shook her head and smiled. "Just kidding you."

"Right." Price nodded absently and looked at his watch.

The phone jangled.

Jo picked up the receiver. "Yes?"

"How's he holding up?" Dees asked.

"Better than should be expected."

Price leaned over her anxiously. "Do they have the plane tickets?"

"You hear?" Jo said into the phone.

Dees sighed. "Everything's set. Plane tickets to Hawaii—the flight leaves in less than two hours. A thousand bucks in an envelope waiting at the American Airlines counter."

Jo circled her thumb and finger and winked at Price. "Great," she said into the phone. "That didn't take long."

"That's because it's *my* goddamn money. Couldn't shake anything loose officially without ten hours' worth of forms. I charged the tickets on my American Express and got the cash out of my savings. Christ." He sounded tired.

"Want me to tell him?"

"Tell me what?" Price asked, hovering nearby.

"Tell him?" Dees said. "I want you to get a fucking receipt. If for some reason I can't get reimbursed, I want to at least take it as a tax deduction. Maybe get the pink slip to his car."

"You're sweet."

"So I hear. Now keep Calender in that apartment. We've got everybody in position just waiting for Devane."

"If he shows."

"He'll show. He wants Calender, wants him bad."

"There's a lot of that going around," she said.

"Huh?"

Jo hung up.

Price snatched the phone and began dialing his grandmother's number. The line was busy. It had been busy five minutes ago when he'd called, and ten minutes before that. "Still busy," he told her and hung up.

"Have the operator break through."

"I'll give it another couple minutes. Busting into a phone call isn't something you do lightly with a woman her age. First thing comes to mind is usually someone's dead. Anyway, she's probably just calling Mrs. Crenshaw to take care of her plants while she's away.''

He collapsed onto the sofa with a huge sigh. ''How long we going to wait for Devane?''

''Well,'' she said looking at her watch, ''let's give him another fifteen minutes. If he doesn't show, we're outta here.''

''Seriously.''

''Seriously? As long as it takes.''

''That could be a long time.''

She smiled at him, pecked him on the cheek. ''You going somewhere, buster?''

''I been asking myself that question for the past seven years.''

''You should have an answer by now.''

''I do, only I don't like it, so I keep asking.''

She snuggled up to him, humming absently with Roy Orbison's ''Crying.'' ''Hey, that's the price of wanting to be famous. You spend half your life worrying that you'll never make it, then when you do, you worry about losing it or getting it back. It's crazy.''

''Easy for you to say. You married into it.''

''Men stink.'' She bit his arm, not hard, but enough to make him wince. ''I had my dreams, too, you know. Even in Texas little girls dream of more than little boys.''

''What was your dream?''

She hesitated, shook her head. ''Never mind.''

''C'mon,'' Price coaxed. ''I showed you mine—now show me yours.''

She mumbled something.

''What?'' Price said.

''A diver.''

"Driver?"

"*Diver.* Like off a diving board." She swooped her hand into a diver's arc.

"Sounds interesting."

"Interesting? Man, it's like flying. You've got your five-meter springboard and your ten-meter platform. You know how high ten meters is?" Her accent crept in stronger with each word. "Well, it's 32′ 9 3/4″, mister. And that's high. And you don't just jump off them things, splash and hitch up your trunks. You gotta do something fancy to knock the judges' eyes out. Hell, when diving was first added to the Olympics in 1904, they called it 'fancy diving.' Crush told me that. Anyway, there's all kinds of things you gotta do with your body while you're falling. There's inward pikes and reverse somersaults and back twists and arm-stand reverse with somersaults. But like the whole time, it's like flying, not falling, like you're aiming at something, hitting the water at fifty mph, the cool water catching you and slowing you down like you were in it together, conspiring." She stopped to catch her breath. "I figured I'd collect a bunch of gold medals, be as famous as Mark Spitz. Posters of me dripping wet in my sexy suit. Stuff like that."

Price nodded. "Did you dive in school?"

"No. Not exactly."

"Country club?"

"Oh, hell, I never dived in my life. I just read about it and dreamed. Actually, I can't even swim."

"You're kidding." He laughed.

She looked disgusted. "That's what everyone says."

"It's easy. I'll teach you."

"That's what Steve promised."

"And?"

She shrugged. "Never got around to it. Not his fault. I didn't exactly push it or anything. Water makes me nervous. I don't even like to drink the stuff. I've jumped out of planes lots of times, but something about all that liquid under you, things swimming around you can't even see." She shivered. "Yeech."

Price chuckled and dialed his grandmother again. Busy. He frowned. "Two more minutes, then I get the operator to break in. Or I go over myself."

"You're not going anywhere. We've got every damn light on in here and the stereo blasting so Devane knows you're home. You're not going to blow it by walking out."

"You've got his face out to every cop in the city. They'll catch him sooner or later."

Jo laughed. "Talk about not knowing how to swim. Gawd. There are about a million wanted fugitives in Los Angeles right now. That includes about thirty thousand felons—murderers and robbers and such. And most of them aren't half as smart as Devane."

Price sighed, leaning back into the sofa. "We wait, right?"

Jo nodded. "We wait."

There was a long silence, and Jo wanted to ask him what he was thinking about, hoping he'd say "you," but afraid he'd say Liza R. She asked, anyway.

He smiled. "Paul Simon."

"Why?"

"Because he's one of the greatest songwriters who ever lived. And he's rich and famous and never seemed to give a damn about either."

"Yeah, well, when he was on the cover of *People* magazine, it was their worst-selling issue in ten years."

He gave her a look. "How do you know stuff like that?"

"I don't know. I just do. An Olympic diver has to be well-rounded."

"She also has to be able to swim."

"First things first."

Price reached for the phone in his lap to dial again, but it rang just as his fingers touched it. He picked it up immediately. "Hello?"

"Price?" The voice was unfamiliar.

"Yes."

"The big-time rock 'n' roll star."

And Price knew. He'd never heard Devane's voice before, but he knew that the smooth, cocky voice belonged to that grinning arrogant face he'd seen on tape. "What do you want?"

"I want to tell you all the lovely things I'm going to do with your grandmother and that sexy little gimpy daughter of yours if you don't do exactly what I tell you. You understand?"

Jo tugged on Price's arm, but he ignored her. Fear and anger enveloped him as if he were locked in an airless closet. "I'm listening."

"Good. Now let's chat, shall we?"

26

Jo punched the tape recorder that was attached to the phone, screwing the earplug into her ear so she could listen in. She hurried over to the kitchenette counter, cupped her hand over the mouthpiece of the remote transmitter and whispered to Conroy on the other end to have the call traced.

"It's up to you, of course," Devane was saying, "but if anyone is listening in to our conversation, I suggest you jerk their chain immediately."

"Listening in?" Price was still stunned from Devane's unexpected call, the knowledge that his young daughter was a prisoner of this maniac.

"Don't fuck with me!" Devane snapped. "I've lived with those people for the past ten years." His tone softened, sounded amused. "Hell, it's your family, Calender. Do what you want."

Jo made a stirring motion with her finger, telling him to keep Devane talking. Price walked over to the tape recorder. Jo sensed what he was about to do and rushed at him, trying to push him away. He elbowed her aside and yanked the wire leading to the phone. She threw the earplug to the floor with a whispered curse.

"Okay," Price told him. "We're alone. What'd you have in mind?"

"Unfinished business. From seven years ago."

"Look, that had nothing to do with you. What happened then was between my wife and me."

"But I suffered, Price." The voice was almost a pained whisper, like a ghost's.

"Let me talk to my grandmother and daughter."

Devane chuckled. "They can't come to the phone right now."

Price waited, taking deep breaths, trying not to think about what Devane had done to other little girls. "I'm listening," Price said.

"I bet you are." Devane laughed. "I'm going to give you an address, and I'm going to give you a time. As they say in the movies, come alone. Don't keep me waiting. I get nasty when I'm kept waiting. Hey, you know something, I think your gimpy little girl kinda likes me. What do you think? Is there a chance in this crazy mixed-up world for a girl like her and a guy like me, a May-December thing?"

"Don't touch her," Price said in a voice so low and hard it even quieted Devane for a moment.

Jo stamped and huffed angrily next to Price, but stopped at those last words. She watched his face, saw his features freeze, his back stiffen. Now he was nodding, saying, yes, yes, he would be there. Asking to speak to Rebecca or Tillie, getting only laughter in response. Then he was hanging up, looking tight and murderous as he adjusted his gun and shoulder holster. He went to the bedroom closet, rummaged a moment before finding what he wanted—a battered black satin jacket with red stitching on the back that said PRICE CALENDER WORLD TOUR, 1977.

"I'm going," he said.

"I know."

He nodded toward the door. "They'll try to follow me. Can you do something about them?"

"Yeah, I can let them do their jobs. They know how to be discreet. Devane won't know they're there."

"I can't take that chance, Jo. He's known too much already."

"So what's your plan." She sounded angry.

"Plan?"

"Yeah. How are you going to take him down, save your daughter's life."

He patted his gun.

"Shit," she sneered. "You'll be lucky not to shoot yourself."

"Look, I'm not saying I'm the best candidate for this job, just that I'm the only one. I'm not volunteering. For Christ's sake, he drafted me. I'm scared to death right now, doing everything I can not to puke in front of you. But that's my goddamn daughter he's got. And it's her bad luck that I'm her only chance."

Jo hugged him tight, felt a tear trickle down her cheek, maybe his, maybe hers. "At least give me the address. That way we'll have some place to start if I don't hear from you."

Price shook his head. "Can't do it."

"Christ, you're stubborn."

"Just practical. You people assured me my family would be protected."

"Dees thought they were safe. Devane has always preferred the direct approach with his victims. I guess he just got smarter."

"Yeah, well, it sure didn't rub off from you people."

"What's with this 'you people' crap?" she said. "Is it us and them now, and I'm with them?"

Price didn't say anything.

She sighed. "Okay, maybe I had that coming. We should have seen this coming, I guess. Or at least covered the possibility." She looked at Price. "Wanna take a sock at me or something."

"A favor."

"What?"

"Can you do something to keep your guys off my tail?" he asked.

"I'll try." She tucked a stray wisp of hair behind her ear. "I'll tell them something. Something."

He kissed her on the lips, wanting to say some words, something binding. He shrugged. "See you."

"Sure."

He gave her a questioning look. "Keep 'em away, promise?"

"Would this face lie?" She smiled.

His smile was forced, but at least he'd made the effort. He waved as he went out the door.

"Squeeze the trigger, don't pull," she called, watching him move toward his car in the dark.

She was speaking into the transmitter as Price backed his car out of the parking stall. "He's gonna rabbit, guys," she said. "Stay on his ass."

DEVANE WAS NOT HUNGRY, but he ate, picking grumpily at the food Tillie Calender served him. Heated leftover walnut chicken, mashed potatoes and ears of corn that looked delicious, but had no taste or smell. He chewed each bite excessively, trying to mash some taste out, but it was hopeless. As in the restaurant, nothing had any taste. Worse, he had no appetite. He ate because he knew his body needed food. But it didn't tell him that any more than it told him when he was hurt. No pain, no hunger, no thirst. "That wound doesn't look good," Tillie Calender said, spooning another helping of mashed potatoes on Devane's plate.

Devane thought she meant his hand, and looked at the torn strip of shirt he'd wrapped around it. Blood had soaked through both sides of the stab wound, but the bleeding had stopped long before he'd come here. "It'll be okay."

"I don't know," she said. "I've seen broken collarbones before. If you don't get them tended right away, could be serious."

He smiled his full set of teeth. "Thank you for your medical advice, Mrs. Calender. Now shut the fuck up before I stick your face down the garbage disposal."

Rebecca sat at the kitchen table with Devane, making her face all mean and scrunchy. "My daddy's going to kill you," she said.

"Rebecca," Tillie Calender snapped. "There'll be no talk of killing." Her spoon rattled against Devane's plate as she plopped on some mashed potatoes.

"Nervous?" he asked, grinning.

"Parkinson's."

He sat at the table, tapping his finger against his watch. Suddenly he pushed his plate away and stood up. "Time to go."

Tillie Calender drew herself straight as she stood in front of him. "Just take me. If you want someone to hold hostage, for God's sake, use me. My grandson will pay you."

Devane stared at her, aware that his hearing was fluttering. The old woman kept fading in and out, sometimes so loud it hurt his ears, sometimes so low he couldn't make the words out, like a distant radio station. It didn't matter. Soon as he finished with Price Calender, he would start the bidding again. Some of those other offers had been pretty good. With the money he'd be able to correct these side effects.

The old woman was still jabbering at him.

"Shut up," he said, and she did. "Let's go, kid. You and me are going to go see your tough daddy."

"He'll kill you," Rebecca said.

Devane laughed. "You can watch him try."

Tillie Calender drifted back to the stove and looked at the pot of water she'd cooked the corn in. The water was still steaming, bits of corn still floating on top. She didn't know anything about this man except that he wanted to have Rebecca. She picked up the pot, burning her hand a little, and spun around, throwing the hot water into Devane's face. Then she attacked him with the pot, hollering at Rebecca, *"Run! Run!"*

Devane had been looking at Rebecca when Tillie Calender had thrown the hot water, so he caught most of it on the right side of his face.

Tillie had counted on his pain to disable him long enough to knock him silly with the heavy pot. But he was smiling at her, his right eye red, the skin puffed with white patches of blisters, when he blocked the pot with one hand as it came whooshing toward his head. He batted it aside. Rebecca, too frightened to run, sat crying.

"Bad move, Mrs. Calender," Devane said. The charming smile that once had the young mothers in his office blushing now looked like a grotesque parody beneath the blistered flesh. "A serious mistake."

"Not my first," Tillie Calender said, standing in her slightly hunched way, holding her quivering hands. She did not look afraid, though she knew now what he intended for her all along.

Devane reached out and took her shaking hands in his own, looking deep into those old brown eyes, seeing she wasn't afraid and feeling a little jealous because this old diseased woman had achieved some of what it had taken many years and millions of dollars to give him: fearlessness.

And as he stared into her eyes, he slowly began to squeeze her hands. Nothing more than a firm handshake at first, then tighter and tighter. She wriggled them, tugged desperately at them, but they were trapped in his powerful fingers like squirrels in bear traps. He squeezed tighter, and tighter still feeling the old brittle bones crackling from the pressure.

The little girl screamed at him, clawing at his back as the old lady lost consciousness.

"Don't be impatient," he told Rebecca as she bawled hysterically, her little fists bouncing harmlessly off his back. "I have something very special in mind for you, too, little daddy's girl."

27

Price saw them after three blocks. A black man and a black woman in an old tan Plymouth Valiant, staying far enough back not to be too obvious but making the same turns Price was making.

He wasn't surprised. Either Jo had failed to convince them with her story, or—and this was more likely—she'd lied to him and told them to follow him. He wasn't angry. Just weary of the lies and deceptions. He had a momentary pang of nostalgia for those lost sixties days of "gut reactions" and "being up-front" and "sharing my feelings," until he remembered how most of that crap had nauseated him even then. In a way he was even touched by Jo's lie. She wasn't doing it just because it was her job, he was certain, but because she felt something for him. She wanted to protect him. The way Trinidad had. Then again, maybe not. Maybe she was just doing her job. He'd been wrong before.

His hands tightened around the steering wheel in frustration and sorrow. Why did others always have to pay for his naïveté. He'd trusted one woman, Liza R, and that had set up a grim chain reaction that was still hurting people. Trinidad, Crush, Rupert Hesse, and now his grandmother and daughter. All he'd ever done was fall in love. Where was the crime?

Christ, what bullshit. He'd seen there was something odd about Liza R even back then. He'd seen the casual neglect of her daughter, the unconscious cruelty to his friends. But she'd always found a way to explain or laugh or make love that made him forget. You were just a kid, he reminded himself. Yeah, he answered back, but so was she.

The tan Valiant followed for another couple of blocks, then turned off into a Del Taco. Maybe I was wrong, he thought, staring into the rearview mirror. Maybe Jo did come through.

Then he saw the blue Ford Escort pull out of an alley and fall in beside him at the light, the driver a middle-aged executive type with silver hair and a pipe. He made a point of ignoring Price's stare.

Price went straight. So did the Ford. Price turned left. So did the Ford. Price made a U-turn. The Ford kept going.

But a white Buick station wagon with an elderly woman driver and five bags of groceries in the back stayed with him for a couple more miles.

"Okay, Jo, you want to play it that way," he said, looking at the cheap plastic digital clock he'd stuck next to the radio. There wasn't much time left and they were using a lot of cars on him. He stomped the gas pedal and shot the Rabbit through a red light, barely avoiding an anxious motorcyclist. In the rearview mirror he saw the elderly woman in the station wagon still sitting at the red light, talking into a car phone. "Son of a bitch," he said.

"SON OF A BITCH," Jo said, after receiving Agent Susan Farley's report. She turned to her driver. "He knows, Jim. Calender knows we're on him."

Agent James Rinehart nodded. "What do you want to do? Drop him?"

"No way. Just keep rotating more cars in. He's got a time limit, so if he can't shake us, he'll have to lead us to the meet." She tapped a button on the receiver. "Conroy?"

"Yeah?" a voice crackled through the speaker.

"Any word from Mrs. Calender's place in Pasadena?"

"Andy hasn't called back in yet."

"Okay. I want to hear."

"You bet."

Jo spoke to several other drivers, receiving directions on Price's movements.

"He's picked up speed," one car reported, "and is taking some crazy chances."

"Stay with him," she said.

"We'll try, Jo."

"Don't try. Do it!" She pointed at the intersection coming up. "Turn right. He's heading west."

"I heard," Jim said evenly.

Jo studied the street map on her lap. "Where the hell's he going? Looks like a figure eight."

The car phone buzzed and she answered. "What?"

"Andy just called in," Conroy said. "Devane was there, but he's gone now."

"How do you know he was there?"

"The old lady," he said quietly. "She's dead. Christ, her hands are like jelly." He took a breath. "The kid's gone, too."

Jo pictured Tillie Calender as she'd last seen her, standing there slightly stooped, hands trembling uncontrollably, but the eyes bright, mind sharp and will strong. She'd been friendly, extrafriendly Jo had thought. Afterward, thinking about Price, Jo had allowed herself to imagine picnics with the four of them.

Or Jo and Tillie on the phone, gossiping about their boy, Price. It was a harmless fantasy, a grown-up woman's version of a high-school girl doodling "Mrs." in front of her boyfriend's name. Now that Tillie was dead, it seemed to sour everything.

"Where is he now?" she asked the lead car. She plotted the coordinates on the map and told all the chase cars that she and Jim would pick up Calender within six blocks and take it from there. The others should stay close.

"You think that's wise?" Jim asked, meaning it wasn't.

"Do it," she said, ending the discussion.

They swerved onto Rivero just two cars behind Price's red Rabbit. Price bolted immediately, darting around cars, ducking into alleys.

"Stay with him," Jo said eagerly.

Jim tried. He bounced over railroad tracks, narrowly missed a head-on collison with a pickup truck, scraped the bottom of his car on parking lot speed bumps. He hung onto Price's car as if they were attached by a long wire. But eventually that wire would have to snap. Once the tail was spotted, all the odds were with the runner. If he didn't kill himself in traffic first.

They wheeled sharply around a corner after Price, but the car slid a little too far, bumping up into the curb and blowing a tire. Jo immediately radioed for the other cars to take over, but one by one they called back. They'd lost him.

Jo sat hunched over the radio, listening to the dead static, feeling a strange nausea, an emptiness, the same kind she felt when she'd miscarried.

28

For the first time since he was eight years old, Price Calender was afraid of the dark.

It wasn't an ordinary dark. The late-night air was laced with tendrils of smoky fog common for the late spring. Streetlamps glowered down at the sparse traffic, necks bent, pumping light through the wispy fog. As Price walked quickly toward the large building, he had the feeling that the night was somehow all wrong, manufactured from someone else's imagination. Almost as if he were tramping through someone else's nightmare.

The Sports Courts was a huge modern health and racquetball club that Price had frequented many times before, usually when he was staying at his grandmother's house, only a few miles away. Tonight he had parked his car down the street and walked the rest of the way, circling around the back of the building as Devane had instructed him to do. His heart thumped against his ribs and he seemed to have trouble catching his breath. Every shadow looked threatening, as if concealing some unknown terror.

The back fire door was open, held slightly ajar by a piece of clothing with tiny horses all over it, which Price immediately recognized as one of Rebecca's blouses. He'd brought it back with him last year when he'd played Atlantic City. It was one of her favorites. An icy cold splashed through his stomach.

Once inside, he stared down the long dark corridor and tried to remember the layout of the club. On this level were about twenty-five racquetball courts, a snack bar, the day-care center, the front desk, the membership office, the pro shop, the men's and women's locker rooms. Downstairs was the indoor lap pool and the kiddie pool. Upstairs, the gymnasium, the weight rooms, the aerobics room, a couple of dozen stationary bikes and the catwalks that ran above the racquetball courts, allowing you to watch the action below. On the roof was a running track.

Devane could be anywhere.

Price pulled out his Walther P-5 and started slowly down the corridor. Like many sports buildings, this one was completely windowless and reasonably soundproof, so anything that happened in here would not be heard or seen by the outside world. They were in the middle of downtown Pasadena, yet they were as remote as if on a deserted island. Devane had made a clever choice, and that depressed Price.

The only light came from a series of tiny bulbs staggered down the corridor, obviously for emergency use. The light was minimal, nothing more than a string of lit matches, but enough to find his way. He noticed, too, that the red lights on the video cameras in the ceiling weren't on. There would be no record for the police of what was about to happen.

He moved cautiously, peeking through the thick glass window of each court, but each court was too dark to see anything. He held the Walther in both hands as he walked, ready to swing it up at anything that moved.

Footsteps. Running.

He sprinted down the corridor, following the sound. One person's footsteps. Heavy, like a man's. He came to the middle of the corridor, where the rest of the building formed a fat T against the long straight line of courts. Price moved slower now, past the challenge courts, where the walls facing the lobby were all glass. Chairs and tables were scattered about for people to take their refreshments from the nearby snack bar while watching others run and sweat and play. Price nearly tripped over one of the chairs as he cocked an ear for any sound.

A door creaked, hissed with compression.

He ran past the pro shop, membership office, front desk. Saw the women's locker-room door hush shut.

Price hesitated, feeling more frightened then he ever had before. Then he entered. The lights were on inside the locker room, and somehow Price found that even more alarming. It was as if Devane knew he had nothing to fear, was only toying with him. An image flashed in Price's mind of Devane easily hefting those four-hundred-pound weights, smiling at the camera, looking so smug and carnivorous.

Price was surprised to find the women's locker room not much different from the men's. Same drab brown lockers with the same hard wooden benches with the same cramped space where no one could change comfortably. He had expected something different, something more sexy. Instead the place just smelled of built-up sweat and pine-scented disinfectant, same as the men's.

He glided past each aisle of lockers, swinging his gun out as if he expected to find Devane there changing clothes. He even stood on one of the benches and checked the tops of the lockers. No one here. He moved on to the showers.

With the lights on, the showers were easy to check, as were the toilet stalls. That left the sauna and tanning rooms next to the spa. Or the stairway that lead up to the weight rooms or down to the pool. Price heard the bubbling of the spa and smelled the woody scent of the sauna as he approached. The spa was almost the size of a kiddy pool, surrounded by two walls of natural stone facing and tropical plants. The hot water splashed down the rocks to form several waterfalls. It reminded Price of the Playboy mansion he'd visited once after his first platinum album. The water bubbled and churned, frothing with white steaming foam. The sauna wall facing the spa was glass, so Price could see no one was in there. Same with the tanning room.

The moist heat had caused sweat to slicker his skin. Even the gun felt slippery in his hand now. He wiped his palms against his pants.

He headed toward the stairway to check the pool. He'd save the weight room for last. The equipment there would make it the most dangerous room. What bothered Price most now wasn't the question of where Devane was, but where Rebecca and his grandmother were. He'd already been through much of the club and hadn't seen or heard them. If the footsteps he was chasing belonged to Devane, the man was moving alone. Where, then, had he stashed Price's family?

As he walked toward the stairway, Price passed the bubbling spa, heard a slight splash, like a trout leaping, and suddenly felt his right ankle caught in a tight grip. He looked down and saw Devane's grinning face rising from the water like some slippery Neptune. His powerful fingers were already wrapped around Price's ankle, squeezing. Without hesitation, Price aimed the Walther P-5, but even as his finger tightened on the trigger, Devane was jerking Price's ankle out from under him. The gun exploded, but by now Price was already falling, and the bullet dived through the water three feet away from Devane. As he fell into the hot water, Price felt the gun fly from his hand and plop into the spa.

The suddenness of the dunking had knocked all the air out of Price, and he struggled now under the hot water, trying to loosen Devane's grip on his jacket. Then Devane was no longer just holding him under, but thrashing him about, shaking and dragging him through the water as if it were some giant washing machine. His face scraped against the bottom, grating skin from his nose. His ear banged his own knee. Price lost any sense of direction, even where the surface was. He opened his eyes, but the hot chlorinated water burned, and he had to close them again. His lungs, empty of air, were starting to spasm, sucking in anything, even hot spa water. Price gagged as the hot water streamed through his nose and down his throat. Then, just as suddenly as it had begun, it was over. Devane no longer had hold of him. Price clawed weakly to the surface. He pulled himself to the edge and hung there, gulping air, fighting the dizziness. When he looked up he saw Devane standing above him, hands on hips, laughing.

He was naked.

Devane's body was slick with water, the muscles smooth and hard as if carved from expensive wood, then sanded and polished for weeks. Standing there, dripping, smiling down from his tower of muscles, Devane looked reptilian. Price noticed the clumps of white burn blisters on his cheek, the ugly mess of chewed flesh and protruding collarbone, the scrape along his ribs, the nasty gouge on his hand. They looked painful, but they didn't seem to bother Devane. If anything, he looked stronger than he had on the tapes.

"Where are they?" Price asked.

"They?"

"My daughter. My grandmother."

"Well, now, your grandmother couldn't make this trip, Price. She's a little old for traveling, wouldn't you say?"

"Is she alive?"

Devane smiled. "I'd worry about that daughter of yours if I were you, Price. She's quite a little looker. Gonna break a lot of hearts someday. With the proper instruction." He winked.

Price didn't say anything. There was nothing to say. The man was insane. He intended to kill Price and Rebecca, may have already killed Tillie. The gun, Price's only defense, was lying at the bottom the the spa now.

"Don't you have anything to say? A plea to my humanity? Something about the sanctity of children, perhaps?"

Price considered diving for the gun—he knew approximately where it was. But how long would it take to find it? Too long. Devane would be on him like a flaming meteor.

Devane took a step closer, his feet planted less than an inch from Price's panting face. He's daring me, Price thought. He wants me to try something.

"Well, Daddy," Devane said, "what's your plan?"

"My plan?"

"To kill the dragon and save the princess. How are you going to do it?"

"Right now," Price said, lifting his head, "I'm taking a leak. I figure the rest will fall into place after that."

Devane laughed, his genitals shaking. He stooped down, grabbed the front of Price's sopping satin jacket in one fist, and lifted Price straight up into the air. Devane stood now, holding Price at arm's length with one hand. When he spoke, his voice was soft and curious, as if he'd forgotten what he was here for. "If you were on a desert island and could only have one food for the rest of your life, what would it be?"

It was an odd sensation to be dangling above a spa, hot water spilling from every opening. "Fettucini, maybe. Or peaches. Fresh peaches."

"Could you describe what a peach tastes like if you met someone who'd never tasted one?"

"I don't know. That'd be tough."

Devane nodded, his eyes drifting for a moment. Then they focused again and he glared angrily at Price. It reminded Price of some kids he'd seen using LSD years ago. "What the hell are you talking about? Peaches?"

Hoping for some element of surprise in Devane's confusion, Price kicked at Devane's exposed genitals. Even though the leverage wasn't too great, his foot caught Devane squarely in the nuts. There was enough force to send most men crawling. But Devane merely blinked and smiled.

"Good for you," he said. "I thought you were just going to curl up and die. But you're going to make a fight of it. That's good." Devane was peering into Price's eyes, frowning in concentration, as if looking for something. He seemed surprised, a little disappointed. "You're not afraid. Just like your grandmother. Nothing."

Price wanted to laugh. Afraid? Of course he was afraid. But then he thought about it a moment and realized that there was something different. He had been afraid when he'd entered the building, practically paralyzed chasing through the locker room. A few minutes ago, while Devane had held him airless under the water, he had wanted to cry and beg. But that had all passed. As soon as he'd realized he was actually going to die, all that mattered now was trying to save Rebecca before his death. And the fear had gone.

The sadness passed from Devane's face and he was grinning again. "Okay, Daddy, I'm going to give you a chance to find your little darling. But every time I find you first, you have to pay a penalty. I break something." He reached out with his free hand, grabbed Price's left arm and twisted it sharply. The arm broke and Price screamed.

Devane shoved him back into the water and ran, his wet feet slapping against cement.

PRICE DRAGGED HIS BROKEN ARM through the water like loose driftwood. Each movement sent thorns of pain deeper into his arm. He ignored the feeling. It took a few groping dives, forcing his eyes open under the hot water, but he finally found the gun on the bottom of the spa. Water poured out of the barrel, and he wondered if it would still shoot. He considered firing a trial shot, but decided he couldn't afford to waste the bullets. Devane was much stronger than he had imagined.

Price was sure he'd heard Devane running up the stairs, but he wasn't about to go after him in the dark. He ran out to the front desk. When he'd been here before, they'd turned on the lights in assigned courts on a panel behind the counter. That was also where the video screen was. If he could turn the cameras on, he could find Devane and Rebecca without searching the whole building.

He ran behind the front desk counter, only to find the video panel's wires torn out. Devane. He pounded his right fist against the monitor in frustration, but the impact sent a rattle of pain across his shoulder and down his broken left arm. Quickly he flipped the light switches, turning on every light in the building except the lobby light near the glass front doors. The room lights went on immediately, but the court lights only flickered slightly, taking a few minutes to warm up.

Price kicked off his squeaking sneakers and tossed aside his black satin jacket. He grabbed a couple of towels from the stack behind the counter and dried himself and the gun off. Then he went hunting.

He climbed the lobby stairs as quickly as his broken arm would allow. At the top there were two ways to go. Left, into the women's weight room with the stationary bikes and leg-weight machines, leading into the gymnasium. Or right, into the men's weight room with the free weights and Nautilus machines, and leading to the catwalks above the racquetball courts. Price went left.

He'd been here dozens of times, running the Nautilus circuit, doing sit-ups on the slant boards, watching the magnificent torsos of the women bodybuilders. One woman had talked him into joining her in an aerobics class for an hour, which he'd staggered out of after twenty minutes, gasping for air. Disgusted with himself, he'd added another twenty pounds to his Nautilus circuit and quit smoking for three days.

He slid along the wall, nosing the gun ahead of him as he scanned the room. Nothing. He paused, giving his heart a chance to settle down. His back was still pressed against the wall separating the men's and women's weight rooms, when the wall above him exploded and a ten-pound dumbbell crashed through, showering him with plaster and splinters. The dumbbell clanged into one of the stationary bikes, denting the wheel. Price ducked just as another dumbbell, this one twenty pounds, hurled through the wall, smashing the glass partition where the weight instructor's desk was. Price dived to the floor and rolled to the doorway, clenching his teeth against the pain in his arm. When he reached the doorway to the men's weight room, he raised his gun to shoot.

No one was there.

Shiny steel Universal equipment stood in some jumbled order on one side of the room. Utilitarian brown Nautilus machines stood on the other side. Free weights lined the back in front of the mirrored wall. Two of the dumbbells were missing from the rack.

Price stood up, the Walther thrust in front of him as he entered the room. The room was eerie without the familiar sounds of grunting and creaking pulleys and the slap of metal weights smacking each other, the loud debates about the advantages of Universal over Nautilus and free weights over both, the big men with swollen chests and tiny waists standing nose to nose in debate. But now the room was quiet. Beyond was the catwalk above the racquetball courts, where players were always calling for help when they'd hit a ball up there, knowing the weight lifters would ignore them.

It was odd to suddenly feel frightened here. This room, and the ones just like it at other clubs he'd worked out at, had always been a kind of refuge. No one was famous in this room. Everyone was judged on the same criteria, strength and determination. No gray areas, no talk about work or the office. He knew a couple of people here, enough to talk to, but he had no idea what they did for a living. Except for occasional pro sport chatter, conversation was limited to how many reps you were up to, how many pounds you could bench-press. The basics. It was a code language, Price had decided, a way of saying, "Today I can withstand this much weight from the world, this much pain, but tomorrow I'll be stronger for it." In this room he'd learned that language, had understood people's obsession with their bodies. Outside, the forces were uncontrollable; in here, at least, the body could be shaped and formed any way you wanted. Price was only a fringe indulger, lifting occasionally, swimming, or playing racquetball. Just enough to keep in shape. But he understood.

He was starting to shiver in his wet clothes. The fear was coming back. He worried that the gun might not fire, that a heavy dumbbell would come streaking at him, crushing his skull into oatmeal before he had a chance to find Rebecca. He thought of the perversity Devane had in mind for her, and rage replaced his fear.

"Daddy dearest," Devane's voice teased behind him, and Price spun around and saw Devane, still naked, leaping from the wall above the doorway, saw the holes in the drywall where his fingers had poked through and held him suspended like a spider. Devane's hand closed over the top of the gun and plucked it out of Price's hand. He released the clip and threw it away, then walked calmly to the Nautilus abdominal machine, lifted two hundred and twenty pounds of weight by moving the chest bar forward with one hand and let it crunch down on the gun, smashing it. "Now that should make us even, eh?'' He laughed and strutted back toward Price. "I warned you I'd have to penalize you if I found you first, Price." He stepped closer, and Price punched him in the nose.

Price was surprised to see the blood spurt out, even though the punch didn't seem to have any other effect on Devane. Still, it reminded Price that the guy was still mortal, still human. He bled. Price threw another punch, this time at the gooey mess where Devane's collarbone protruded. Blood sponged onto Price's fist from the wound, but the blow didn't stop Devane.

"You dumb fuck," he said. "You can't hurt me. No one can." And to prove his point, Devane held up his hand with the stab wound, put the little finger of his other hand against the gouged palm and poked the finger into the hole, all the way through the hand. Price winced at the sight, and Devane laughed. He pulled out his finger, covered with blood, and held both hands up to Price. "So go ahead, tough guy. Let's see your stuff."

And Price surprised Devane by hitting him again. He threw a solid right into Devane's stomach, then brought his right up into an uppercut that caught him on the chin. The force of the blows rocked Devane, but nothing more. Except made him angrier. Price ran to the wall with the free weights and lifted a five-pound dumbbell. As Devane ran toward him, Price threw it, bouncing it off Devane's thigh. A dark bruise welled up immediately, but it didn't slow Devane's pace. Price reached for another dumbbell, but Devane was on him, grabbing him by the broken arm.

"You know what's going to happen, Price? Huh?"

Price was swooning from the pain, and Devane slapped him on the cheek to get his attention. Price felt each burning finger imprint as if they had been sizzling brands.

"Pay attention, Daddy," Devane chided. "Eventually I'm going to bust every bone in your arms and legs. You won't even be able to crawl, just lie there like a squashed snail. Then I'm going to make you watch while I fuck your daughter every way there is. Or maybe I'll make her watch while I fuck you. I haven't made up my mind." He held the fingers of Price's left hand and snapped them all backward until they cracked. Price yelled as each finger broke at the joint. "And one to grow on," Devane said breaking the thumb, too. Price slumped to the floor, tears of pain filling his eyes. "Well," Devane said, "I've heard you play guitar, and I think this little adjustment can only help your technique." He walked away, then ran down the stairs.

Price pulled himself halfway up, stopped to throw up, then hoisted himself up the rest of the way. He needed a weapon. He looked around, trying to think, but his brain seemed stuffed with cotton. He slapped his broken arm and the pain jolted his brain with energy. A weapon. What would make an effective weapon against a man like that? He checked the gun, but that was smashed beyond hope. He couldn't carry a dumbbell around with him. Besides, that hadn't worked before.

Devane's voice taunted from downstairs. "She's waiting, Daddy. She wants me."

In desperation, Price pulled one of the metal pins that held the stacks of weights on the Nautilus machine. It was about six inches long and thick as the shaft of a dart. With just the right amount of timing and strength, he might be able to drive it through an eye or throat or chest. At least it was something.

He walked carefully down the stairs, the pain in his arm and hand only a minor throbbing at the back of his mind. He kept the metal pin concealed in his right hand. Slowly he stalked the corridor, passed the pro shop and snack bar, until he saw the first glass racquetball court, with a large A above the door. This was where the club's best players challenged one another to grueling matches.

This was where Price fround Rebecca.

29

The sight shocked him. Not so much finding her, as what Devane had done to her.

Her long strawberry-blond hair had been hacked off into short spiky clumps resembling those of the punkers Price saw around the recording studios sometimes. False eyelashes were pasted awkwardly onto her eyes, and heavy red rouge spotted her cheeks. A large hunk of white adhesive tape covered her mouth, but thick red lips were outlined over the tape with dark lipstick. She was wearing only her undershirt and underpants. Her skirt, shoes and socks were in a pile in the middle of the floor between the painted red lines. Her leg brace was on top of the clothes. A lacy black garter belt, much too big for her, had been cinched around her waist. She cowered in the corner, her hands tied behind her back with panty hose. When she saw Price, she tried to climb to her feet, but without the brace, couldn't. She started to crawl toward him, tears streaking the black mascara down her cheeks, shame and relief in her face.

The first time Price had passed by it had been dark, and he'd been chasing the footsteps. He hadn't noticed the heavy ten-foot glass showcase Devane had dragged from the pro shop to block the door. Tables and chairs were stacked on top, which he quickly threw aside. But with only one good arm to use, he couldn't budge the huge showcase itself, filled with dozens of cans of racquetballs, T-shirts with the club's name, gloves, aerobic shoes. He tried every angle, but it was no use. He'd have to go in from the top.

He ran down the corridor again, up the stairs, through the weight room and onto the catwalk overlooking the court. From here he could see the walkways, forming a T, overlooking all the courts. Now all he had to do was somehow ease himself over the railing, hang by one good arm, drop about fifteen feet to the hard wood floor, and maybe the two of them pushing outward against the door might be able to move the heavy showcase. If not, at least he'd be there with Rebecca when Devane came. Somehow he'd find a way to kill that bastard, even if he had to gnaw his way into Devane's chest and eat his damn heart.

"It's all right, honey," he called down to Rebecca. "I'll be down in a second." She grunted tearfully, and a pain wrenched his heart greater than the pain from his broken arm or fingers. "It's all right," he repeated.

"Liar," Devane said, appearing suddenly behind him. His magnificent body looked a little ragged, like a marble statue of a Greek god that's been chipped and scarred by vandals. The collarbone was oozing something thick; the skin on his stabbed hand looked gray next to the rest of his body; the bruise on the thigh was dark; and some of the white blisters on his face had opened. But the power was still there. "Shouldn't get her hopes up," he said sadly. "That's not really nice."

He stood ten feet away from Price, in no hurry to move. Price squeezed the metal pin in his hand, getting ready, picking the spot where he'd plunge it into Devane. Even naked and battered, Devane exuded an odd charm. He smiled, and Price had the feeling he was about to say it'd had all been a terrible mistake, that they should be buddies. When Devane spoke, his voice was friendly. "There's so much to know, Price. So very much. Most people don't realize that. Or if they do, they ignore it. But there's a fucking universe of information and knowledge. There's a difference, you know. Between information and knowledge." He paused, looking now like a brilliant professor delivering a lecture to a hushed crowd of undergraduates. "Information? Did you know that in 1980 the volume of domestic intercity freight and passenger traffic totaled over 2,503,000,000 ton-miles? And that 37.24% of that was from railroads? In 1945 there were 2,000,000 job-related disabling injuries. A family earning less than $5,000 consumed .54 quadrillion BTU's in one year. In the 1960 presidential election, Kennedy got 49.7% of the popular vote and Nixon got 49.5%. Eugene Debs ran for president in 1920 on the Socialist ticket and got 919,799 votes. Shakespeare purchased a house in Blackfriars in 1613. In 1830, deer hides in the West went for about thirty-seven cents a pound...."

Price watched Devane rattle on, trancelike, as if he were reading everything from an imaginary blackboard. None of the facts followed any pattern, just random bits of information, like a trivia quiz. Price turned slightly so his right hand was hidden. He eased the metal pin between the middle fingers of his fist. He would try to punch it into Devane.

Devane sighed. "The thing is, I can't remember what a peach tastes like." And suddenly he was on Price, flying at him with one giant leap.

Price brought the metal pin around and punched at Devane's heart with all his might, but in the turmoil he missed. The pin punctured Devane's right side, and when the two men rolled apart, the pin was still sticking in his side. Devane pulled it out, examined the wound. A little blood leaked out, but it was a minor wound.

"Resourceful little bastard, aren't you," he said with a smile. "But now it's time to say goodnight, Gracie. I have a date with your daughter, and it's not nice to keep a lady waiting." He hopped to his feet, looking as fresh and confident as ever.

Price struggled up, fighting the pain and depression. He took a weak swing at Devane and clipped him on the chin. It didn't do any more damage than anything else he'd done, but he wound up to do it again.

Devane punched him in the chest, which sent Price staggering back to the floor. It was an awkward punch, probably the only reason his ribs hadn't all caved in. Devane was an awkward fighter, inexperienced, but with his enormous power, Price didn't find any hope in that knowledge.

"Still the amateur, Devane," her voice teased from behind them. Liza R, pointing her shiny 9 mm Star Model 28 gun, came slowly down the catwalk. She gestured at Devane's penis with her gun. "At least you're dressing more for the part. Hello, Price."

Price remained seated, back leaning against the glass partition that overlooked the court below. "Happy anniversary."

She laughed. "Let's see, it would be our seventh. That makes it wool or copper. Right?"

"Maybe I did make a mistake about working with you," Devane told her with a smile, pouring on the charm.

"You made a lot of mistakes." Liza R leaned against the wood railing that capped the top of the glass partition. Price was between her and Devane. "You made a mistake by hanging around trying to kill him," she said, pointing at Price. "That was dumb. Where's the profit in it?"

"Revenge," Devane said.

"Jesus." Liza R laughed and shook her head. "First, you made a mistake by killing the wrong person with that silly poison. And then, when you finally do get a hold of him, you turn it into some primitive tribal rite. Some bullshit voodoo. You should have just killed him and been done with it. Look at you. You're a mess."

Devane put his hands on the railing, looking hurt, like a scolded child. "Maybe you're right."

"No maybe about it, doc."

He looked over at her, grinning. "Then let's kill him and get out of here."

Price said, "He's got your daughter down there."

Liza R walked closer, one hand on the wooden rail, the other on her gun. When she was close enough, she peered over the edge to the court below and saw Rebecca.

Price studied her face for some reaction, but there was none. It was the same as when he'd kicked Devane's balls. Still, he had to try. "You know what he intends to do to her?"

Liza R shrugged. "I'm glad I got to see her in such a situation. I was curious about how I'd react. You know, all you hear about outraged mothers lifting cars and throwing two-hundred-pound men who threaten their babies. I wondered if I'd feel that same power. But I don't." She smiled, pleased.

Price was calculating the distance to Liza R, whether he'd have a chance of grabbing her gun before she shot him, or, having gotten the gun, if he'd have enough time to shoot Devane before those powerful hands crushed him to death. He decided he couldn't possibly make it, but that he would try, anyway. What other choices did he have?

"So what about our deal?" Devane said.

"Deal?"

"Our partnership?"

"Oh, that. That was a one-time offer. You could have had an easy shot, but you went for the three-point play. Tough luck. It's going to take all my considerable charms just to convince the KGB I had nothing to do with your killing Alexei. Besides, you were so childishly predictable. I knew once you'd run from me that you would still go after Price. And since we knew he was being watched, even you wouldn't be stupid enough to risk getting near his apartment. The only thing that could draw him away from his guards would be his family. I simply drove there and waited for you, following you here." She gave him an annoyed look. "I had expected you to have killed him already. Now it looks like I'll have to do both of you."

Devane shrugged. Then the shrug turned into something else, a sudden yanking on the wooden railing that ran from under his hands to where Liza R was leaning. The rail lifted in a long ten-foot hunk, knocking her off balance. Price raised himself onto his haunches to spring at her just as she fired the gun twice. Even off balance she managed to pump one into Devane's hip. The other splintered the wooden railing that he was swinging toward her head like a baseball bat.

The impact of the bullet kicked Devane's leg out from under him and sent the railing wild, whacking the floor. Liza R was falling, so that she had to stick out her gun hand to catch herself. That was when Price leaped at her, driving his elbow into her throat and pulling the gun from her hand. Another elbow into her jaw sent her head into the carpeted catwalk. Price rolled free just as Devane, balanced on one knee, swung the railing again. It whistled through the air. Price flopped facedown and squeezed the trigger. The deafening roar cracked his ears as the bullet drilled through Devane's stomach.

Devane smiled and started to swing again.

Price couldn't believe it. He'd seen the bullet enter the stomach two inches from the navel. But Devane didn't respond. His movements were slower, but his body didn't go down. No shock, just a bloody hole. Devane smashed the railing into Price's broken shoulder. The shock of pain sent a razor through his brain, blinding him for a second. When his head cleared, Devane had struck his other arm, batting the gun over the railing into the empty neighboring court below.

Devane turned his attention to Liza R, who had dug a switchblade from her purse. She flipped the blade open and stood hunched with both hands wide, her teeth bared like a wolverine. Devane poked the railing at her. She backed up. "Come on, toots. Come here and I'll liberate your head from your shoulders."

Liza R looked at him, then straightened up and smiled. "I think not," she said. "No profit." And with a wave she ran the other way, toward the back exit where she'd come in.

Devane looked surprised, and Price didn't wait for him to recover. He ran straight toward Devane, dipping his right shoulder as he plowed into his chest. The collision slammed Devane's hip against the partition, and he flipped over the edge, dropping into the court with Rebecca.

Price lunged to the edge. The fifteen-foot drop had seriously damaged Devane. He was sprawled face-down; his left leg was at an awkward angle, apparently broken. Jagged streams of blood streaked the wood floor around his wounded hip. There was a big hole in his lower back where Price's bullet had emerged. Dark liquid glistened in his scalp.

And he started to get up.

Rebecca made hysterical yelping sounds behind her taped mouth as she watched the bloody naked man crawl toward her. His huge white smile was marred some by a couple of missing teeth and the pink foam at his lips.

Price thought about running back down the stairs, trying to move that showcase again. But if anything, he was even weaker now than before. Maybe he could retrieve the gun from the next court and shoot Devane through the glass wall. But he couldn't be sure the thick glass or cement walls wouldn't deflect the bullet, maybe hit Rebecca. Besides, there wasn't time. She was scampering away from him, using her legs to propel herself along the floor on her backside. But Devane kept coming, leaving a slick red trail behind him as he crawled.

Price swung one leg over the partition and, holding on with only his right hand, managed to lower his body until he was hanging there by one hand. He opened the fingers and dropped to the floor. He hit the floor hard, trying to roll so his legs would absorb most of the shock. His left arm felt as if it had been sawed half off.

Devane's head turned slowly. He saw Price and began to rise, hoisting himself up with great difficulty. Blood flowed freely from his wounds, yet he was still smiling. "Incredible, isn't it?" he said. "It'll still be a long time before my nervous system realizes how badly I'm wounded. That should be more than enough time, don't you think?'' He lumbered toward Price with clumsy steps that reminded Price of Rebecca first trying to walk with her leg brace. ''Amazing,'' Devane continued happily, as if Price were his biographer. ''I feel no pain, no fear of death. In some ways I feel stronger than ever.''

He was right, Price thought; he did look stronger, his eyes brighter. Price looked around the court, but there was nothing to use for a weapon, no escape. Devane was coming, and Price had no choice but to face him.

Price used his speed, running around behind Devane and kicking him in the wounded hip. The jolt seemed to hurt Price more than Devane, but the blow dropped Devane to his knees.

''Didn't hurt,'' he told Price. ''Try again.''

Price kicked him again. Blood sprayed onto Price's bare feet. Devane's body jerked, but he merely laughed. Then he slowly started to get up. Price kicked him again, but this time Devane caught the foot around the ankle and yanked Price to the floor. Devane kneeled like a religious devotee, and without turning, he dragged Price toward him, reeling him in. Price kicked at Devane with his free foot, delivering several rattling thumps to the hip and collarbone. Devane seemed to buckle at one point, stopped pulling Price toward him, though he kept a tight grip. He took a deep breath, then started again.

Price clawed at the floor, fingernails skittering over polished wood. But it didn't help. As he slid across the floor closer to Devane, Price's hands snagged Rebecca's clothes, felt the cool metal of her leg brace. His fingers closed around it just as Devane's fingers closed around Price's throat. Price jammed the brace up into Devane's face, but that didn't seem to stop the crushing pressure at his throat. Again and again he stabbed at Devane's face. Devane's fingers tightened, and there was no more air. Price felt his jabs becoming weaker, heard the muffled whimpering of his daughter somewhere behind them. Wished he had enough air to at least apologize to her for letting her down. His eyes closed and he forced them back open. Then he saw her beside Devane, lying on her back and kicking at him with her tiny bare feet. Her head rocked from side to side as she kicked out at him with energetic thrusts. Her right foot kept snapping into Devane's broken collarbone, and soon Price felt the left hand around his throat weaken. He renewed his jabbing with the brace and felt hot dry air scrape down his throat as he took his first breath.

Devane turned angrily toward Rebecca, slowly raising his hand to strike her, and Price shoved the battered stainless-steel brace into Devane's face. He didn't have enough strength to knock him out, but it was enough to knock Devane off balance. He tumbled off Price toward Rebecca.

"Get back!" Price yelled at Rebecca. But too late. Devane's hand stretched out and closed around her skinny throat, pulling her across the floor toward him. She struggled at first, clawing at his fingers. Price, too, pried at the fingers, but couldn't open them. He saw Rebecca's eyelids flutter and close.

"No!" he yelled. "No!" He quickly straddled Devane's chest. The brightness had gone out of Devane's eyes as his brain finally recognized the damage.

"Amazing." Devane smiled, holding Rebecca's limp body by the bruised throat. She wasn't moving.

Price, staring into Devane's cold flat eyes, raised the leg brace over his head and brought it down again and again and again. . . .

30

"Jersey stakes, lady," the Puerto Rican kid sneered.

"Sure," Liza R said. "Winners' outs, clear everything passed the foul line."

The black kid with the comb stuck in his hair shook his head. "We talkin' *jersey* stakes, mama. You understand?"

"Losers give their shirts to the winners, right?"

"Yeah, right. Don't think we gonna let you off cuz you a chick. You gonna have to strip it off same as the dudes."

Liza R smiled. "I'll remember."

The black kid with the comb winked at the Puerto Rican. "You on, lady." They slapped each other's hands above their heads and laughed. "Gonna see some white titties today, Raoul."

It was a two-on-two game. Liza R and Dino against Raoul and Kenny, who called himself "Kenya." Dino was a half black, half Italian sixteen-year-old, six foot one, with remarkable hand speed and a sweet hook shot. Liza R had played with him before. Kenya and Raoul were both six-footers, but with more bulk on their bodies than Dino. They'd never seen her play, so that was going to be her edge. They'd be sloppy, condescending.

Kenya shot for outs from the top of the key. The ball swirled around the rim and hopped out. Liza R brought the ball in.

Neither team was ever more than a point ahead or behind. Raoul worked the inside, muscling Dino but getting frustrated by the hook shot. Kenya played Liza R tight, too tight, doing more with his hand than the usual hand check on the hip. Still, he was good, forcing her to shoot a little farther outside than she liked. The result was a thirteen to eleven tiebreaker.

Kenya looked at her with a cocky leer. "Come on. Pay up."

Raoul was leaning against the post, catching his breath. "Fuck man, let it slide."

"Fuck you, Jackson. We won. The chick knew the rules." He grinned at her. "Need some help, mama."

Liza R smiled at him. "Never have." And she pulled her T-shirt over her head and tossed it to him. She wore a lacy yellow bra underneath. Dino handed his torn shirt to Raoul.

"Nice tits," Kenya told her.

"You know just what to say to a woman," she said.

Raoul got a lingering eyeful before he sheepishly tossed Dino's shirt to her. "It ain't right."

Liza R tossed it back. "You won. Now how about another game?"

"Fuck, lady," Kenya said. "What you gonna play for now. Your panties?"

"Okay," she said.

"Shit," Dino said, shaking his head. "Not me."

She took Dino aside. "A hundred bucks, win or lose."

He shrugged. "Okay."

Liza R walked up to Kenya, her breasts less than three inches from his sweating chest. "Well, you up to it?"

"You mean, we win, you give us your pants."

"Uh-huh. Pants and bra. And if you lose, you give us your shirts and pants."

He thought about it, a slow smile splitting his dark face. "Shit, yeah."

The game was rougher this time. Kenya didn't try any of his fancy reverse lay-ups or finger rolls, just straight no-nonsense basketball. Dino was outrebounding Raoul under the basket and setting good screens for Liza R's fall-away shot. Kenya started to get a little rough, charging into Liza R, knocking her over onto the asphalt. He apologized with a crooked grin, then knocked her down again a few minutes later. It was all over in twenty minutes.

Afterward they stood around, hands on knees, sucking air.

About a dozen neighborhood kids had gathered to watch the white lady in the bra play. Playing for jerseys was a schoolground tradition around there, a nonviolent variation of gang warfare where you tried to take a rival gang member's jacket, his colors. But they hadn't seen anyone play for pants before.

"Let's go," Liza R demanded, her voice harsh. "Strip."

Kenya was having trouble catching his breath. He glared at her. "No fucking way, cunt."

"Wanna bet?" Her smile was cold and threatening. Several onlookers began to jeer Kenya, call him names. "Well?" she said.

"Fuckin' cunt," he spat. He yanked his shirt off and stepped out of his denim cutoffs. His underpants had holes in them. "Enjoy it, lady."

"Small pleasures," she said.

He threw the clothes in her face. The crowd hooted.

She turned to Raoul. "You, too, man. Let's have 'em."

"But . . ." Clearly he thought his earlier gentlemanly gesture was worth something. He didn't know Liza R.

She paid Dino off and carried her basketball across the playground. The bruises around her jaw from Price's elbow had just begun to clear up, and now she'd have more on her leg from Kenya knocking her down. Well, at least she'd managed to come out of that whole Masked Dog mess with something. It had taken all of her persuasive powers, but the KGB finally accepted her story about Devane's killing Zinov, Denisovitch and Alexei. And that she had killed Devane herself. They'd even paid her for the execution. Not that they'd had any choice, especially after losing Alexei. They would need her even more now.

She entered Washington Square Park and thought of Price Calender. A moment of regret clouded her face as she wondered what it might have been like to stay with him. He had more strength than she'd realized. But he had too many silly notions. Now he was just a nuisance who could identify her. Someday soon, when his government bodyguards had disappeared for good, she would pay him a visit. Not clumsily, like Devane. Quick and professional and he would be dead.

A few of the old men playing chess under the tree looked up as she walked by, staring at her sweaty legs. She turned to acknowledge their lusty stares, when the basketball she was holding to her chest exploded, knocking her to the ground. Her ears rang from the explosion and she felt a sharp pain in her chest. She laughed to think a defective ball could do all that. She started to get up, only she couldn't. Her legs wouldn't move. There was blood on the front of her T-shirt. A hole in her chest. She looked terribly confused, staring at the bleeding hole as she died.

31

Price searched under the newspaper where he'd last put them. They were gone. "All right, you little monster, where are they?"

"Guess."

"Uh, in the toilet bowl?"

Rebecca giggled. "No! Don't be gross."

"In the attic?"

"You don't have an attic."

"Well, that leaves only one place." He walked to the sofa where she was sitting. "Behind your back."

"Yup." She pulled her hand out and held up his new glasses. She tried them on. They slid off her nose. "They almost fit."

He leaned over and kissed her on the head. "Try that on, instead."

She rubbed her head. "Guys are so mushy."

Price laughed. He sat back down at the portable electric piano and began to play chords with his right hand. His left arm and hand were in a thick white cast. He hummed a melody with the chords. "How's that sound?"

"Like 'Duke of Earl,'" she said.

"Yeah. That's what I thought, too."

"Start with the C minor."

He did. "That's better. Maybe you should write the songs."

"I thought Barry Manilow wrote the songs. That's a joke, Dad."

"Barry Manilow writes the jokes."

She giggled.

"Now put some of that sun screen on, I don't want you to burn out there."

"Cripes, this is number fifteen. I might as well be wearing jeans and a coat. I'll never get a tan."

"You don't tan, sweetheart. You burn, just like—" He caught himself before he said "your mother." It had taken the past two weeks to get her settled down after her ordeal, Trinidad's and Grandma's death. The only fortunate thing was that she hadn't been able to hear the conversation on the catwalk, didn't know her mother was still alive.

"Burn like what?"

"Like my toast. Now slop that stuff on nice and thick."

"Yeah, yeah." She did, though accompanied with heavy sighs.

Price continued to play the chords, stopping occasionally to jot the notes down. He had no great expectations from the songwriting; it was just a way of killing some time while he recuperated enough to find out if he'd be able to play the guitar again. The doctors were "cautiously optimistic." In the meantime, the guys in the group brought the piano over. He'd started by writing some sentimental crap about his grandmother, then some more sentimental crap about Trinidad. None of that had worked. He hadn't sorted out those feelings yet, and until he did, they deserved better.

The knocking on the door wiped the pout off Rebecca's face. "Time to go," she said.

"Let's answer the door first, okay?"

"Okay."

Price smiled. Around kids there was no such thing as a rhetorical question. They answered everything.

He opened the door. Jo bustled in with her arms full of bags. "Help."

Price took one.

"All right now, this is the fried chicken, potato salad—German, folks, so forget the mayo. Here's some wine for us, the best that $3.79 could buy, and some Dr. Pepper for the bathing beauty over there."

"He's making me put all this goop on so I don't get a tan," Rebecca complained. "Number fifteen, for cripes' sake."

"You'll thank him someday."

"When?" she asked seriously.

"When you're my age and your face is all wrinkly around the eyes so that guys like your father make cruel comments."

"Hi," Price said, kissing her. "I missed you, too."

"It's only been ten days. And we talked every night on the phone. On *my* credit card."

"On Rawlings's."

"Yeah, but I have to explain it at the end of the month."

"By the end of the month, he'll probably have figured it out for himself. You get all your reports filed?"

"Yup. Ten days' worth. I'm sorry it took so long, Price, but there's no way to hurry the process. Endless meetings going over every detail. Cross-meetings with the FBI and Secret Service." She threw up her hands and sighed. "Let's just forget it. How's the arm?"

"Fine."

"Hand?"

"Okay."

She leaned against him and gave him a kiss. "Hey, what're these." She pulled the glasses out of his pocket.

"His new glasses," Rebecca explained.

"When'd you get them?" She tried them on. They slid off her nose.

"While I was at the hospital, getting my hand and arm put in a cast. I figured since Rawlings was paying, I might as well get these while I was at it. Only thing is, I can't find a place to keep them where I won't lose them."

"How about on your face?"

He shook his head. "Nah, I don't really need them exactly. Just for reading and stuff."

"Sure." Jo looked at Rebecca. "Guys are so vain."

"And mushy," Rebecca added.

Price sat behind the electric piano. "Too bad you can't stay."

"Not so fast, buster. My luggage is in the car. This is just the stuff for the beach." She stood behind him and put her hands on his shoulders. "What's this? A new Price Calender song?"

"Maybe. Eventually. If I can ever get it to stop sounding like 'Duke of Earl.'"

"I like 'Duke of Earl.'"

He began playing the song, humming the melody. "That's all I've got so far. What do you think?"

"It certainly doesn't sound like 'Duke of Earl.' More like 'Leader of the Pack.'" She laughed, bit his ear and whispered, "I love it," in a way that he knew she meant it.

He stood up. "Okay, everybody ready for the beach?"

"Yeah," Rebecca said.

"Yeah," Jo said.

"Good, because today's the day we teach junior G-person, Jo Dixon Montana, to swim."

"Yeah," Rebecca said.

"Noooo," Jo said.

"We'll see. Let's get going before the sun goes down. Rebecca, bring the beach bag."

She got up, the shiny new brace encasing her left leg. Her hair was shorter, in an attempt to correct some of the damage Devane had done to it. She brought her father the large canvas bag. Price started transferring the food and drinks from Jo's paper bags into the beach bag. He picked something out of the bottom of one bag and held it up. "What's this?"

She shrugged, took it from him. "A basketball."

"Once maybe. Not anymore."

"It exploded. This is all that's left."

He gave her a quizzical look. "What are you going to do with it?"

"Nothing," she said. "It's just a memento. That's all."

"Of what?"

She smiled. "A hell of a lot."

"I didn't know you played."

"There's lots about me you don't know. Yet."

They finished packing and sent Rebecca ahead to the car. When they were alone, Price held her tightly in his arms.

"How is she?" Jo asked.

"Better. Therapy helps. Won't go to sleep unless I check the room out first. Closets, under the bed. Never closes the door anymore when she goes into another room. But all things considered, she's doing damn well."

"She looks good."

"You, too."

"Gawd, I missed you," she said, kissing him. "Ouch, that cast hurts my ribs."

"How long can you stay?"

"A week."

"And then?"

She smiled, kissed him again. "Ask me then."

32

Dees wheeled his car into Rawlings's gravel driveway, pretending his Honda Accord was really a Porsche 944. He pulled next to Rawlings's Audi 5000 and decided that would be okay, too.

Rawlings's place was an old Virginia farm barn converted into a house that was now worth more than the farm it had originally been a part of. The woods surrounding the house were thick and green. Dees was impressed.

Rawlings answered the door. "Come in, Dees. You haven't been here before, have you?" He knew damn well he hadn't.

"Hmmm," Dees said, "this isn't where the Christmas party for section chiefs was held, is it?"

"Yes."

"Then I haven't been here before."

Rawlings grinned. "Drink?"

"Something cold that won't freeze my fillings. I'm getting a toothache."

A slim woman in her early fifties walked into the room. Like Rawlings, she was wearing a tennis outfit. Only he looked ludicrous in his, like a bear someone thought would be funny to dress up. She looked attractive and lively, certainly not someone who'd be married to Rawlings for thirty years.

"This is my wife, Glenda. This is Dees."

"No first name?" she asked.

Dees smiled. "We're not allowed. Budget cuts, you know."

"Very good," she said, laughing. "Something for you gentlemen to drink?"

"Gin and tonic?" Dees asked.

"Two," Rawlings said.

Dees saw her turn and, when she didn't think he was watching, wink suggestively at her husband. Rawlings blushed slightly and gave her a dopey grin. The whole exchange nearly floored Dees; to think that these two actually got it on together.

Rawlings lead him into the study, where they sat without speaking until Glenda Rawlings brought the drinks and left, closing the door behind her. The study wasn't anything like Dees had expected. He'd thought to see framed and autographed photos of Rawlings shaking hands with political muckety-mucks. Maybe some crossed swords, dueling pistols or such hanging on the wall, Richard Helms's biography tucked into the bookcase, a wet bar. Instead there was a big desk with a plastic cube of photographs of kids—apparently grandchildren—a wire basket filled with old tennis balls in the corner, and a lot of dog-eared tennis magazines on the desk.

"How'd Jo handle the assignment?" Rawlings asked.

"Excellent. We sent her in with two crack people, but she insisted on being the trigger herself. Hell of a shot, too."

"Aftereffects?"

"Minimal. She seemed, I don't know, relieved. Not just that Liza R was dead, but that Calender was safe. She's with him now."

He shrugged. "That's her business."

Dees waited. Rawlings had called him up at home on a Saturday and asked him to come right out—something he'd never done before. There must be a reason. Something important.

"Well," Rawlings said, finally getting to the point. "I got word about the promotions."

Dees leaned forward, nearly spilling his drink. "Any in our section?"

"One."

Dees waited. Rawlings looked a little sad, which he decided was because Dees was getting the promotion instead of him. To be honest, Dees had to admit that Rawlings had been the key behind the success of the mission. Success, hell. They'd been lucky. Still, they had pulled it off. Devane was dead.

"This isn't the Academy Awards," Dees said. "You going to tell me, or what?"

Rawlings sighed. "Godfrey got it."

Dees gaped. "Huh?"

"He's been promoted to section chief over at S division. They'll be rotating someone from outside our section into his job."

Dees nodded. He considered questioning it, getting mad, resigning, going to *The Washington Post*, pissing on the director's desk. Instead he nodded. He'd been around long enough not to be surprised.

"Wanna toss that record on for me?" Rawlings gestured at the stereo. He was closer to it, but stared at his drink as if he didn't know his way around the room and might get lost.

Dees walked over to the stereo and flipped the lever. The turntable whirled and the arm floated to the first cut. A lively bass was joined by drums, a couple of gui-

tars, then that unmistakable voice. It was Price Calender, singing "Off-ramp Life." Dees noticed that the
album cover was tattered, as if it had been around a
while.

The two men listened silently, sipping their drinks,
not looking at each other. Finally Dees said, "The
bastard's not half-bad."

"Yeah," Rawlings said, "but I hear he can't play
tennis worth shit." He finished his drink and looked at
Dees. "How's your tennis, Dees?"

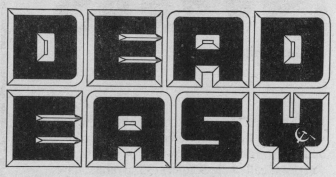

**Nile Barrabas and the
Soldiers of Barrabas are the**

SOBs

by Jack Hild

Nile Barrabas is a nervy son of a bitch who
was the last American soldier out of Vietnam
and the first man into a new kind of action. His
warriors, called the Soldiers of Barrabas, have
one very simple ambition: to do what the
Marines can't or won't do. Join the Barrabas
blitz! Each book hits new heights—this is
brawling at its best!

"Nile Barrabas is one tough SOB himself. . . .
A wealth of detail. . . . SOBs does the job!"
—*West Coast Review of Books*